Our Justice

John W. Howell

Published by Keewaydin Lane Books
Editor Harmony Kent
Copyright © 2015 John W. Howell
Keewaydin Lane Books Port Aransas, Texas
ISBN: 978-0-9969115-2-8

Dedication

Our Justice has been a labor of love to bring the story of John J. Cannon and his challenges with Matt Jacobs to a satisfactory conclusion. For those of you who have read *My GRL* and *His Revenge*, you have become acquainted with the personality and quirks of the man. John is far from being a classic hero. He started out on this journey simply wanting to buy a boat and try his hand at becoming a charter captain. As readers, you have been supportive and gave him the courage to persevere against what were at times, oppressive odds. Therefore at John's suggestion, I am dedicating this book to all of you as a thank you.

The dedication is a thank you for the encouragement, the reviews, and the kind words for the past three years. I hope you enjoy the third book in the John J. Cannon Trilogy.

Acknowledgements

Our Justice is a piece of fiction written out of the author's imagination. Port Aransas is a real place with real people, but the events described, characters developed, and places visited are purely fictional with no intent to depict reality. I want to thank all my beta readers for reading the book in its pre-edited stage and for making very meaningful comments which served to enhance the story. I believe you should be sainted. I also want to thank C.S. Boyack for providing the kind and supportive endorsement displayed on the back cover. A special thanks also to editor Harmony Kent, who continues to exercise her craft in such a way as to teach while improving the readability of my story. She is a saint. I also want to thank Jo Robinson for her fine formatting work that creates an excellent visual effect for Our Justice. Finally, as always, a thank you to Molly McCormick for her continued support, and to Abagail McCormick for being a super person.

Chapter One

I finally get a chance to give Ned Tranes, the police chief, a call. I've been back in Port Aransas for three days and have been so busy putting my house in order and haven't had a moment to call my own. The first thing that I need to do is to order all-new furniture. The goons working for Jacobs—the guy who wants me dead—made a mess of it. They shredded every piece of fabric on the upholstered furniture and took an ax to anything else made of wood. All my clothes lay in a pile on the floor, looking like an angry lover had chopped them up with shears. I really did *not* appreciate the frozen food left to thaw on the kitchen floor. Since I'd been gone for over a week, the vegetables and meat had reached an advanced state of decay when I got home. I can still remember the smell, even though it's been cleaned up for weeks.

My FJ 40 Toyota Land Cruiser was in no better shape. I guess there are about six holes in her body where one of Jacobs' sharpshooters shot to kill, but missed out on the opportunity. I'm thankful that nothing important was hit on the vehicle, and nothing important on me as well since I only took a bullet to the hip. I called the guys over at Wimberley Four Wheel, and they came with a wrecker and picked her up. The guy said it would take about six or seven days to repair the damage. Most of the repair is cosmetic and, except for the bullet that passed through the brake master cylinder, could have been put off. I guess I'm a softy when it comes to the FJ, so I just told them to fix all of it, and we would be done.

Ned and I agreed to meet for lunch today. I'm heading there in a rental car. I have to say, it's much newer than my FJ but doesn't have the same cache. The worst part is not being able to drive on the beach when I want. The FJ has four-wheel drive and can never be stopped in the sand. This Ford Focus wouldn't make it ten feet on the beach before becoming bogged down hopelessly.

I arrive at police headquarters at quarter to twelve, which gives me a few moments to duck into city hall across the street, since Ned and I agreed on twelve o'clock. Ned is a man of precision and punctuality. To arrive early would only cause him to alter his schedule in his belief good manners necessarily dictate the need to pay attention to me. I don't want to interfere, so I'll take care of registering my FJ first since the sticker expired at the end of the month. I walk into city hall, and to my relief, there is no one in line. After a glance around, I walk up to a window that has a sign over it indicating it's the right place for titles, registrations, and tax collections. A windowsill with a nameplate indicates that Betty Kent is on duty.

A person sitting at a desk across the room from the window, whom I assume to be Betty, rises and walks to the window. "Yes, sir. Can I help you?"

"Why, yes. I need to register my FJ."

"Well, we can help you with registrations. Do you have the paperwork?"

"Yes, it's right here. The state mailed it to me." I look up to see a kindly woman smiling at me. "Oh yes, you knew that, didn't you?"

Her smile never leaves her face. "In Texas, all of the registrations are mailed. So, yes, I knew that." She chuckles and reaches for the papers, which I release to her care. "Um. It looks like you bought your vehicle while ago."

"Yes, yes, I did. Is there a problem?"

"No, there is no problem. Everything is fine as long as you have not been issued a citation. Have you?"

"Gosh no. Actually, I haven't been driving the vehicle lately. Not because of the expired sticker, but because I've been out of town for a while."

"Well, when we're finished, you'll be legal again." She gives me another big smile and returns to the desk. After a minute on the computer, she calls out to me, "If you have a check handy, I can give you the amount."

"Yes, I'm ready."

"Sixty-five fifty. You don't need to fill in the name; I have a stamp. I'll need the check number."

"It's 1702."

She makes a few more keystrokes and comes back to the window. "All set," she says.

I thank her, take the registration, and then go through the door. I think about how long the process would have taken back in San Francisco. A visit to the DMV would take upwards of two to three hours. Today, I got in and out of the Port Aransas version of the DMV in less than ten minutes. I'm so happy to be living in a small town.

Of course, I say living here since I still don't know if my leave of absence extension request has been approved. Originally, I got a six-month leave, and have asked for another six. Peters, the partner back at the law firm, seems to have something against me taking time off. The last time I talked to him, I had to put on a hair shirt to get through to him. He gave me some kind of bullshit to the effect that he wasn't sure if the other partners would grant my request. It's so stupid since these leaves of absence are a matter of standard operating procedure.

I finish crossing the street and glance at my watch. Three minutes to go. What the hell—I can disturb Ned for two or three minutes, and it won't kill him. I go into the police station and announce myself to the sergeant behind the desk, "John Cannon to see Chief Tranes."

"Yes, Mr. Cannon. The chief is expecting you. Please, go right in. I think you know where he can be found."

"I sure do, Sergeant. Thank you." I reflect on the last time I came here. Ned and I were working on the murder of that poor young woman, Gerry Starnes, who sold me my first boat. I say working but, in reality, I was the prime suspect since they found me unconscious next to her body. It seems like ages ago, but it's only been two months. Since that time, I've been held captive by a group of terrorists, helped stop their attempt to blow up the Annapolis Midshipmen, got named a national hero, kidnaped again and almost forced into subverting the American political and financial systems, finally escaping with Ned's help, and have now come back home.

In the bargain, we captured Paul Winther, who is the number-two man behind Ralph Jacobs, the most diabolical billionaire on the planet. It is my hope that Winther will start talking and see the wisdom of turning state's witness against Jacobs. Ned doesn't think such a situation will ever happen. He believes Jacobs and Winther have an ideological score to settle with the Western world, and they will never give up their fight until they are dead.

I reach Ned's office and wait by the doorway for him to notice me. He's on the phone and seems to be deeply involved in the conversation. I can't make out the discussion since all Ned seems to say is "bullcrap" over and over. He finally hangs up without saying goodbye, and then looks up and gives me a big welcome wave. "Hey, John. Come on in."

I go in and sit where Ned points. "How are ya, Ned?"

"Just great. The question is more like how the hell are you?"

"Doin' just fine. I've got my house set up pretty well. Wimberly picked up the FJ yesterday and said it will take about six days."

"Whoa, that's fabulous. I would've thought it would be longer. How many damn holes were in that thing, anyway?"

"About six or so, I guess. Where do you want to go for lunch? I'm buying."

"I don't care. Wherever you'd like is good for me. I was on the phone with that dickhead from the prosecutor's office."

"Yeah? What did he want?"

"He's starting to sound like he's working for the defense. He's beginning to think he doesn't have an iron-clad case against Winther, so he's thinking of makin' a deal."

"A deal? What kind of deal d'you make with a murderer?"

"That's what I told him. He said he could offer Winther an accessory plea for co-operation. You heard my response, 'bullcrap.' Winther's never going to give up Jacobs to save his own ass."

"Why does the Federal prosecutor have this one, anyway? Shouldn't this be in the hands of the military since Jacobs and his band seem hell bent to declare war on the US?"

"Yeah, you would think so, but the executive branch seems to feel these terrorists should get a fair and open trial."

"Well, that's a noble gesture, but dealing with these cutthroats, such nobility can only lead to more bloodshed. I still have nightmares about the young girl in the phone store who lost her life only because these guys were trying to get me."

"You're preaching to the choir, John. I'm kind of glad I was de-activated from the FBI and am a simple small town police chief again. I don't have to deal with this whole thing anymore."

"Lucky you. I still have to appear as a prosecution witness. Also, let's not forget that Jacobs is still on the loose, so he could still be interested in seeing me dead. I'm sure that when he got wind of the fact his little plan to discredit the US backfired, he started making a plan to get even."

"Yeah, and that's why the Secret Service has you under observation twenty-four-seven."

"You know, I don't even know they're there most of the time. Of course, Ramon reminds me how he got assigned to this. As he would say, 'salt blown pile of cat litter.'"

"Yeah. What happened to him in Washington?"

"I think the reason he was re-assigned had something to do with allowing a sniper to get a shot at Stephanie."

"You would've thought, with all the agents around her at Arlington, that never would have happened." He shakes his head. "Let's get some lunch. We can gab some more over food."

Ned comes around his desk, and we head out to my car.

"What the hell is that?" Ned says.

"My rental Ford Focus."

"I thought the Secret Service would be driving you around."

"Oh, they offered, but I'm not comfortable being driven. Call it a control thing."

We get in the Focus, and the car is way too small for Ned. "You can hit that lever under the seat and push yourself back," I say.

"Whew, that's a little better. I thought my knees would obstruct your view out of the windshield." Ned laughs that great deep laugh he gets when he thinks he's said something funny.

"Okay," I say. "So, this isn't a big SUV, but at least it has four wheels."

"You sure?" More laughter from Ned. "I don't see the Feds anywhere. Where are they?"

"See that guy on the bike over there?"

"Yeah."

"He's an agent. If you look beyond the corner, you can see the big SUV, which will pull out and follow us. I don't guess you saw the guy standing outside the station, did you?"

"The one with the little dog?"

"Yup, that's the one."

"You've got to be kidding me. Part of the agent's job is to be close enough to you to take a bullet if need be. These guys are playing it way loose."

"I feel a little like a goat tied to a stake as a way to attract a lion."

"You may be right. I wouldn't think they'd want to take the chance and see you knocked off in hopes of catching some gun for hire. When we get back to the office, I'm going to give this guy … what did you say his name was?"

"Agent Ramon."

"I'm going to give agent Ramon a call and let him know he needs to be a bit more attentive to the fact that you're a target and also a valuable witness."

"Not to mention a nice guy."

Ned breaks into a wide grin, and I start the car and pull away from the police station. We head up Avenue A, and on the way, decide to eat at the Café on the corner of Cotter and Alister Street. I reach Alister and turn on my signal for the left turn. The café is about a mile up. Ned says something that I ask him to repeat.

"John, I don't like the looks of that SUV across the street," he says.

The first time didn't register, but now I see what he's talking about. The SUV sits broadside to the street in the parking lot. The blacked out windows make it impossible to see who's inside. My heart pumps faster to prepare me for a fight or flee decision.

"Make a U-turn," Ned says. He sounds calm but reaches for his gun. I turn the wheel of the Focus as hard as I can to the left and the punch the accelerator. The rear end of the car spins around, throwing up sand and dust and making a horrendous screeching noise. Now we're heading back down Avenue A. No sooner do I start my maneuver than the SUV makes a hard left and bolts across Alister, obviously to chase after us. Ned keeps telling me to speed up, and I worry about hitting some innocent person who might get in the way. I lay on the horn until Ned tells me to knock it off. "We're only a block from the station, and I really don't think that the horn is helping. Just keep an eye out and go faster."

I see out of the corner of my eye that Ned is on the phone. Hopefully, he's calling in reinforcements since it looks like the SUV is gaining on us. Just as the rear window of the Focus blows inward, he finishes the call. Hundreds of pieces of glass hit Ned and me. Luckily, it's shatterproof stuff, so we're mostly okay cut wise. Ned crouches down and fires three quick shots with his 9MM. In the mirror, the SUV swerves to the left and almost explodes after it rams a parked car. "Stop," Ned yells.

I slam on the brakes, which nearly tosses Ned through the windshield. "For shit's sake, I don't have a seatbelt on, junior, so take it easy. Just stop and turn around."

"You think those guys are still alive? The way that SUV went into that parked car, I would bet the driver is no longer with us."

"Yeah, I bet you're right. Just in case, though, slow down and stop fifty feet before them."

I slow the Focus and come to a stop. Steam rises from what used to be the front of the SUV. The entire front end has been driven into the parked car, which looks like an old Cadillac—good and heavy, which doesn't bode well for the SUV.

Ned gets out of the Focus and stands behind the door with his gun aimed at the SUV. "Don't see anyone moving," he says. "I'm going to approach the vehicle from the right. You stay here."

He didn't need to remind me to stay out of the way. By now, I've learned to let the professionals handle the sticky situations. Ned moves off to the right and walks at a slow pace up the slight grassy incline, which ends at the side of the surf shop. It's obvious that he isn't going to approach the SUV directly. I have to assume the line of fire for the guys in the SUV is severely restricted, since the way the SUV came to rest on the parked car, it's as if it was parked that way on purpose. They'll have to sight and fire out of the side windows, which will be tough since all the windows are up. Just when I thought there was no one alive in the SUV, a loud blast from inside blows out the rear side window and onto the grass. Ned falls down on his stomach, and I'm not sure if he's been hit. While I sit wondering, a round of automatic fire erupts from the SUV, and the bullets stitch a line slightly above Ned, throwing up pieces of brick and mortar in a reddish haze.

I punch the accelerator on the focus and steer into the rear of the SUV. The airbags deploy, and the impact to my head leaves me dazed. A couple of seconds later, the bags deflate, and while still seeing stars, I attempt to open the door and get out. Something tells me to move quickly, and then I realize that the smell of gasoline is everywhere. I must have punctured the fuel tank. When I lift the handle and push against the door with my shoulder, nothing happens. I realize I am also still in the seat belt and think this is why I can't move. I unlatch the belt and shove hard on the door and still cannot open it.

As I am beginning to feel nausea from the gas fumes, I see someone in the back of the SUV. He is looking directly at me and has what could only be described as an insane grin on his face. He slowly raises the automatic weapon, and it is clear he intends to blow my head off. I raise my hand with the universal sign of wait a minute and then hold my nose. His eyes go wide as he suddenly comes to understand what I am trying to communicate. His face is broadcasting what his mind must be doing in calculating the result of a muzzle flash in the presence of all this gasoline. His insane grin turns to a serious expression and then a lighter look as he gives me a little two-finger salute. I take it to mean *thank you for saving my ass from an inferno*. He then disappears from the rear of the SUV.

I waste no time lunging for the other door. I grab the handle and, this time, the door pops open. I more or less slide out of the Focus and go behind it. I look up to where I last saw Ned and to my relief he is no longer there. If he's hit by the initial blast, he's still okay enough to move.

"John." Ned is yelling. "Get the hell away from the car. Run as far away as you can." I take off running and do what I think is a clever serpentine maneuver as I go. Hearing the distant sound of sirens in addition to my own heartbeat in my ears gives some element of comfort. I look back over my shoulder and can see Ned on the very corner of the surf shop using it for cover as he points his weapon at the SUV. I pull up and stop running. It is clear the people in the SUV do not want any more shooting, and all Ned has to do at this point is keep them from running away. From this distance, I barely hear him shout for the occupants to come out of the vehicle. They don't follow Ned's orders.

A police car and EMS unit pass me and come to a stop short of the cars. The police car then makes a maneuver and positions crossways on the street. Another, up at the intersection, does the same thing. The scene is now cut off from the rest of Port Aransas. The police officers get out of the car closest to me and take up a position behind it, facing the Focus and SUV. They each have what appear to be shotguns in addition to their side arms. Ned holds his position and continues to yell at the occupants to come out. One of the guys says something that I can't hear. Ned's response tells the occupant, in no uncertain terms, to cut out the crap and come out of the vehicle.

Ned's words work, and the rear door of the SUV swings out, and then the guy attempts to slide out with his hands on his head. Ned and the police officers rush over and pull the man into a standing position. They put cuffs on him, and Ned lets an officer take him to the patrol car. Ned motions for me to come closer and meets me halfway. "We should stay here. No telling if that gas will find a way to ignite."

"How many were in the SUV?"

"Looks like three. The other two are gone, according to our prisoner. I want to thank you for smashing into the back of their vehicle but, as police chief, I have to let you know what a dangerous thing that was to do."

"Yeah, I didn't think of that. I thought they'd shot you."

"Well, a lot of glass from the shotgun blast came my way, but none hit. The worst part was all that dust from that automatic. I still have it in my teeth. Gritty as hell."

"Who do you suppose these guys are?"

"We'll find out when we get him to the station. Right now, the fire department is on the way, and we need to make sure this mess doesn't turn into a fireball. Oh, I hope you took out extra insurance on that Focus. Looks like it's totaled."

Ned and I laugh, and can't seem to stop. The insurance comment just isn't that funny, yet we continue for five minutes. Finally, we get our breath and watch as the fire department and EMS guys go to work removing the bodies and taking care of the fuel spill.

The two guys supposedly looking after me show up at last. Ned asks them if Ramon is still in charge. They confirm that he is.

Ned says, "From my point of view, you guys are doing a shitty job. Where the hell were you?"

One of the agents stammers something about loose surveillance. Ned cuts him off and lets them know he is going to have a discussion with the higher ups. They both look a little nervous. Ned tells them that he'll drive me home, and they should contact their boss and tell him to expect a phone call. They both turn and walk away slowly.

Chapter Two

"Get in. I'll give you a ride home," Ned says. "I'll need to do some paperwork at the station. You want to catch dinner later?" We both get into the Police SUV before I have a chance to answer, and when Ned finally closes his door, I ask, "Your wife coming this time?"

"Nope, she's at her mother's for a week. It'll be just us."

"Aw, too bad. I would like to meet her sometime."

"You're kidding me. You haven't met Geneen?" Ned starts the car.

"No, the last time you were babysitting me, she was also at her mother's. Of course, that was when it looked like the Jacobs team was going all out to kill me, and you got her out of Dodge, so to speak."

"I think they're still going all out if those guys in the SUV are any example."

"You think they're Jacobs' men?"

"Well, not his men per se, but I would be willing to bet he hired 'em. I know I'm going to have a problem getting the live one to talk. The last time we had a run in with Jacobs' boy Winther, he never said a word." Ned puts the vehicle in gear, and we pull away from the scene.

"Any idea when Winther is going to trial?"

"I understand his lawyer is asking for a change of venue. Seems they don't think they can get a fair trial in Texas."

"How did you manage to get the trial set up in Texas, given the fact that most of Winther's crimes occurred offshore?"

"Yeah, it took a bit of doing, but I convinced the Federal prosecutor, seeing as you were living in Texas at the time you were kidnaped, and this would be the best place for the trial since you're the victim."

"So, this is a trial of Winther. What about Jacobs? He's the man behind all this terrorism activity."

"Don't forget that Jacobs has billions, and it'll not be easy. If I can get someone in his operation to turn state's witness, we may be able to bring him to justice. Our justice. Well, here we are." Ned puts the gear lever into park and leans back in his seat.

"Thanks for the lift. What time should I be ready for dinner?"

"I'll swing by at six-thirty. That sound okay?"

"Well, beggars can't be choosers. Sounds great." I reach for the door and start out of the vehicle.

"Okay, see you then. Try not to get kidnaped or shot until I get back. Your handlers should be lurking here somewhere."

"I promise." I dismount and let the door close. Ned smiles and pulls away.

This late in July, the temperature rests around eighty-nine degrees. Being near the Gulf has the advantage of about ten degrees cooler than inland. The weather forecast said that the temperature is supposed to hit over a hundred in Corpus Christi. Sounds like a perfect day for a swim.

When I look around for the Secret Service agents and can't find them anywhere, I unlock my door and feel the cool of the house against my moist skin. It feels good compared to the heat outside. After climbing into swim trunks and grabbing a towel, I'm ready for the beach. Up and over the boardwalk, my feet touch the hot sand, forcing a quicker move to the water. I enter the surf at a pace that sends the spray flying, and drop into the cool water to get used to the temperature as fast as possible. It works well, and the Gulf feels almost warm now that I'm in all the way. Once there, I lean back and do a relaxing float while watching some Pelicans drift overhead.

The salt water buoys me up, and I could fall asleep just bobbing around. I know it is impossible, and with that thought, it's time to get out and take a shower. Slowly, I make my way back to the shore and pick up the towel. While drying myself off, and for no apparent reason, I think of Sarah again. Even though we made love, she had no feelings for me at all. She's the type of woman who goes through life doing whatever she needs to do to survive. Sarah made love to me knowing the entire session was being recorded. The worst part was sending some photos to Stephanie for no other reason than to make sure Stephanie and I would never have a relationship. So far, her plan has worked. Sarah is on the run with Jacobs, and Stephanie and I have nothing going on. I would have liked to get to know Stephanie better, as she and I also had a consensual moment of pure bliss. The pictures Sarah sent threw cold water on that idea. So, the best I can hope for is that Stephanie will somehow find it in her heart to forgive the fact that I made love to Sarah. Until then, all I will ever be is an acquaintance with which Stephanie shared beautiful moments.

Ned told me Sarah was also the one who called him to come get me in Ecuador when he lost track of where I was. That certainly doesn't sound like someone who hates me. The thought of Sarah actually liking me sends a chill through my body. Not a bad chill, but one which has a pleasant danger tinge to it. I have to get over her and concentrate on the fact that she's loyal to Matt Jacobs, and nothing is going to change. Why did she call Ned, though? She didn't have to and was clearly far away from Ecuador when she placed the call, and safe from the authorities, for that matter. Yet she took the chance of getting caught by Jacobs when she rang Ned. Damn, the old thrill is there, and there isn't much I can do about it. I shake the memories from my head. I can't keep thinking that Sarah and I could have a future. And a future with Stephanie is doubtful. I have to get rid of these thoughts before I believe myself to be the loser that such thoughts breed. I almost trip on the stair. "Wake up, John," I say aloud.

I open my back door, and then pick up my watch from the table. A nice shower and a nap before Ned picks me up sounds in order. Then, seeing (or maybe just sensing) movement in the front of the house, I say, "Who's there?" Right after I said it, I wish I hadn't. For definite, someone is in my house, and they may have a gun. How many movies are there where the dope walking into a trap yells "who's there?" and the audience groans at the stupidity?

I crouch down and look around for something to use as protection. The floor creaks, and whoever is in the house is moving toward the rear where I'm hidden. With a need to move quickly, I shoot to my feet and grab the back door knob, throwing the door open, and then run outside. I'm not sure where I'm going, but it's a damn sight better to be away from whoever is trespassing in my home. After I run over the boardwalk, I turn onto the beach and move into a jog, hoping I'll run into someone who will help me. About a hundred yards further on, I hear a snap like a twig on my right side toward the Gulf. Before I can look over, I hear the shot of a gun behind me. The snap was the bullet missing me by a fraction. Finally, the shot sound catches up to the speed of flight of the bullet. I turn, and a guy stands on the beach with his arms extended, holding a gun and aiming for another shot. I break to the left and pick up speed until I'm near the dunes. It will be rough going once I get over the dune, but that's a better bet than staying to stop a bullet. I look as I break and see the guy has stopped aiming and is now running toward me. Dressed in black, he looks way out of place in the bright sunshine.

At the dunes, I crawl up and over the top. From there, I keep running and only now realize I'm still barefoot. Dry scrub, with some cactus thrown in for good measure, makes up the undergrowth on this side of the dune. The jog to Twelfth Street, about a city block away, will be painful. A few cars pass by on Twelfth, and I probably made the right choice in getting off the beach. When I look behind, I see that the man in black has just made it to the top of the dune. It looks like he may not follow me, but I can't take any chances. I continue to move as fast as I can through the scrub, although my momentum slows. Another snap passes my ear, and the sound of the gun is close behind. The son of a bitch is trying to kill me from the top of the dune. I thank my lucky stars he doesn't have a rifle, as at this range, a pistol hit would be a lucky shot indeed. Right away, I want to take back the thought since tempting fate like that would dictate the guy would have the luckiest shot possible given my arrogant belief he won't be able to hit me.

Another snap gives me the courage to think that I may just make it. Another glance back shows him still on top of the dune, but not in the stance necessary to aim his weapon. I almost laugh out loud that crazy kind of laugh you make when you know you've cheated death. I believe the guy has given up, and slow my pace a little. The pain of my journey hits me all at once. When I look down at my feet, dark red streaks stain all around my shins. The underbrush has cut me a thousand times. Now it feels almost unbearable to walk. However, I have no choice but to continue. I still have my watch in my tight fist, and I put the leather band in my mouth, so I can bite down on the strap and (maybe) go the distance. Actually, thinking about the leather and biting it, takes my mind off my excruciating pain. Must be why it works. My mind drifts over what I plan to do next. I'll stop a car and ask them to call Ned. I'm sure, since he's the Police Chief, that whoever I run into will be willing to do it.

At Twelfth Street, I look both ways. There are no cars in sight. Just as I think I must be doomed, a car comes around the corner from Avenue C. I wave my arms and walk out into the middle of the street. The car speeds up and goes past me while the occupants look away. They must think I'm some kind of crazy person or a drunk or both. When I glance down at my feet, it looks like I have stockings from the knee down. The cuts are so numerous that my legs have the appearance of patterned knee-highs. What a picture for anyone coming along to see—a guy in board shorts, no shirt, with dripping knee-high socks, and holding a watch in his teeth. I'm not sure I would stop either.

Worried that the guy with the gun will get into a car and come get me himself, I try and get out of sight. A house across

Twelfth offers possible refuge, and I make a run for it. It may be someone's home, and I can borrow their phone. While I cross the street, another car comes around the corner. I wave for them to slow down, but like before, they speed up. The phone is my only chance. I look at the house. It will take a long wide stairway climb to reach the front door. My feet drip splotches of red. The owner won't be pleased to have someone track up their wooden stairway with blood. The better part of valor is to go around back.

Quickly, I walk around to the side of the stairway. A fence surrounds the property. With a limp, I get to the gate and feel relieved to find that it's just vinyl with an easy-open latch. I lift the latch and open the gate. Collections of plants in pots and some nice palm trees dot the yard. The shade feels good, and I almost want to sit in one of the chairs under the tree and take a nap. That's a no go, though; I'd better get help before the shooter man catches up with me. One nice thing is that I can no longer see the street, and anyone on it can't see me either. A hose lying on the grass tempts me to rinse off my legs and feet. Best not. Too much of a liberty with someone else's stuff, and it'll waste precious time. A back door stands on the same level as the yard. This is good since I won't be messing up a set of stairs or a porch, and any climbing will be torture. A knock on the door ignites the sharp barking of a small dog. Probably a dachshund—they can bark all day long without let up. Someone inside yells for it to shut up. Yeah, like that'll happen. The door swings open in a savage way, and a look of irritation settles on the woman standing in the doorway holding a fuzzy little dog that is nowhere near being a dachshund. "Can I help you?" she says. Finally, the dog stops barking. The woman waits for a logical answer.

"Someone's just shot at me, and I ran across the brush from the beach. I'm all cut up. Would you be so kind as to call Chief Tranes at the police department?" Logical went out the window with that one.

"Uh. You say someone's shooting at you?"

"Yes."

'Why would they do that?"

"I'm not sure." Impatience sharpens my voice. "It might have something to do with terrorists."

"Wait a minute. Aren't you that fella who stopped those guys from blowing up the Naval Academy Midshipmen?"

"Uh, Yes. Yes, I am."

"You poor dear. Please, come in."

"No, I better not. My feet are a mess, and I don't want to get your place dirty."

"Never mind my place. We need to get you some help."

"If you'll make the call, I'll just sit over by that table. Could I use your hose?"

"You need a drink? Let me fix you one."

"No, I am all right. I just need the police."

"Okay, hon, you rest over there, and I'll call the chief."

The door closes, and I hope she doesn't forget. Of course, she did recognize me, so I don't think her memory is all that shot. Not sure why her memory came into question. She does look old enough to have memory problems. Now I'm rambling. With a sigh, I pick up the hose and turn on the tap. The cold water feels so good on my tortured feet. I rub my legs and wash the cuts. Fewer cuts line my legs than I thought. The amount of blood made me think I would lose a limb. The little cuts are on the surface, and the capillaries made the quantity seem more. The cold water makes the stinging go away.

When I'm done with my legs, I hobble over to the chair and sit. I run the water over my feet. Splinters stick out of the sole of each foot. I'm not sure I can get them out, but I try and pull the obvious ones. One by one, I win the battle. The cold water helps to numb the foot slightly, which makes scraping the splinter out more bearable. I finish those that are removable and make a note to myself that a doctor visit is in order.

"I talked to the chief, and he's on his way over here. Are you sure you don't need a drink?"

"No, I'm just fine."

"Those are nasty looking splinters. You'll need to get them looked after."

"Yes, thank you."

"You finished with the hose? If so, I'll turn it off for you, so you don't have to get up."

"That would be nice. Thank you, and yes, I'm finished."

"I can't imagine why anyone would want to shoot you. You're a national hero." The woman takes the hose from my hand and drags it back to the tap, which she turns off.

"I don't know if 'hero' is the right word."

"From what I hear, you and the Navy Seal fella saved the lives of those Midshipmen and all the people who would have been gathered at the Intrepid museum."

"Jason Savard is the name of the Navy Seal."

"He died, right?"

"Yes, he did. He was shot and didn't make it."

"How did that make you feel?"

"Lousy."

"Yeah, I'll bet it wasn't easy. I hear the President gave you a medal."

"Yeah, he sure did. Unfortunately, I got it in the mail 'cos when I went to Washington to pick it up, those terrorists tried to kill me there as well."

"So you never met the President?"

"Nope, not even close."

"Wow, that's a shame."

"Do I hear sirens?"

"I think you may be right. The chief said it would only take a couple of minutes."

As we finish talking, Ned's SUV pulls up in front of the house.

"Well, I must get going. Thank you for your hospitality and the conversation." I get up and try to leave. The net effect of the cuts, splinters, and shock hit me like a ton of bricks. Quickly, I sit back down with a strange feeling that I'm about to throw up. Not a good thing in front of this fragile old woman. I fight the urge and put my head down between my knees.

"You rest for a minute, son. I'll get you a cold cloth."

Finally, I hear the jangle that I know to be Ned's keys. "John. What the hell happened?"

"Some guy was in my house, and when I found out, I ran out the back door, and he followed me."

"How did you get so cut up?"

"He was trying to shoot me, so I ran through the brush to get away."

"You get a look at him?"

"Only over my shoulder. He wore black and didn't have a rifle or automatic."

"Could you tell what kind of weapon?"

"Not real clear on that. I don't think it was a revolver. Could be a 9MM since I didn't see any sun glint off it."

"Makes sense. How many times did he shoot?"

"Um, I guess two, but there could have been more."

"Only two? I'll bet he picked up the casings then. We'll probably never know the kind of gun. Come on, John. Let's get you home and put something on these cuts."

"Just a minute. The lady of the house went inside for a cold cloth."

"I'll go tell her we need to leave. Be right back."

While Ned takes care of the old woman, I think back on the last time someone was in my house. They left tracking devices in my shoes. I'd better remind Ned so we can look to see if there's another set anywhere.

Ned returns. "Okay, no problem, she knows we're leaving."

"I didn't get a chance to thank her."

"It's okay. I thanked her for you."

Ned and I go to his vehicle. The bottoms of my feet are killing me, so I take it slow. We get in. "Boy, thank God you're here. Don't think I could walk back home." I shake my head. "Do you think the guy was in my house to plant a transmitter like the last time?"

"Good question. I should get one of the experts from the bureau over to check it out. When we get to your house, let's be careful about what we say."

"I thought you were no longer attached to the FBI."

"They told me in no uncertain terms that I'm never released. They want to know about anything funny going on. It appears that the prosecutor has friends in high places and doesn't want anything to go wrong on his case. Long story short, I still work for the FBI. Since this is something that could fall under the definition of funny, we need to let them know."

"Yeah, I understand."

"Where were those two idiots from the Secret Service?"

"I don't know. I looked for them when I got home but didn't see them."

Ned picks up his radio mic and asks for a secure connection. He then asks the person on the other end to call the FBI and ask them to meet us quietly at my house. Without saying anything further, he replaces the mic. "That should do it. I didn't want to use a cell phone. You never know who's listening."

"The radio is secure?"

"Oh yeah. We have private frequencies, and they're scrambled, so it's hard to tap into the conversation."

We reach my house, and Ned pulls into the driveway. "Stay here. I'm going inside alone. Anything happens, pick that mic up again and tell them to get here quick."

"Okay, but be careful."

Ned eases out of the SUV. He goes to the door and pulls out his weapon. Then he looks back at me and makes a sign like a key turning in the lock. I shake my head, so he knows the door is unlocked. A few steps bring him next to the door. He puts his right hand on the knob while holding his weapon aloft in his left. Almost before I realize it, Ned has opened the door and gone inside. If anyone is in there, they wouldn't have heard him coming. It always amazes me at the skills Ned has when it comes to law enforcement. Despite being such a big man, he moves with the grace of a dancer. I wait for any alarming sounds from inside the house, but so far, nothing.

The hair on my neck stands up when Ned's form fills the doorway. I feel so glad that it's him. He motions me to come in. To get out of the SUV proves more painful than I'd imagined. The gravel that makes up my driveway feels like fire on the soles of my feet. I can imagine what walking across burning coals must feel like as I finally reach the front porch and go inside.

Ned stands in the living room. "Well, John, welcome home. Looks like we should get you into a bath and see how bad those feet are." Ned raises his finger to his lips as a reminder about possible listening devices or intruders. I nod so he knows I understand.

"Yes, Ned." I sound like a poor actor in a radio drama. "You stay here, and I'll go and take care of these feet." I raise my eyebrows, and Ned gives me a look intended to tell me to be natural. I nod understanding and shuffle off.

The hot water feels good. I lean back in the tub and try to relax. Ned says something that I can't understand, so I yell for him to come into the bathroom. He comes through the door and averts his eyes. "I just wondered if you had any hydrogen peroxide."

"Yes, in the cabinet. I used it the other day on some bites."

"Not snake, I hope." Ned turns to the cabinet and pulls out the bottle. "Any cotton balls?"

"They should be under the sink. I think I put them there the last time I used them."

"Oh yes, here they are. I'll leave these two things here so you can get them when you get out of the tub. Try to wash your legs and feet with soap. Do you have a washcloth?"

"Yeah, it's here in the water.'

"Good. I'm not sure what's in that underbrush, but I'm sure a good cleaning will help prevent an infection."

I smile. "Thank you, doctor."

"You're welcome, and I only play one on TV." Ned smiles back, and then leaves.

I rub my legs and feet with the washcloth, and then do it again after I fill the cloth with plenty of soap from the bar. The cuts feel better after the good cleaning. Once out of the tub, I see most are minor. A few could get nasty if infected, but for the most part, I came out okay. After I get the splinters out, I dab the hydrogen peroxide on the wounds. A visit to the doctor won't be necessary. I slip into flip-flops, which lessen the pain in the soles of my feet. Once dressed, I go back to the living room.

To my surprise, there are others in my house besides Ned. "Hey, fellows," I say. To a person, they all raise their finger to their lips. I get the idea quickly to shut the hell up.

"Hi John," Ned says. "Here are some of my friends who wanted to meet you."

All of them speak at once in some sort of greeting. "Hi, you guys," I say again. "Nice meeting you."

Ned comes over and takes me off to the corner. "Let's go outside for a minute." He then steers me toward the back door. We go outside to the back yard. "Show me where the guy took a shot at you."

"We have to go over the boardwalk. Follow me." I take the lead, and we go up and over the boardwalk. I walk out onto the beach a few yards, with Ned following, and stop. "Right here is where he took the first shot."

"You sure?"

"Pretty sure. I was running down the beach when I heard the shot. Actually, I heard the bullet go by first."

"You looked at the guy before or after the shot?"

"I saw him take aim, so I would say before."

"Okay, if your feet can stand it, let's fan out and see if we can find a cartridge. It will be brass. If it's here, we should see it, but like I said, I doubt it will be."

"Why so sure?"

"I think this was professional, and those guys don't usually leave anything behind that could ID them."

"Makes sense. I'll go this way."

Ned and I fan out and start looking for a shell casing. If the guy left any behind, there could be two or more. I meander down the beach until I'm about at the spot where I cut over to run to the dunes. I start back on a line more toward the dune and parallel to the route I just took. I look down and turn my head left and right, but don't see anything that looks like a casing. Nearby, Ned performs a similar maneuver to me. We almost come together at one point, and he asks, "You see anything?"

"Nope, I sure haven't." We keep looking for about ten minutes more, and then Ned waves me over.

"I'll have a team do a more thorough job, but I still don't think anything is here. We should probably get a metal detector and give the place a clean sweep. Let's go to the house and see what the boys found in there."

As we walk back toward the house, I can see Ned is wrapped up in his thoughts. He isn't talking much, which isn't unusual, but he seems distracted. "You okay?" I say.

"W-what? Oh yeah, I'm fine. I'm thinking about the need to protect you, and I'm sure, Stephanie Savard as well."

"Stephanie? She has no connection to the case. She's just the sister of a guy killed trying to protect his country."

"Don't forget Jacobs had her kidnaped and held to try and get her brother to do what they wanted. Also, they had a sniper shoot her in the head in Washington. I think there are a lot of reasons Jacobs could want her."

"Name one."

"Didn't you and she have an affair?"

"We had a one-night fling."

"Jacobs thinks it's more than that."

"How so?"

"Didn't he have Sarah Barsonne seduce you and send the pictures to Stephanie?"

"Yeah, but your analysis made it out to be a simple case of trying to make sure my life was miserable."

"And why would he think Stephanie not having a relationship with you would make you miserable?"

"I see. He thinks Stephanie and I could have been an item."

"Right, and if Jacobs thinks you care, he'll also think you can be manipulated if he were to be able to get to Stephanie and threaten to do something dire if you don't co-operate."

"You know what? He's right. I wouldn't want anything to happen to Stephanie because of me."

"I know that. So, she ought to be protected."

"Can you put us away in the same place?"

"John, you're speaking like an evil person." His soft smile doesn't quite take the sternness out of his words. "You should get it through your head that, if there *was* something between you and Stephanie, it's over. You and your short arm made sure of that situation."

"You sound pissed."

"No, not pissed. Stephanie had feelings for you, and you pretty much screwed that pooch. I like the Savards, so I have a soft spot when they get hurt. I can tell you, Stephanie got hurt. I don't blame you. You and she didn't have a committed relationship, but to see her face when she gave me those pictures made me want to punch you in the nose."

"Sorry. I've hurt you as well. It's the last thing on earth I would want to do."

"Yeah, I know it, kid. I'm just telling you the truth about how I feel. I like you, too, so I won't punch you in the nose, don't worry."

"I'm not worried. I just hate to have something like this come between us."

"Don't worry, John. Nothing will come between us."

We reach the house. One of the team members waits on the back porch. "Where's the boss?" Ned says.

The guy's thumb indicates that the boss is inside. Ned thanks him, and we go into the house.

Ned walks up to the leader. "So, speak to me," Ned says. "Tell me these guys have put another transmitter in John's house."

"Well, you know what?" the guy in charge says. "We've turned this place upside down and haven't discovered anything. We did find a few prints and have taken them for analysis. The guy forgot to wipe his feet as well. He left some footprint residue. Looks like he was in a quarry or something before he came here."

"A quarry? How do you know that?"

"Well, there seems to be granite dust that he dropped off his shoes. At least, we think it's granite dust. We'll know for sure when we get the samples back to the lab."

"Anything that can identify whoever was here?"

"Naw, not much. I suspect the prints are someone Mr. Cannon knows, or are Mr. Cannon's, since no self-respecting assassin would leave forensic evidence behind. We'll know for sure after the analysis."

"You got a pocket print analyzer?"

"Yeah, we have one."

"Let's rule out John and me now so we can see if we have a real set or not."

"Good idea. Hold on." He turns and walks over to another agent. They discuss something and the other agent pulls what looks like an iPhone out of a case on the floor. The agent points and looks like he is giving instructions on how the thing works. The head agent holds up his hand and indicates that the other agent should follow him. They both return to Ned and me.

"This is agent Rollins. He understands this thing, so he'll do the analysis."

Rollins takes Ned's hands one at a time and rolls his fingers on the screen. He lets go and comes over, then wipes the screen and does the same to me. "It'll be a few minutes," he says.

Ned asks the head agent, "So, what will you get from the granite dust?"

"Well, again, not much on the individual, but at least we may be able to determine the location of his last stop before here."

"You're telling me it will be like the old needle in a haystack."

"Oh, I'd say more like a needle in the universe."

"Well, do your best." Ned looks down. What's he thinking? Rollins comes over and verifies that the fingerprint samples belong to Ned and me. He also tells us that a partial print doesn't belong to either of us. "Can you identify the partial?" Ned says.

"Yes, possibly. Interesting, though—we found the partial print on the doorknob. It could just be that the perpetrator broke his vinyl glove while opening the door."

"How do you know he wore a vinyl glove?"

"We found a small piece of it on the stoop. Another thing: we found a trace of blood on the knob. It looks as if the guy twisted the door knob, and something ripped the glove and gave him a cut."

"Oh, I can explain," I say. "That door knob has a small piece of steel on it from an old scrape. I've cut myself on it before. If you don't know about it, when you twist the knob, it catches your thumb."

"Tell me how it catches your thumb?" Rollins says.

"If you're not careful and reach for the knob with your right hand, the sliver of steel is just where your thumb wraps around the knob. I always open the door with my left hand to avoid it. I've been meaning to fix it since I moved in."

"How can you avoid it with your left hand?"

"I'm not sure. It's the way the fingers wrap on the knob as opposed to the thumb."

"So, you don't think about how you grip the knob; you just do it?"

"Yes, I suppose that's true."

Rollins turns to Ned and the head agent. "The guy is right handed, and there just may be a way to match his DNA from the small sample. Of course, unlike the TV shows, it will take about six to eight weeks for the matching. The partial print will be a bear as well. I don't see any real distinguishing marks on it, but it's helpful to know it's a right thumbprint."

Ned thanks the agents, and then walks with them to the door. They spend a few minutes talking, and then Ned says his goodbyes. He shuts the door and comes back to the living room, where he sits on the couch heavily. "I don't think we'll ever find out who was here today."

I sit in the chair across from Ned. "It's not so important who was here shooting at me, but why."

Ned looks at me and shakes his head. "Right, but I'd still like a name."

A knock sounds at the door. Ned jumps up and puts his finger to his lips. He pulls his weapon out of the holster and holds it by his side. He opens the door to surprised looks on the faces of two Secret Service Agents.

"Where have you been?" Ned says.

Chapter Three

The two agents explain something about being called off the case. Ned asks them what they're doing here, and they tell him they're sorry for the way things turned out. We all shake hands, and they go away.

Ned suggests we go to dinner, and we do. We have a little discussion about the agents, and I think Ned feels it is good riddance. Ned and I finish dinner, and he drops me off at my house again. He wonders if he should come inside to check the house before he leaves. I offer to buy him a beer if he's so inclined. He smiles, "You know, a nice cold beer might be just the thing to top this day. Also, I'm going to have an officer come over here tonight."

I don't say anything about the officer and just nod. We get out of the SUV and start up the driveway. I'm not sure if I see something at the corner of the house or not. "Ned, take a look at the corner of the house to the right."

He whispers, "Yeah, someone's there. Get down."

As I move to the ground, flashes come from the dark corner. Ned grunts like someone just hit him in the stomach, and then falls to the ground and rolls over close to me. "Take my gun and start shooting." He reaches out, and I can see his gun and also a lot of blood.

I take the gun from his sticky hand and fire toward the corner of the house. A dull moan tells me that I've likely hit something other than the building. I get up and hold Ned's gun out in front of me, as I've seen the police do on TV. After a quick move to my left, I run toward the corner of the house, only closer to the bushes in the front. I don't want to be a big target while I make my approach toward the gunman. When I reach the corner, I make out an arm with a gun in the hand. Though the arm is outstretched on the ground, it could be a trap, so I step on the wrist. When I do, the hand opens, and the gun makes no sound when it slips to the ground. With the muzzle of Ned's gun at the person's head, I say a line I've heard before, "One move and you are a dead man."

Upon looking closer, I can say that my line was a little redundant. I haven't seen too many dead men in my life, but this guy looks dead to me. Still wary, I pick up the guy's gun and sprint back to Ned. When I get there, Ned is still on the ground. "Ned, can you hear me?"

"Call 911. I need to get to a hospital."

"Should I drive you?"

"No. No offense, but we both need to stay alive."

I dial 911 and speak to the dispatcher. I tell them where we are and that the chief has been shot. The dispatcher sounds upset and lets me know that EMS and a car are on the way. "Please, stay on the line, Mr. Cannon. I need you to give me some idea of Chief Tranes' condition."

I assure the dispatcher that I don't intend to hang up. I sit on the driveway and look Ned over. He seems to be bleeding a little less, which I take as a good sign. "Ned, the dispatcher wants to know about your condition."

"Uh, tell her I've been better, but it's not too serious." He pauses. "And, John, try to make it believable. The dispatcher is my wife, Geneen."

"Oh my God. I had no idea."

"Tell her."

"Mrs. Tranes? I just spoke to your husband, and he told me to tell you that he's been better, but it's not serious."

"I heard him, Mr. Cannon. Please, don't let Ned die. He is the love of my life, and although he's one tough son of a bitch, this is just the kind of nightmare I've had for years. Please, promise me you won't let him die."

"I promise, Mrs. Tranes. I promise." I look down at Ned, and he seems to be sleeping. "Ned, for Christ's sake, wake up."

"I'm awake. Just resting my eyes."

"Your wife will kill me if anything happens to you."

"I don't envy you."

"Mrs. Tranes? Your husband's holding on. How much longer for the EMS team?"

"You should be hearing their sirens now. He's okay, then?"

"He's holding. I don't know how badly he's injured, and I don't want to move him."

"I understand. Do I hear the sirens?"

"Yes, thank God. They're pulling up now."

"Stay with me, please."

"I will, Mrs. Tranes. I will."

A police car pulls up to the front of the house. The doors fly open, and two officers come running. I look up and say, "Where's the EMS team?" Panic raises the pitch of my voice.

"Right behind us," the first officer says. "How bad is it?"

I make a motion, pointing to the phone, and the officer's eyes widen, as he comprehends that Mrs. Tranes is on the other end. He bends down and checks the chief, and I'm not sure if what he says next is the truth or for Mrs. Tranes benefit.

"He looks like he's in pretty good shape, considering."

Mrs. Tranes says, "Oh, thank God."

"There's a guy over by the corner of the house. I shot him after he shot the chief."

The officer tells his partner to check it out, and he remains with the chief. "You shot him, huh?"

"Yes, with the chief's gun. Oh, here're the EMS guys. Mrs. Tranes, the EMS guys are here."

"Thank you, Mr. Cannon."

The second officer comes back. "He's dead. Shot once in the head, from the way it looks."

The first officer makes a whistling sound, which I take to mean that he's impressed.

"I think I shot four times."

The second officer says, "That may be true, but one of the shots hit the man just about dead center of the forehead. I would say nice shooting, but sounds like it might have been a fluke."

"Never mind that," says the first officer. "Let's get the crime scene secured. Looks like the EMTs have things under control. I'll need to take the chief's gun, Mr. Cannon."

"I understand." The chief's blood covers the gun and my hand. "Do you have something to protect yourself from getting blood all over you?"

"Yes. Let me worry about that. Here, just give it to me."

I hand the gun to the officer, who takes it with a pen through the trigger housing. He's handling the gun as if it is evidence.

"I'm staying with the chief," I say.

"Good idea," says the first officer. "You can keep Mrs. Tranes advised along the way. We'll catch up to you at the hospital."

The two officers go back to their car and pull out various things to secure the scene. I see the first officer put the chief's gun in a plastic bag. The ubiquitous roll of yellow tape is the next thing out of the car. Another car arrives, and I start to feel more comfortable and that all will be well.

"Mr. Cannon?" The EMT causes me to jump.

"Yes?"

"The chief is stable and ready for transport. I understand you're to go with him."

"Yes, that's correct. Mrs. Tranes? You still there?"

"Yes, I am, but since I heard Ned's stable, I'm going to hang up and head for the hospital. Ask the young man which one."

"Which hospital we going to?"

"We'll go the closest—Corpus Christi Medical Center. They also have the best trauma group."

"Mrs. Tranes—"

"I heard. Thank you so much for bearing with me. I'll meet you there."

"All right, then I'll see you there."

I follow the EMT. Ned is already in the ambulance. With a grunt, I get in, and the EMT closes the door. The other EMT works on Ned. Not wanting to take him away from doing what he can for Ned, I keep quiet.

"Chief Tranes has lost a lot of blood," he says. "I've started a shock pack and some plasma. I think he'll be fine. I'm a little worried about the placement of the shots, though. It looks like he got hit about three or four times, but I can't be certain."

"I-is he in danger?"

"Well, the chief's a tough one, and he seems to be resting okay, but I'd never say there's no risk. We just need to get him to surgery as soon as possible."

"Why aren't we taking a helicopter?"

"Unless we couldn't move Ned for some reason, the ambulance is faster."

Almost on cue, the sirens start, and we are off on the twenty-mile ride to the hospital. I never realized how unstable a ride it is in the back of an ambulance when you're not lying down. Each turn threatens to throw me down onto the floor, and I have to remain mindful of the potential. I look out the front window. A patrol car races ahead of us, making sure that we get there as quickly as possible.

My mind wanders back to when I fired at the guy. How many times did I pull the trigger? As hard as I try, the sequence of events doesn't separate one from the other. The man fires at Ned. I get the gun and fire back. I should be able to recall the number of shots. There were four. At least, in my mind, I think I heard four shots. I can't remember Ned's gun bucking four times, but I do recall four sounds. It amazes me that I hit the guy at all, let alone in the center of the forehead. There'll be some good-natured ribbing about my ability as a marksman when Ned gets better. Let me hope that Ned does get better to give me some ribbing.

"John, you there?" Ned says at a near whisper.

I move over toward his stretcher. "Yes, Ned, I'm here."

"Did I hear officer Runyan correctly?"

"About what?"

"You hit the shooter in the middle of the forehead?"

"Yep."

"That's some shooting. How many times you fire?"

"Four, I think."

"You think?"

"Yeah, I can't remember."

"Well, that's okay. It only takes one. Besides, you're not exactly trained in the police arts."

"You need to take it easy and rest."

Ned coughs a little, then says, "I'm proud of you. You stepped up. That guy would have kept shooting 'til he got us both. Nice job."

"Thanks. Now, quit talking."

Ned chuckles but says no more. The EMS tech watches the monitor, and then turns to me with a concerned expression. Wary of alarming Ned, I don't ask if everything is okay. I suspect it isn't, but there's not much I can do. The tech breaks the tension when he says, "He's going into shock."

Ned looks at me, and I tell him, "You're going into shock, and he's hooked you up to some juice that'll help prevent it."

Ned coughs again. "I feel like I'm gonna throw up."

"That's a symptom of shock," the tech says. "Lift his feet. Let's get some blood into his hard head."

I grab Ned's feet and raise them above his head.

"That feels better," Ned says. Then he passes out.

I look at the tech. "What's going on?"

"His body is shutting down to try and conserve its resources."

"Is that normal?" I hear concern in my voice.

"Yes, perfectly. This IV should stabilize him in a few minutes. His pulse is strong, and none of the bullets hit his heart. So, from a wound standpoint, he's no worse off than if he had a severe cut. We have the bleeding under control, so now we just have to wait."

"How long do I need to hold his feet up?"

"I have no good news for you there. You need to hold them until we get to the hospital."

"What would you do if I weren't here?"

"I'd raise the foot end of the gurney."

"And you're not doing that for what reason?"

"I didn't want to mention this while Ned was awake, but a bullet nicked his carotid artery and broke loose when we put him in the ambulance. The only thing keeping the bleeding under control is my hand on Ned's neck, and I don't want to let go."

"Oh my God. What can I do to help?"

"Just hold his feet. We don't need Ned shocking out right now."

Sweat pops out above my upper lip. Is it from having to hold what are becoming increasingly heavy feet, or concern about how long it might take to get to the hospital? To add to my misery, a droplet runs down my forehead and into my eye. I don't have a free hand to wipe the sweat away, and it burns my eye. I try to wink in the hope of clearing away the salt water. The more I try, the more the sweat burns. I shake my head, hoping it will help. The tech looks my way. "Sweat in the eye," I say.

"That's a bitch." He doesn't sound like he has any sympathy at all.

To try and ignore the burning in my eye, I concentrate on Ned. His eyes are closed, and his breathing sounds labored. His face no longer has the ruddy glow I'm used to seeing, and his facial muscles look as if they've turned into dough. Ned looks puffy and not well. His paleness contrasts with his bright Hawaiian shirt, which appears blotchy due to Ned's blood. He looks so vulnerable. I say a little prayer that he'll be okay. What will happen if Ned doesn't pull through? I'm not concerned about myself, but imagine the effect of Ned's death on the community. Everyone in town knows and loves him. He's a revered and visible symbol of law and order.

I shake my head to get rid of the negative thoughts. Of course, Ned will make it. Just thinking it makes me feel better. We turn into the hospital grounds. When we pass the sign for emergency intake, I sigh with relief. The ambulance comes to a hard stop, and hospital personnel pulls the rear doors open.

"We got this," a guy in a white coat yells at me. I let him take Ned's feet and try to squeeze as close as possible to the side of the ambulance to give them room. The EMS Tech provides a status report while the staff pulls the gurney out of the ambulance. The tech stays with Ned, telling the medics that he needs to keep the pressure on Ned's neck. The whole entourage moves through the double door and into the hospital. I sit down on the floor of the ambulance and take a minute to catch my breath. The driver comes around and asks me if I'm okay. I tell him I am and move to exit the ambulance. With my feet dangling over the back, I pause. The driver takes one look at my face and tells me to lay down for a minute. Events finally caught up with me, and I feel as if I'm made of lead. Just keeping my head upright takes an immense effort, so I take the driver's suggestion and lie back on the ambulance floor. He breaks something under my nose, which hits me like a slap in the face. I bolt upright. "I'm awake."

"You're in a bit of shock, yourself. You should feel better in a second."

He's so right. I feel like running around the block. "What is that stuff?"

"Fairy dust," he says. He returns to the front of the ambulance, grabs a clipboard from the cab, and goes into the hospital.

Chapter Four

The chairs in the corridor prove as uncomfortable as my worry for Ned. A doctor in surgical scrubs makes his way toward the two double doors that separate the treatment area from the relatives' waiting room. Geneen Tranes looks up when he approaches. We both rise and wait. The doctor comes up to Geneen and talks even before getting close, "Mrs. Tranes?"

"Yes, I'm Geneen Tranes."

"Your husband's going to be okay. We were able to stop the bleeding and repair the tissue damage from the bullets."

"Oh my god. Thank you so much." Geneen reaches over and grabs the doctor in what has to be a painful bear hug.

"Uh, Mrs. Tranes, you don't have to thank me. Your husband is resilient, and he had the will to live, which helps immensely in cases like this. I must caution you, though, he will need to take it easy for the next few weeks. I don't want him to drive a car or exert himself. He can walk a little each day, but that's about it. I have written some instructions for you. We will keep him here for about three days to make certain everything is okay. Do you have any questions?"

"No, doctor. I'm just glad he's okay."

I step forward. "I have one if you don't mind."

"Yes, Mr. Cannon, what is it?"

"How many times was he shot?"

"Four. Quite a number, given the fact his assassin missed any vital organs. A bullet nicked his artery, and that could have been serious. The EMS tech did a great job."

"Wow, that's a lot of hits. You say nothing vital?"

"That's correct. The bullets patterned around the vital organs. Seems almost on purpose."

"Mmm, strange."

"Well, if you'll excuse me, I need to get to another surgery. I'll be checking on Mr. Tranes each day. If you have any questions, please give me a call. Here's my card. He'll be asleep for the rest of the night. I would suggest that you go home and get some rest. You can see him tomorrow."

"Thank you, doctor," Geneen says.

"Yes, thank you, and I'm glad you were on duty."

"My pleasure." The doctor turns and goes back through the doors.

I glance down at Geneen. "What do you think? Would you like to go home?"

"Not on your life. Let's find out where they've taken Ned. We'll go to his room."

"Good idea. I'll check."

I walk over to the nurse's station and ask where he is. The nurse tells me Ned is in intensive care, in the A wing of the hospital. She instructs me to follow the yellow line on the floor, and it will take us there. I thank her and go back to Geneen.

We follow the line until we come to an area marked *Intensive Care,* and a sign on the door telling visitors to check in prior to entering. The check-in desk stands in a waiting room off to the left. Geneen and I go stop at the desk.

A nurse behind the desk raises her gaze. "May I help you?"

Geneen identifies herself. "Is it okay to go in and see Ned?"

The nurse says, "You can go in for fifteen minutes once an hour, and he can only have one visitor at a time and only once during the hour."

"You go ahead," I say. "I'll wait right here."

Geneen's smile looks worn and worried. "Thank you."

The nurse gives her a pass with the room number, and Geneen goes through the door into a hallway.

"When she comes back, if you want to see Mr. Tranes, you will have to wait forty minutes."

"Yeah, I get it. Of course, if Mrs. Tranes wants to go again, then I'll have to sit out another hour. Right?"

"Yes, sir, that's right. Sorry. House rules."

"I guess the rules are for the patient's protection, so I don't mind."

"You're very understanding. There's coffee over there. Please, help yourself."

She points to a small table with coffee service. A cup will hit the spot right about now. I go over. It's one of those machines where you select your coffee, and it brews it right there. The day is definitely picking up. It even has Splenda and creamer, so I'm set. I put in the coffee and hit the medium button. The aroma gets my mouth watering. While I wait for the machine to finish, someone enters the waiting room. I pull my coffee out from under the spout.

"Mr. Cannon?"

When I turn, I see a uniformed officer standing there. "Yes?"

"I wonder if you would mind answering a few questions. My name is Officer Buell, and I am investigating the shooting."

"Which shooting? The one I did or the one aimed at Chief Tranes?"

"Well, both, actually, but my main concern is the one for which you were responsible. The other will take a little more investigating by some higher pay grade types."

"Why, is something wrong?"

"No, it is just a little complicated. Someone else needs to go over the chief's shooting with you."

"That makes sense, I suppose. Would you like some coffee?"

"That sounds good."

45

I show the officer how to make the coffee and busy myself with the creamer and Splenda, and then I walk over to two chairs with a corner table between them. The officer gets his coffee and follows. He has a clipboard, which makes a nice tray for his coffee. We each sip our drinks, and then he says, "So, tell me what you can remember about the shooting."

I relate the facts as I remember them. Ned goes down, and I grab his weapon and fire three times.

"Excuse me. Are you sure it was three times?"

"Yes, I'm quite sure now. I've been over it in my head and remember pulling the trigger three times. I must say, I did think it was four, but now I'm convinced it was only three."

"Why did you think it might have been four?"

"Well, I thought I heard four shots."

"The evidence at the scene appears to corroborate your belief."

"Evidence? What evidence?"

"First of all, we could only find three spent rounds from Chief Tranes' service weapon."

"Yeah, I didn't pick anything up; I was too busy with the chief."

"Secondly, there are three strike points in the corner of the house."

"What's a strike point?"

"Oh, sorry. That's where a round hits something."

"There were three in the house?"

"Yes, that's right."

"So, I never hit the perpetrator?"

"So it appears."

"Who shot him, then?"

"I told you it was complicated. We don't know right now."

I take a sip of coffee and lean back. This is information I had not expected. I'm a little relieved that I didn't kill anyone, but can't imagine who would show up and start shooting at someone who was shooting at Ned. I'm almost positive it wasn't one of his force. "I didn't see anyone around there at the time."

The officer nods and says, "It looks like the round was a different type than what would come out of Ned's service weapon. It appeared to inflict maximum damage. We will have to let the ME … uh, medical examiner—"

"I know what ME means."

"Oh. Sorry, of course, you do. I forgot you're a lawyer. Well, anyway, we'll let the ME decide, but I can tell you that a nine-millimeter bullet didn't make the exit wound I saw at the scene."

"So, where did the shooter come from?"

"He may have been using a high powered rifle and could have been quite far away. We're looking at the surrounding neighborhood to see if anything shows up. Also, we're going door to door to see if anyone heard or saw anything."

"They must have heard the shot if I did."

"Well, that's a funny thing about the sound of gunfire. Two or three shots can sound like a bunch when the sound bounces off houses and things. My bet is that the guy had a sound suppressor on his rifle. If not, I'm sure we would have had a call about it before now."

"Did anyone call on the original shots?"

"Yes, we had about four calls."

"Maybe one of them heard a rifle as well."

"We'll check that out."

The officer finishes his coffee and thanks me for talking. He tells me he hopes the chief will be okay, and I thank him for his concern. We shake hands, and he leaves the waiting room. I sit in deep thought about the other shooter. Then Geneen sits next to me and apologizes for disturbing me.

"How's Ned?"

"He seems to be holding his own. He's still under from the surgery, so it's hard to tell. His signs look good, though."

"Would you like some coffee?"

"That does sound good right now. I'm exhausted."

"I'll get it. You've been under a lot of strain for the last few hours, and you can use a pick me up."

"Yeah. How about a double? ..." Geneen grins. "I guess coffee will have to do."

I get up and go to the machine and make her a cup. "Anything in it?"

"I like it black, so no, thank you."

I hand her the coffee, and she takes it with two hands. She shakes as she brings the paper cup to her lips. When she takes a sip, her eyes meet mine. I wish I knew what to say to her that would make her feel better. "Ned's a strong man." It's all I could think of right then.

"I know he is, and it's hard to see him in a vulnerable state." She takes another sip, and the coffee appears to have some magical power—the color flows back into her cheeks, and she looks much younger than just two minutes ago. "I've come to rely on Ned a great deal, and I don't have a clue what I would do without him."

"Well, I don't think we have to worry. The doctor says he's doing great."

Geneen continues to drink her coffee and doesn't seem to want to talk anymore. I shut up and go to the machine for another brew. While I return, she mumbles something that I can't hear. "I'm sorry, but I didn't get what you said."

"It's okay," she says. "I was just wondering aloud on who would want to kill my husband."

"There are some real nasty folks who've been trying to eliminate both of us."

"Oh, you mean that Jacobs fella."

"Yes, he's the one."

"Ned told me he has a lot of money."

"Yeah. I think he's in the Forbes top fifty worldwide."

"How much do you think?"

"Around eight billion dollars."

"You would think, with money like that, he would have better things to do with his time than to try and kill a couple of Port Aransas citizens."

"He believes that Ned and I are capable of bringing him to justice, and he wants to hedge his bet that we won't be successful."

"So, he's using his money to hire people to kill you both?"

"It's a bit more complex. He's using his money to fund terrorist activity designed to further his cause. Ned and I have been in the way, so he believes he'll get away with additional terror if we're out of the picture."

"I just think, if you have the money to do this kind of thing, you should use your funds to do good rather than evil."

"Yep. Unfortunately, Matt Jacobs believes he's doing the right thing. He believes his mission is a true calling from his god, and that if he fails, he'll have failed in finding a place of eternal glory."

"So, his is a righteous mission in his eyes?"

"Exactly."

"I'm afraid that this isn't over, but just beginning. I fear for my husband and you, John Cannon."

I reach around her shoulder and pull her closer. She puts her head on my shoulder. "I think I can speak for Ned when I say you don't have to worry. Money doesn't buy smart, and so far, all the money spent by those guys on various schemes has been totally wasted."

"I hope you're right."

I let go of her shoulder and can see she has been only slightly comforted. She still looks troubled. "Is there anything I can do?"

Geneen shakes her head. "I think not. You probably should go home and get some rest. I'm going to stay here in case Ned wakes up."

"Do you want me to call anyone?"

"No, I think everything is under control. I'm just worried about my husband."

"I understand. Please, call my cell if anything changes or you need anything. Anything at all."

"Do I have your number?"

"Not sure. Here, let me put it in your phone."

Geneen reaches into her purse and pulls out her phone, which she hands to me. Quickly, I program my number and contact information into it and hand it back. "Please, call if you need me."

"I will. Thank you. Now, go along."

I give Geneen a hug and leave the waiting room. The door hisses shut behind me, and I get the feeling I'm running out on Ned. I know the feeling is silly, but maybe I should just sit here with Geneen. The day has been hectic, though, and the rest will do me good. Although I feel somewhat guilty, I call a cab and look forward to climbing into bed.

Chapter Five

I wake with a start, and before I even open my eyes, the past day's memory slams into me. With a sigh, I sit upright and try to shake the feeling of loss surrounding Ned's injuries. He isn't dead, but I feel a sense that some part of Ned will be gone forever, and it makes me apprehensive. Is it a concern for Ned or concern that he might not be up to the job of bringing Jacobs to justice? I keep thinking about the concept of justice, and in Jacobs' case, I'm not sure what it means. Should he be put in jail or worse? His plans resulted in the death of innocent people like Gerry Starnes and that poor girl in the AT&T store, but is that enough to ask for the death penalty? I don't like the idea of Jacobs being able to live while others had to die on his whim. At the same time, I'm not sure I'd like to see him put to death. A long prison sentence would be something Jacobs deserves, and he wouldn't serve contentedly. Jacobs is the kind of person who needs to have his own way always. Having him confined to a Federal facility might be the perfect punishment. Although he'd be alive, for Jacobs, it would be a living hell.

My cell phone rings and snaps me out of my revengeful thoughts. "Hello?" Sleepiness slurs my voice.

"Yes, Mr. Cannon. This is Vincent Herron of the District Attorney's office."

"Uh … yes, Vince. Which District Attorney?"

"Melvin Compos, the Federal prosecutor."

"Oh, yes. I've heard of him. Done some fine work on white collar crime. You calling from Austin?"

"Yes, yes, I am. We, here, are wondering if we could get some time with you to discuss the Jacobs matter?"

"Yes, I would be happy to discuss Jacobs. You say 'Jacobs matter;' has he been charged?"

"As of today, no. We would like to go to the grand jury and get an indictment, but before we do, we want to hear from you about what you know of his activities."

"Have you talked with anyone else?"

"No, you'll be our first. We would like to know from you about anyone else we should talk to as well."

"Who are you planning to interview?"

"We don't normally discuss other witness testimony, but in this case, I think you can know who is on the list. There are only four: Sarah Barsonne, Paul Winther, Sammy Speale, and Clive Gibbons."

"Do you have Sarah in custody?"

"Not yet. We think she and Jacobs are together, but we can't be sure. Paul Winther is a tough one. He doesn't want to talk even if we promise him some immunity."

"You do know that anyone on Jacobs' team who talks ends up dead."

"Yeah, we figured as much. Look, I don't want to spend any more time on the phone since we never know who's listening, so I would like to come to Port Aransas and meet with you."

"I would be happy to meet with you. Please, don't take this wrong, but you'll need to bring some ID, and I'll have to talk to Mr. Campos once we're together. I've been hoodwinked by Jacobs' team before, so I don't trust anyone."

"I understand fully. How's tomorrow sound?"

"Sounds good. What time and where?"

"How about we meet for lunch and then go wherever you say."

"Okay. We can meet at Judy's for lunch. It's on highway 361. We can go to my house after, where it's private."

"Sounds great. I'll see you at Judy's at, let's say, eleven-thirty. That okay?"

After I confirm the venue and time, we disconnect. I need to call the DA's office to verify the identity of Mr. Herron. I'm not falling for any more phony Federal agent or other scams. It interests me that the Feds believe Sarah and Paul will turn state's evidence. There isn't a one in a million chance it will happen. Jacobs has a way of complete control of the people who carry out his dirty work. He must hold some threat over them that keeps them totally loyal to his cause and him personally. Simply avoiding additional jail time won't convince Paul or Sarah to give Jacobs up. I'm not sure even a full immunity deal would yield that result.

Right now, though, it's time to get out of bed and get on with the day. My first order of business is to find out how the chief is doing. I don't want to call Geneen but can't see any way out of it. Maybe I'll call the hospital and start there. I can always call Geneen later. She's most likely tired enough to be taking brief naps between the times she can visit. I look up the hospital number in the phone book and punch it in. A kindly sounding voice directs me to the nurse's station, where another kindly voice tells me there is no additional information available on the chief. The nurse advises to contact the family.

With a sigh, I hang up and call Geneen on her cell phone. Surprisingly, she answers on the first ring. She sounds tired but lets me know everything is well with Ned. She also tells me that Ned is awake, and it would be great if I could come over. Geneen plans to go home for a few hours to get some sleep, which will be good for her. When I agree that it's a good idea, she seems relieved. With the promise of going to the hospital sometime today, I hang up.

Since I have that appointment with Vincent Herron, I should probably go to the hospital first thing. First, though, I want to give the District Attorney's office in Austin a call to see if Vincent is who he says he is. I'll shower and get dressed and then make the call. A cup of coffee is high on my agenda, so I head to the kitchen. I punch the coffee machine and wait for a fresh cup to come drooling out of the spigot. The aroma takes me back to a time when life wasn't so hard, and the only worry was not missing an exam. The smell of fresh coffee always reminds me of the coffee shop at the corner of campus where I would grab a cup of espresso on the way to class. It's been a long road since then, and now I'm worried about getting Jacobs to face the music. With a chuckle at the major difference between the two worries, I head for the shower.

After dressing, I sit at the kitchen table and do a search on Vincent Herron. After wading through a bunch of Herrons, including the birds, on the search results, I find him. He is with the DA's office in Austin. Actually, he's the head Assistant District Attorney and is pictured along with Compos and a few others. It won't be necessary to call, after all. Once I've shut down the computer, I grab my keys and head out to my brand new rental car. The ride to Corpus Christi should take about fifteen minutes. Since I can only visit the chief for fifteen, I shouldn't have much trouble getting back to Port A in time to meet Vincent.

I pull out of my drive and make my way to State Highway 361. The traffic is quite light, which surprises me. Of course, it's a quarter to nine and most everyone should be at work by now. Still, the tourist season is in full swing, and I'd expect a lot of cars on the road toward Port Aransas. Although I'm heading in a reverse tourist commute direction, the other side doesn't seem particularly busy. The new rental Focus has a decent radio, so I turn it on and select the XM station that plays songs from the nineties. Songs I grew up with, and which I still love. I never got into the Spice Girls, but thought Gwen Stefani was terrific in No Doubt and fell in love with Alanis Morisette. Right now, R.E.M's *Losing My Religion* is playing. On auto-pilot, I listen to the words and forget about my concern over Jacobs. Lulled by the songs, in no time at all, I find myself in the visitor parking area of the Memorial hospital.

I arrive just in time for the fifteen-minute visiting period. Upon finding no sign of Geneen, I go right into Ned's room. I half expect to see Ned near death with tubes and things connected to him. Instead, here's Ned sitting up drinking something out of a cup. "Hey there," I say.

"Hey, yourself. Good to see you. Come over and have a seat."

"You look good. Great, in fact. What're you drinking?"

"Soup. At least, I think it's soup. The doctor said I could start on this, and if everything goes well, graduate to lime Jell-O."

"You've made a nice rebound. They told me you didn't get hit in any vital areas. Glad for that."

"Yeah, me too. The shooter should've been better than that. Of course, he might have been way better and did this as some kind of warning."

"Did anyone brief you on the fact that it's probable that a sniper shot the shooter?"

"No, I didn't hear that. Tell me more."

"I don't know much more than that. The forensics team is going over the area with a fine-tooth comb and hopes to come up with something more substantial."

"Yeah. Knowing Jacobs' team the way I do, it's doubtful they'll find anything."

"How's Geneen this morning?"

"Okay. I told her to go home and get some rest. Poor dear stayed up all night."

I nod. "No one else has come in to talk to you?"

"Nope. They think I need my rest. I can take about another day of this, and then I need to get out of here. I hope you're not planning on staying here all day."

"I wouldn't flatter myself so much if I were you. I have an appointment with an assistant DA at eleven-thirty."

"Which assistant DA and what do they want?"

"Federal, out of Austin. He wants to see what I know and if I can help with the case. Apparently, he has four witnesses, and I think he wants to check me out to see if I would make a good fifth. Although, one of the witnesses is Sarah Barsonne, and he hasn't located her yet."

"Of course not. She's with Jacobs." Ned gives me a piercing look. "Have you called Stephanie Savard yet?"

"No. Why?"

"Well, I think you should."

"Isn't she mad at me?"

"That's no reason not to call and, at least, see how she is. She took a bullet to the head for you, and it would be a nice thing for you to allow her to shit all over you if she so desires."

"Okay, okay. No use getting your dander up. I'll do it today."

"Good deal. How about your work? Have you called to see if your leave can be extended?"

"No. That's a good idea as well. Man, you sound like my father."

"I don't have much else to think about lying here."

A nurse comes in and tells me in hushed tones that my time is up. I bid Ned a goodbye and promise to see him later. I'm not sure how long the hospital will be able to keep him, so I don't say exactly when I'll return.

"Call Stephanie," he yells to my back.

I raise my phone in my hand as a promissory symbol and leave his room. As his door eases shut behind me, I figure this would be as good a time as any to call Stephanie. A flutter in my stomach makes itself known. A sign that I feel concerned about what she'll have to say. I don't doubt she'll be angry, but I have to face her sooner or later. The idea that Jacobs sent pictures of Sarah and me having sex to Stephanie makes my face flush.

Seated on one of the chairs in the waiting room, I pull up Stephanie's contact information. Since no one else shares the room, I get on and make the call. When she answers after the first ring, I'm surprised into silence.

"Hello, John," she says.

"Hey, Stephanie. I want to tell you how sor—"

"No need to apologize. You and I made no commitments to each other. We were, and are, free to see anyone we wish."

"But, Stephanie. What Jacobs did wasn't right. You should never have been put in such a position."

"I agree with that, but again, you weren't the one who sent the pictures. You were just the pawn in the game."

"You can say that again. Sarah took me in, for sure."

"Yes, it does happen. I hope you've learned something from all this."

"Well, if you mean some people aren't what they seem, I thought I was old enough to have learned that lesson already."

"It doesn't appear that the lesson took hold."

"I deserve that. Good point. How are you feeling? Not to change the subject, which I desperately want to do."

"I feel great. Fully recovered."

"That's excellent news."

"I understand the government is trying to make a case against Jacobs."

"Yeah. I'm not sure how tight it will be, but they're trying."

"Well, for one, I hope they nail the bastard."

"I join you in that hope."

"Sorry, but I was just walking out the door. I'm going to be late for a doctor's appointment if I don't step on it."

"Nothing serious?"

"No, just a check-up to make sure my head still works. I'm glad you called and would like to talk again. Give me a call sometime, okay?"

"Yes, I will. Thanks for taking my call. Please, take care of yourself."

"I will, John. Goodbye."

By the time I say, "Goodbye, Stephanie," she's already gone, and I doubt she heard my farewell. She didn't sound as upset as Ned led me to believe she was. If anything, she's rather understanding of the whole thing. Of course, she said we were free to see anyone we wanted. This means she doesn't feel committed to me in any way. Not to go all OCD, but now Stephanie's calmness worries me. Certainly, it means she's written me off and has no feelings for me at all. Of course, she did say she wanted to talk again. Still, she may have only said that to get me off the phone. She did seem in a hurry to disconnect. The doctor appointment might have just been an excuse she made up. Oh God, I so need to get a grip here. I can't imagine a person would want to have a relationship with someone who casually sleeps with another woman. To make it worse, said casual sex took place after Stephanie got shot in the head by the men who worked for the guy whose girlfriend I slept with. My face burns up.

What must Stephanie have thought when she opened those photos? Did she feel betrayed, or hurt, or angry? If we ever do speak again, I'd like to ask her. Yeah, right—I'll never ask, and we probably won't speak again. Something in her voice registers, which I didn't think about until just now. When she said that we must talk again, and then "give me a call sometime," I had the feeling you get when you hear someone tell you goodbye forever. If she really wanted me to call, she wouldn't have said "sometime." She would have been more definite like "next week or tomorrow." As it is, it *was* a goodbye salutation. It makes me sad to think I could have prevented this by not wanting Sarah so much. I feel like a moth to the flame. And, although I did get burned, oh but what a fire.

A glance at my watch shows me that I need to get moving if I'm to make my appointment. I have to give Stephanie high marks for her class and dignity in giving me the brush off without so much as raising her voice. What a woman. With a shake of my head, I get up and leave for the parking lot.

Chapter Six

With a couple of minutes to spare, I reach Judy's. I always hate to be late and, in this case, I would feel it if I strolled in after the appointed time. Jacobs' prosecution is one of the most important things in my life right now, and I don't want anything to get in the way of making that a reality. Judy greets me when I go through the doorway. She shows me to a table where Vincent is already seated. When we approach, Vincent gets up and offers his hand.

"Vincent Herron. So very pleased to meet you. You are like a hero to our group."

With a blush, I take his hand. "You're too kind. I'm so pleased to meet you. Jacobs needs to spend some quality time at taxpayer's expense, and your office is the place that will put him away."

Vincent, rightfully, wants to let go of my hand quickly. I didn't mean to come off as a zealot, but that's the impression I make. Vincent sits, and so do I. Judy leaves two menus and lets us know Chas will be our waiter. I thank her, and she leaves.

"I didn't mean to sound like a lunatic just then."

"Forget it. If I had been through as much as you at the hands of Jacobs, I'll bet I would sound like a lunatic too."

"You're very kind. I hope I can be of some assistance. I'll make myself available as much as you need me."

Vincent smiles, and the edge comes off. "What's good at Judy's?"

With a smile, I tell him, "The seafood enchiladas are to die for."

He looks around and asks, "Do you come here often?"

"At least once a week."

Herron looks satisfied, and I think he takes my recommendation more seriously now he knows I come here often.

Almost like Chas is reading minds, he appears. "Can I get you gentlemen something from the bar to start?"

"A bit early for me," Vincent says. "You go ahead, John. I'll just have water, thanks."

"Very well, sir. Mr. Cannon?"

"I'll join Mr. Herron with water." I look at Vincent and ask, "You ready to order?"

He orders the seafood enchiladas, and I order the same. Chas nods and moves away.

I decide to hit Vincent between the eyes. "So, tell me about your case against Jacobs."

"To tell you the truth, we don't have much. We have the two guys who were in Ecuador with you." Vincent pauses to look at notebook lying on the table. "Ah, here it is. A Sammy Speale and Clive Gibbons. Unfortunately, their statements are limited."

"What do you mean, limited?"

"They can attest to the fact that Paul Winther was part of a scheme to discredit you, but they have no evidence that places Jacobs at the head of the operation. They never saw him, and nor did he talk to them directly. I questioned them carefully, and other than what they heard from you, they have no first-hand knowledge of Jacobs' involvement. They will make excellent witnesses against Winther, but useless ones for Jacobs."

"I don't understand. They were there. They heard Winther talk about Jacobs."

"That is all true, but when push comes to shove, they will not be able to testify to the fact that Jacobs was, indeed, behind it all. A second-year law school student would be able to punch through their story without a lot of effort. Remember, we are trying to get Jacobs. Not Winther. He is all these two guys have as eyewitness testimony."

"Think you could get Winther to co-operate?"

"Boy, that would be great. So far, he has not given any indication that he is ready to turn on Jacobs."

"He's a dead man if he does."

"With Jacobs in jail and under a witness protection plan?"

"The government isn't able to keep Jacobs from running his business no matter where he is. Besides, Jacobs will be free on bail and will do whatever he wants."

"Not if we can get a charge of terrorism against him."

"That would be good if it were possible." When Chas approaches with our lunch, I pause the discussion. We each order more water and, once delivered, Chas disappears. Vincent takes a forkful of the enchilada, and his expression tells me he is pleased.

"Wow, this is good."

"Best in the state."

We eat in silence for a few minutes, and then Vincent speaks. "Tell me all you can about your direct knowledge of Jacobs' activities."

The instruction takes me aback until I remember that the job of the assistant prosecutor is to test the evidence to determine its strength and how it will hold up in court. I begin by giving Vincent a complete rundown of the attempt by Jacobs to destroy the Annapolis Midshipmen while moored in New York harbor. I explain meeting Jacobs on the cargo ship and listening to his diatribe against America and me.

Vincent interrupts with a question, "Was there anyone else present during your discussions with Jacobs?"

"Yes. Paul Winther."

Herron mumbles something along the lines of "go on," and I continue with the story about Jacobs kidnaping me and flying me to Ecuador.

Again, he interrupts, "Who was with you?"

The more it becomes clear that all my interactions with Jacobs were in the presence of either Paul Winther or Sarah Barsonne, the more nervous I grow. I give him their names.

He makes a note in his book and then asks, "Anyone else?"

"No. Just those two."

"And this Barsonne person is the one you had sex with?"

My face burns and my jaw drops. "How did you know that?"

"We talked to Ned Tranes a couple of days ago, and he filled us in."

"What else did he tell you?"

"Nothing much. He just let that drop while we were chatting. How is he, by the way?"

"He's fine. What does sleeping with Sarah have to do with anything?"

"Right now, nothing. I can see a defense attorney down the road asking you a question like, 'Isn't it true, Mr. Cannon, that the only reason you are accusing Ms. Barsonne of terrorism is that you wanted to have an affair with her, and she cut it off?'"

"Shit. So that whole thing was a method of providing a cover should Sarah get caught."

"Got to admit, it was smart. I'm not saying a jury would buy it, but with you as the only witness against her, it makes her case stronger. Did Speale or Gibbons interact with Sarah?"

I try to think of a time when we were all together. Nothing comes to mind. "No, I don't believe so."

"So, it's your word alone that she was even in Ecuador."

A sinking feeling settles in my stomach. It's the same feeling I used to get when I couldn't think of an answer on a test in school. I had the answer, but it was locked away somewhere and needed to be hunted and found. "Yes, I would say it is just my word." I lay my fork down, as I've lost my appetite. Jacobs has worked me over and will now remain a free man to wreak havoc on others. The last time I saw him was during the video conference between the two of us. The same video conference call where I saw Sarah's earring and her walking away from the camera. "Wait," I say, too loud. "There was a video conference between Jacobs and me where Sarah was in the room as well. We talked about the plan, and I made a proposal to Jacobs, which he was going to consider. Could be that a recording of the conference is still available at the studio in Ecuador."

Vincent looks surprised but interested in what I'm saying. Lunch finished, he steeples his hands beneath his chin. "How long was the video conference?"

"Had to have been ten minutes or so. Is that studio still under US control?"

"Yes, it is still considered a crime scene, and the Ecuadorians have generously allowed our team to remain."

"Can you call someone?"

"Yes, I think that is the right thing to do. Excuse me for a moment." Vincent takes out his cell phone and makes a call. From his side of the conversation, it sounds as if he's talking to someone in charge of the investigation. He gives instructions to have the people in Ecuador check all the videos to see if there is a recording of the videoconference. When he's done, he excuses himself and asks, "When was the conference call?"

I have to think for a moment, and then remember that it was scheduled for six o'clock in the evening and started a few minutes earlier. It had to have been the day after I got there. I tell this to Vincent, and he nods and goes back to the call. He relays the information and excuses himself one more time. "Do you know the day and date?" Vincent looks apologetic, but I can tell he would like the information to eliminate any extra work on the part of his team.

"I think it was a Tuesday. When Jacobs' team took me and flew me to Ecuador, we arrived on a Monday. Now that I think about it, the date was Monday the eighteenth of July. No, wait, Monday was the nineteenth of July. Yeah, that's right. I talked to him on the twentieth of July at around six."

Vincent returns to his call. He tells the other end to look on both sides of the twentieth. Not too much more is said before he disconnects. He looks at me and says, "That should narrow down the timeframe a bit. It will make it easier for the techs to go through any recordings they find. I'm not sure how many are there, but when the force took over, there wasn't much time for Jacobs' guys to destroy any evidence."

"Yeah, Ned mentioned that the team was able to secure the whole facility and the contents of all the computers. My guess is that there will be a central communication module in the broadcast center that should be the repository of all the discs."

"My guy in Ecuador said the same thing. So, maybe we will get lucky."

"I sure hope so. Would you like some coffee?"

"Coffee sounds real good."

I signal Chas, and he comes straight over. I order two coffees, he picks up our plates, and in no time at all, comes back with two cups and a silver pot. He pours us each a cup and sets the pot on the table. Then he asks if there will be anything else, and Vincent and I both decline any dessert. Chas is gone as fast as he arrived.

Over coffee, we discuss the next step, which will be for the team in Ecuador to finish their search for the recording of Matt Jacobs. Pending the outcome of the search, Vincent may have enough to go to the grand jury for an indictment. Vincent also wants to question me further about events since he is quite pleased in finding out about the video conference and thinks I will have more to offer. "You may know some things you don't even know you know," he says.

"I'm sure there are a lot of things I don't know, but I'm more than willing to do anything to get Matt Jacobs."

"Tell me about Sarah," Vincent says.

He is so blunt that my cheeks flush anew. I take a sip of coffee. "What do you want to know?"

"I know you two had sex?"

"Yes." My face gets hotter.

Vincent leans forward. "I believe Ned said the episode was recorded."

"Yes. Yes, it was."

"Do you know why?"

"Jacobs wanted to use the recording to make me look like a fool with Stephanie Savard."

"How do you know this?"

"He sent her a CD with the episode, as you call it."

"What was the reaction?"

"Stephanie was hurt but seems to understand that they designed it to embarrass me with her."

"I still don't know why Jacobs would think that such a move would harm you."

"Stephanie and I also had sex."

"How would he know that?"

"I'm not sure, but a member of the Secret Service acted pretty strangely while he was protecting us."

"Strange how?"

"After Stephanie and I finished dinner ... oh, wait, we were having dinner in her room."

"Uh, okay."

"Our rooms adjoined with a common area in between. The agent's last name was Ramon, and I never got his first. He said it would be okay to have dinner together."

"Hold on. When was this?"

"When Stephanie and I were in Washington to accept the award from the President."

"I recall that the award was never given. Miss Savard got shot at Arlington Cemetery during or before her brother's burial service."

"Yes, that's correct. It was before."

"Okay, go on. Sorry to interrupt."

"Anyway, Stephanie and I had just finished dinner, and we called room service for dessert. A knock came at the door, and Stephanie went to look through the peephole to make sure it was room service. The peephole was blocked. We called Agent Ramon, but he didn't pick up. It was like he was off duty or something. Later, he blamed some kind of transmission interference, but neither Stephanie nor I trusted him after that."

"So, you're saying Agent Ramon could be on Matt Jacobs' payroll?"

"Yes, I feel there was something off about him."

"What do you mean, off?"

"It's hard to pinpoint, but he was way too controlling with us, and then not to be reachable just didn't make sense."

"Okay, we will need to look into Ramon's background. This is getting us somewhere. So, you and Stephanie had sex, and then what?"

"Well, we liked each other a lot, and I think that before I messed up, and Jacobs threw it in her face, we could have gone somewhere with the relationship."

"But what did Jacobs hope to gain by sending the CD of you and Sarah?"

"I can only believe that he wanted to make certain that, once he was finished with me, I would have no life whatsoever."

"Sounds evil to me, and I don't think it was his only reason."

"Okay, so what's your opinion?"

"He wanted to send the CD to Stephanie so that she and you would understand the power he has over you. If you think of an intimate act such as sex between two people being exposed, you have to believe other parts of people's lives can be exposed as well. I think Jacobs was sending you or Stephanie a message that he can expose any detail of your life that he chooses."

"This's a deep analysis for a prosecutor. Are you sure you aren't a shrink?"

Vincent laughs. "No, it just seems strange to do something that vile without a reason other than to break two people up. Do you have anything to hide?"

"Not that I'm aware of. No."

"How about your firm? What will your partners say if they are asked the same question?"

"They would agree that I have nothing to hide."

"It might be worthwhile talking to them. Are you still on leave?"

"Well, I am for now. I put in for another six months, but I'm not sure it will be approved."

"Why wouldn't it?"

"Originally, I put in for a year, which is standard policy, and they restricted it to six months."

"How long have you been off?"

"Only two months, but I want to know I have more time well in advance."

"What's the name of the partner giving you trouble?"

"Peters. Gerome Peters."

"I'll have a chat with him and the other partners."

"That will be a good thing."

"I think we are about finished here. Most likely, I will want to talk some more later."

I tell him I will be available anytime, and then give a sign to Chas for the check. Chas, as usual, hops right over and lets us know he will take care of the bill. I reach for my wallet, but Vincent grabs the check and pulls out a credit card. "This one is on the government. This is official business."

"Thank you," I say.

Chas comes back and takes the card. As Chas lays the card statement down, I take a final sip of coffee. Vincent signs and gathers his things. I get up and wait for him to rise as well.

"I feel better about getting a case together against Jacobs," he says. When he gives me a smile, I feel better too. Hopefully, the boys in Ecuador can come up with something. We shake hands, and then leave Judy's. Vincent tells me he will be in touch, which with any luck will be sooner rather than later. I watch him get in his car, and then turn to walk across the parking lot to my vehicle. My next stop is a visit with Ned since the day is almost three-quarters gone.

Vincent's starter motor begins the familiar noise, but a concussion that knocks me to the concrete cuts it short. In total blackness, I hear, see, and feel nothing.

Chapter Seven

I wake to a loud humming in my ears. It feels like having an electrical transformer in my head. From the restaurant, Chas runs toward me. When I turn to my right, I can make out Vincent's car—a ball of flame. The heat reaches me all the way over here. I can't hear any sounds other than the humming, and it feels like someone has punched a mute button on a slow motion movie. I can still see Chas running, but it seems as if it will take him forever to reach me. When I try to get up, I realize that I'm almost totally paralyzed. The best I can do is move my head slightly to the right and left. My arms and legs don't respond to the signals my brain sends. Hopefully, it's not a permanent situation, but I just can't seem to get my limbs to respond.

Finally, Chas reaches me and says something that I can't understand. He leans closer and, at last, his words come in through the humming sound.

"You okay, Mr. Cannon? You okay?"

My voice rasps and breaks when I say, "I'm okay. Go and check Vincent."

Chas heads toward Vincent's car. The heat won't let him go too much further. He puts his arm across his face and makes a valiant effort to get nearer. Then he gives up and comes back to me.

"I can't get any closer. Judy has called 911. I don't want to move you, but can you tell me where it hurts?"

"I don't have any pain. I can't hear too well, but my real concern is fading ... I can move my arms and legs again. I couldn't at first."

"We'd better stay here until the EMS guys get here. I don't think your friend knew what hit him. You should have seen the blast. It was like a fireball. The sound wasn't too bad. Didn't even knock out the windows, which is a surprise."

"You know about explosives?"

"I worked in the oilfields before coming to Judy's. We used to do some dynamiting, and I can tell you, a blast like that should have blown out every window."

"Knocked me flat on my face."

"Yeah, I know, I saw you go down. Thought you were a goner."

"So, knocking me down and not breaking the windows sounds contradictory."

"Not really. You were close to the car. Had that been dynamite, you would have been in pieces."

"Glad they used something else."

Chas looks back toward the restaurant and makes a signal. Probably to tell them that I'm still alive. Judy comes out of the door, holding a cloth.

"Judy's bringing a wet towel. It will be good to wipe your face. You have a bunch of sand on it, which will get into your eyes. Oh good. I hear the EMS."

I reach up and grip Chas' elbow. "You've been so nice. Thank you."

"Don't want to lose one of my best customers, now, do I?"

I have a feeling Chas has real concern for other people. Obviously, he got into the restaurant business for a reason. The pay in the oil fields is twice what he could earn at Judy's. Whenever he waits on me, I have the feeling he enjoys his work. Judy arrives, and she and Chas make a fuss about getting the sand wiped off my face. Judy keeps saying she's sorry, and I keep saying everything will be fine. Of course, she'll need a new patch of the parking lot. The burning car may just dig itself to China before it's all over. I haven't had a moment to think about poor Vincent. When it finally hits, the anger takes hold of me. The realization that Jacobs has once again used brute force to eliminate a threat to his security sets in. I get this lost feeling again, which is a signal of the fear I have that Jacobs is going to get away with all he has done.

The EMS and fire crew pull into the parking lot. The EMS team comes to my side. They tell Judy and Chas to back away, which they do quickly. One asks me my name, and then takes my vital signs. The other comes up with a huge bag, which he snaps open. It doesn't take them long to determine that it's best to go to the hospital for observation. They explain that it's quite common to have some kind of delayed response to a blast. Also, one tech tells me that I have blood coming out of my right ear. He assures me that it is probably nothing, but should be checked out. I want to see Ned, so a trip to the hospital isn't all that bad. The guys get a stretcher out of the van and use a slip sheet to move me to it. They must think I might have some kind of spinal injury. Next, they immobilize my head.

While they work, they comment about the fire. One tech asks me if I knew the guy, and I tell him yes. "He is—er, was the Federal assistant prosecuting attorney."

"Wow," the tech says. "Someone sure wanted him out of the way."

The two techs lift me into the van. I tell Chas, and Judy thank you, and then they close the door. We pull out of Judy's and proceed to the Memorial hospital. What with Ned being shot, I've been there a lot lately.

*

It seems to take only a few moments to get to the hospital. I have a suspicion that I fell asleep, but am grateful to be here so soon. We pull into the receiving area and, before I know it, I'm on a table behind a set of curtains. I am having difficulty with time. Events come in jerks instead of free flow. One minute, I'm in an ambulance, and the next, on a table. A person in white looks at me, so I ask, "Everything all right?"

70

"The doctor will be here in a minute. I understand you were close to an explosion. Oh, excuse me, I am Nurse Warren—the ER nurse—and I'll be taking care of you."

"Nice to meet you, Nurse Warren. My name is John Ca—"

"Yes, Mr. Cannon. I know who you are. I was the first person to see you when you were admitted after that poor girl was killed in Port Aransas."

"I'm sorry, I didn't remember."

"You were out cold and had no idea where you were. How about now? Do you know where you are?"

"I do. I'm in Memorial Hospital. I must say, though, I lost track of time getting here."

"Thanks for telling me. We'll have the doctor check you out. Any pain?"

"No."

"The EMS tech said you had difficulty hearing. How is that going?"

"I can hear pretty well, but I still have a low-level hum in my head."

"Was the hum louder before?"

"I'll say. It was more like a transformer hum, only real loud."

"Okay. Don't quote me, but it's a good sign the sound is getting lower."

"Don't quote you?"

"You know, malpractice."

I refrain from going into my background at this time—knowing I'm a lawyer will probably shut down any conjecture on her part. I appreciate the comment about the sound getting lower.

"I know you're a lawyer, but I thought you should know your symptoms are looking good."

So much for my being low key. "How did you know?"

"Seriously, Mr. Cannon? You're one of the most famous people around here and probably in the world. The President gave you a medal."

"I haven't received it personally from the President."

"Oh yeah, but you will. I read in Time magazine about all the trouble you and Ms. Savard had in Washington. Now, you relax. I'm going to see what the holdup is with the doctor."

Now that I'm alone, I have time to think about what this latest attack on Vincent really means. Matt Jacobs must know the government isn't going to simply give up looking into his foul deeds just because he murders the Assistant Prosecutor. Maybe he's so arrogant as to believe he can control the government. Who's to say? Vincent seemed like the kind of guy to keep going until he put a case together. That's why Jacobs took him out. The one thing I can't understand right now is why he didn't take me out as well. Maybe he thought we would be in the car together, and he would get both of us. It doesn't make any sense for Jacobs to live and take Vincent. Maybe the hitman made a mistake. This all makes no sense right now.

"I'm back," the nurse says.

"I can see that. Is the doctor coming?"

"Yup. He'll be here shortly. Let me take your blood pressure and temp."

Nurse Warren goes about her task without a word. Normally, I would ask about the blood pressure, but right now I'm sure it is too high, and I worry that the hum in my head is some kind of incoming stroke. The thought that if I were going to stroke out, I would have done it already comforts me a little. In the end, I ask about the BP. "How's it look?"

"A bit high, but nothing to worry about. Your temp is fine."

"All good information. Thank you."

"So, what have we here?" says a guy who looks to be a doctor.

The nurse jumps in and explains that I've been in an explosion. She lets him know about my time lapse, hum, and high blood pressure. He nods and stuffs something in my ear, and then a flashlight moves across my eyes. "I think you'll be okay. Your pupils are responding well, and I don't see anything in your ears except some slight tissue tears from the explosion. You're a little swollen, and that is to be expected. A little time and the swelling will go down, and when the contusions in your ears heal, the hum will go away. We could take an x-ray of your head to be sure there is no internal brain damage, but you aren't showing any symptoms. You will need to watch the swelling and let us know if it gets worse."

"What about the high blood pressure?"

"My opinion, you're under stress, and it is normal for the body to react. Blood pressure is part of the natural way the body gets ready to defend itself. So, you should be back to normal before the day is over. I don't see any reason why you can't go home immediately."

"I appreciate that, Doctor. You mentioned an x-ray?"

"Yeah, we'll take a picture, and then if it looks normal, which I suspect it will, you can be discharged. Nurse Warren will call radiology, and they'll be here shortly. I'll be on the floor until the films come back. Nice seeing you, Mr. Cannon." The doctor is gone before I can respond.

"What's the doctor's name?"

"Oh, excuse me. I wasn't paying attention. I was making some notes."

"The doctor's name. What was his name?"

"Doctor Samples. Isn't he the nicest?"

I don't answer, and Nurse Warren doesn't wait for a reply. She goes over to a phone and orders a head shot from whoever is on the other end of the call. After she hangs up, she tells me they will be right over. Then she finishes the notes, gives me a nice smile, and disappears. The x-ray only takes a few minutes and, as the doctor suspected, it doesn't seem that I have anything wrong. I get dressed and go to the patient discharge area, where I pay my co-pay, and then I go to the reception area. I ask for Ned's room and, to my surprise, they've moved him out of intensive care. Now he's on the fourth floor. The young woman at the desk points in the direction of the elevators. I follow her directions and, after a quick ride up, find myself at the door of Ned's room.

"Knock, knock. Can I come in?"

"Hey, John. Welcome. Come right in. I'm so pleased to see you." Ned's eyes go wide. "Whoa, what happened to you?"

"Explosion. How'd you tell?"

"You should see your face. You look like you went ten rounds with a much better fighter."

"I haven't seen a mirror. I'm bruised, I'll bet. The doctor said I have swelling but didn't mention what I look like."

Ned shakes his head. "I'll say you're bruised. You look like one of those dolls made out of women's nylon stockings. What the hell happened?"

"Do you remember Vincent Herron, the Deputy DA?"

"Yeah, nice guy."

"He got blown up in Judy's parking lot right after we had lunch."

"You're shitting me."

"No. That's how I came to look like this. The power of the explosion knocked me flat on my face."

A mixture of horror and anger crosses Ned's features. "Why in the hell would anyone kill Vince?"

"Jacobs."

Ned stares at me, and his Adam's Apple bobs when he swallows. "Man. Just as you said that, I wondered if Jacobs had a hand in this. I can't stay in this hospital any longer. Get my clothes. We need to get out of here and start going through the evidence."

"You can't leave. You got shot four times. You need to rest."

"Nothing vital. Remember when the doc said all those shots hit nothing important?"

"Yes, I remember."

"I've been laying here thinking about how that could have been part of a plan. If I took four shots at some guy and I was a trained killer, all four of them would have gone through the heart or, at least, something vital. Don't you see? I was supposed to be out of the way when Jacobs took out Vincent."

"Why not just kill you, then?"

"Good question, which has no answer right yet. Anyway, get me my clothes. We need to get on this case."

I go to the closet and pull Ned's clothes off the hangers. I ask him if he has any underwear, and he tells me to look in the drawer. Sure enough, his boxers are there. I pull them out and hand them to Ned. He excuses himself, and I can see he is still in pain as he shuffles to the bathroom. Not connected to any drips, it's probable that he's close to discharge anyhow. That feels comforting, as there would be no way for me to stop him from leaving.

I hear something muffled from behind the bathroom door, and assume Ned is grumbling about how difficult it is to get dressed with all the bandages he has in place. He opens the door and, to my surprise, is dressed and looking normal.

"You got a car?" he asks.

"No. I came in an ambulance just like you."

"Damn. I'll have to call one of the guys on duty and have him come get us."

"We can take a cab."

"That will cost over fifty bucks."

"I'm good for it."

"Now that you mention it, it doesn't make much sense hauling an officer all the way here just to turn around and go back to Port A. Okay, let's get a cab."

I reach for my phone. Only then do I realize it's not in my carrier. It must have been blown off me, and is probably under some car tire in Judy's parking lot. "My phone's missing."

"Use mine. It's on the nightstand there."

I dial Triple-A Cab, and they tell me it will be fifteen minutes. I tell the dispatcher we will wait at the main entrance of the hospital. I'm almost finished when a nurse walks in and demands to know what's going on. Ned explains we're leaving, and the nurse throws a fit. She orders Ned to get back into bed, and instead of following the order, he walks toward the door. Never have I seen anyone get as upset as this nurse. She threatens to call security, and Ned just keeps walking. I follow, and the scene reminds me of a movie I saw once where someone shoplifted a bag of chips in a convenience store, and the irate owner followed him out of the store. Ned reaches the elevator and pushes the main floor button. The nurse keeps ordering him back to bed until the elevator arrives. Ned and I get on, and the door closes. We can still hear the nurse as we descend. "She's mighty upset," Ned says. We both laugh at the ridiculousness of his understatement.

The door opens, and we face a serious looking guard and what appears to be a doctor. Ned looks at the guard and says, "Excuse us. We need to leave."

The doctor holds up his hand. "Chief Tranes," he says. "I don't think you're ready to leave the hospital, and I suggest you return to your room. If you don't, this hospital cannot be responsible for your recovery."

"I understand, Doc, but we have an important case that needs our attention. So, again, if you will, please excuse us."

The guard stands firm and looks as if someone's given him orders not to let us pass, then he steps in between the doctor and Ned. "You do know I'm the chief of police in Port A, don't you?" Ned says.

"No need to play the police card," the doctor says. "Y'all can leave, but neither the hospital nor I will be responsible for any complications as a result of this action."

"That suits me fine, Doc," Ned says. He turns to me. "Let's get out of here."

Ned and I walk past the guard and the doctor, making our way to the front door. Outside, the cab waits at the curb, and it's a relief that we don't have to stand around while all the people staring continue their eye feast at our expense. We go through the automatic sliding doors and jump into the cab. It didn't occur to me that this might not be our cab. My tension eases when the driver asks, "You Mr. Cannon?"

The run to Port Aransas takes the usual fifteen minutes. I think back on when Ned drove, and he cut the time in half. Of course, the cabbie has to obey the laws, so north of one hundred miles per hour is not within his comfort zone. On the way, Ned calls his office and asks his team to go over my car to see if they can find anything unusual. He tells me he can't believe that Jacobs would only blow up the Deputy DA. When we get to Port A, Ned asks the driver to drop us at Judy's, where I assume my car still waits. With some relief, I see it in the lot, and we instruct the driver to pull over. I pay for the ride, as Ned struggles to get out of the cab.

"You okay?"

"Yeah, just a little sore that's all. Let me call my team and check to see if they've looked at your car." Ned gets hold of someone who gives him information; he says little but thanks whoever is on the other end. When he's done, he looks at me. "You got the keys? My team says they found nothing unusual about your car. No evidence of any explosives or timing devices."

"Yes, right here."

"Go ahead and unlock the doors, then. I still don't trust that there isn't something wired up on it. Stand back and hit the remote."

I activate the remote to unlock the car. We both stand still for a minute. Slowly, Ned goes to the passenger door.

"Well, here goes nothing." He yanks open the door, and all stays quiet. Then he stops and looks toward the restaurant.

"Is that Judy waving her arms?"

"It is. Wonder what she wants."

"She's coming this way, but do me a favor and meet her. I can't take any more delays. I'd like to get to the station and find out what our boys know about the explosion. I imagine we have a ton of evidence by now."

"Okay. Make yourself comfortable. I'll see what she wants."

"Comfortable? I'm going over this car with a fine tooth comb. Do you have a remote starter?"

"No. This model doesn't have one."

"Okay, go head Judy off. I'll deal with the car. Give me the keys."

I leave the chief and head toward Judy, who's walking on the central walkway to the restaurant. We get closer, and she has a smile on her face. We reach each other, and she says, "God, John, I'm so happy you're all right."

"Thanks, Judy. I'm fine."

"How's the chief?"

"Oh, mean as ever, but a little sore."

"I found your phone after the EMT guys took off with you. Here." She holds it out to me.

I smile and take it. "Oh, you don't know how glad I am to see this. Thank you so much."

Judy mumbles something about it not being any trouble, and then gives me a hug. She tells me to take care of myself. I promise to do that. Then I give her a hug back, and we say goodbye. With the scent of Judy's perfume on my mind, I walk back to the car. Ned waves me to get in.

He asks, "What was that about?"

"Nothing. Judy found my phone is all. Everything okay with the car?"

"Looked like she had more on her mind than just your phone." Ned grins, and then grows more serious. "I looked in the trunk and under the hood. Seems normal to me."

I blush in spite of the ridiculous innuendo and wish she did want more. Still, I keep up a front. "For heaven's sake. She's at least five years older than me."

"Uh huh. Go ahead and start her up."

I put the key in the ignition and start the car. We both sigh at the normal sound. Ned enjoys making me uncomfortable. I squirm and mumble, "Just returned my phone." Then I put the shifter in drive, and we head to the police station. The ride takes about ten minutes, and all the while Ned keeps this grin on his face. Every time I look in his direction, he smiles bigger and nods. Clearly, he feels better and thinks he has something to rib me about for the rest of the day. Not wishing to fuel his warped sense of humor, I say no more about it.

When we reach the station, Ned barely waits for the car to come to a stop before he opens the door. Before I can throw the lever into park, he's out on the pavement. I exit myself. Already, Ned's through the door, and I feel a little like a kid trying to catch up to Dad. When I enter the cool station, the sergeant waves at me to go to Ned's office.

Ned is on the phone, talking to one of his officers. He tells the listener to gather up the evidence notes and meet him in his office in five minutes, and then he hangs up. "You want some coffee?"

I nod. "Sounds good. Who was that?"

"The lead officer on the case. I asked him to get the team together and come talk to us."

Ned gets up from his desk, and with a little trouble, starts for the door. "Where're you going?" I say. "I'll get the coffee."

Ned agrees and returns to his chair. He sits heavily, and the squeak of the leather sounds like a protest. Ned lets out a groan, which I'm sure was extemporary. I make my way to the coffee service and get us drinks. When I get back, three officers sit at Ned's conference table. I give Ned his coffee and find a chair.

Ned explains to the group that he would like to review the evidence from the explosion in some detail, as well as ask questions. The officers look at each other, and then one asks, "Did we do something wrong?"

Ned laughs, and then says, "I'm interested in the case, as it was a Federal officer of the court who got murdered. I expect a shit-load of help will arrive at any minute from Austin and probably Washington. I need to understand exactly what we have before I shoot off my mouth. Nobody's done anything wrong, so don't go trying to withhold anything, even if you think it's immaterial. Any more questions?"

The officers get up and file out without saying anything.

I say, "They're a nervous bunch. Why are they on edge?"

"Probably because I wasn't at the scene to secure it. These guys have little experience with murder. Although, I must say, since you came to town, the opportunity to learn has certainly gone up."

"Haha, I'm laughing. Do you think someone messed up the scene?"

"I won't know that until I see the evidence collected. You and I ought to go back to Judy's after we've seen everything. We'll have a better idea of what we face if we do."

"Am I still deputized?"

"Of course. It's like a marriage. You don't get to start over every time something interesting comes along."

"Just checking."

As we finish talking, the first officer comes back into Ned's office, followed by the other two.

"We have it all in these three evidence boxes," he says.

"Put them on the table. We'll start with the one you're holding."

"Yes, sir." The officers place the boxes on the conference table in a line, with the one in the first officer's hands placed closest to the end of the table. The officer puts on a pair of cotton gloves and lifts off the lid. We all move closer to look inside.

"Tell us what you have," Ned says.

"Well, sir, here is the first evidence envelope." He pulls out what appears to be a plastic baggie. "This is the detonator device. Although it's burned badly and melted somewhat, we feel certain that a crude device, triggered by a cell phone, detonated the bomb."

"What makes you so certain?"

"Look here. You can still make out that this blob is a cell phone. A cheap throwaway, but a cell phone nonetheless. On the back, see these marks where the body of the phone was attached to something? I'm guessing it was secured to a board of some kind and wired to the explosive."

I lean in and say, "I remember seeing the same kind of device attached to a bunch of explosives on my boat before Jacobs blew it up. "And, Chief, this looks like the same kind of detonator used by Jacobs' men when they tried to blow up the Midshipmen."

Ned continues to look at the device and, without looking away, says, "That figures. If it's the same people. I don't want to rush to judgment, though. What else is in there?"

The officer places the bag with the cell phone down on the table and pulls out another from the box. "Here are some fragments of the explosive itself. It's C4."

"Chief," I say. "I know we shouldn't rush to judge, but Jacobs' guys used C4 on my boat."

"Yeah, I understand. We still need to keep an open mind."

Without being asked, the officer sets the bag down and pulls another from the box. "This was found in what was left of the trunk of Mr. Herron's car. It looks like the remains of a golf ball. See this little patch of covering? This is where the ball sat on the floor of the trunk. The heat was so intense that the rest of the ball melted—"

"All very interesting," Ned says. "What does this golf ball tell us?"

"It gives us an idea of the temperature of the explosion and combustion. This ball material melts somewhere south of 500 degrees. That's some heat."

"And what does that give us?"

"Not really sure. I think, if there was a question of the source of combustion, we could use the ball as a gage."

"Okay. I get that."

I say, "If Vincent plays—er, played golf, all it means is that he had a ball in his trunk. If he didn't, then we need to figure out why it's there. All in all, a good find by your team."

Ned makes a note in his book and nods affirmation. The first officer smiles at me. The chief seems like a hard taskmaster. We go through the remaining boxes and see a pair of Vincent's shoes, blown free of the carnage. Also, his briefcase wasn't found. Instead, they recovered hundreds of fragments that looked to be cindered leather. With the exception of his proof of insurance, which had been in the glove box, his papers all got destroyed. Though mostly intact, the proof of insurance resembles a piece of parchment paper. It feels nauseating to realize that Vincent's remains are shredded and burned and that some of his bones melted into the steel of his car. Pictures of the car show the intense heat. The frame has crumpled into a flat mass of steel. There's no way to determine the kind of vehicle just from looking at the pictures.

Ned says, "So, we have nothing that can be traced to the origin."

"No, sir," the first officer says. "We don't have enough left of anything to get a serial number or product code."

"It figures. These guys know what they're doing. Okay then, that will be all."

The officers rise and file out of the conference room. I look at Ned, who studies the golf ball. Finally, he speaks, "It bugs me that these guys know so much about getting rid of people."

"I agree. Especially since we have little unique evidence among all these pieces."

"Except it isn't even definable as separate pieces. We have one big blob here."

"The blob, in itself, should tell us something about how these guys operate. Couldn't we somehow cross-reference a similar explosion and trace the method to the perpetrators?"

Ned looks up from the ball. "You might have something." A glimmer of a more optimistic attitude crosses his face. "I'll get in touch with the FBI lab guys and see if they know of another explosion like this. Who knows, we might get lucky and get a name or some other piece identifying these guys." With some effort, Ned gets up and leaves the conference room. He walks down the hall with me close behind and enters his office, where he grabs the phone and buzzes the sergeant. When he answers, Ned gives instructions on securing the evidence in the conference room, and then hangs up. "I can't believe we all walked out of there and left all that stuff lying around. I think those bullets have addled my brain."

I laugh and say, "I don't believe that. You just had other things to think about."

Ned snaps out of his momentary funk and dials the phone again. He connects with someone named Uri, and I understand from the one-sided discussion that he called the FBI. He asks this Uri guy to do a full search of the database to find any similar circumstances where a building, car, or whatever has been blown up with little or no residual evidence. He mentions high heat and little blast field, and then the conversation ends.

Ned puts the phone down and looks up at me. "He said it could take a couple of days. There are a lot of files to go through."

"A lot like this one?"

"No, just a lot of cases that need to be sifted through. They don't categorize 'em by crime, so he's to do a keyword search, and that takes time."

"Okay, so what's our next move?"

"I don't know about you, but I'm famished."

"You want me to go get something?"

"Let's go over to the café and grab a quick bite. I'd like to see if we can do anything else tonight after we eat. Can you drive me there and then back here to the station?"

"Of course. I'm at your disposal. In case you haven't noticed, I'm not that busy right now."

"Did you call your firm?"

"Yeah. They, or rather Peters, is sitting on the decision. Funny thing, though."

"What's funny?"

"One of the last things Vincent said was that he'd talk to Peters."

"About what?"

"For one thing, to get more information about me. I got the feeling he was going to put some kind of pressure on Peters in addition to getting information. You know the old 'we will need John available' kind of thing. I reckon that he was going to try and get my extension approved."

"What the hell? Do we need the President to call Peters?"

"You can do that?"

"No, but it would be cool if I could."

We move out of Ned's office to the open air. When I take a deep breath, I can almost taste the Gulf. We get in my rental and go the two miles to the café. I always wonder why the café has no name other than *café*, which is lit in neon. Must be some reason. I'll have to ask Ned about it. We go in and take one of the tables by the front door. The waitress comes over and says, "Hi, gents. The special is meatloaf with mashed potatoes, gravy, and peas."

Sounds good to me and I let her know I'll have a plate. Ned orders a fish sandwich and fries. She asks if we want anything to drink, and we both order water. With a smile, she leaves us to turn the order in.

Across the table, I meet Ned's eyes. "I've been meaning to ask why this place has no other name but café?"

"Used to be called Shorty's Island café. Shorty died, and his widow took his name off the sign. I think she meant to replace it with something else. It was the Island café for a couple of years, but then the sign busted on the word Island, and she took Island off for good. The only thing left is café."

"Mmm. I thought it would be a bit more colorful than that."

"Well, sorry to disappoint, but that's the truth."

"Who are those two guys over there? Don't turn around to look right at them. Pretend you're looking around."

Ned drops a napkin and leans down to pick it up. Although the guys sit directly behind him, he catches a glance. "The guys by the other window, you mean?"

"Yeah."

"I don't know. Why?"

"They keep looking over here like they're worried about you and me."

"What do you mean, worried?"

"You know. Like they've just pulled a bank robbery and are sitting in a café and in walks the chief of police kind of worried.

"I doubt they even know I'm the chief. I don't have a uniform and am not carrying my weapon in plain sight."

"All the same, they look worried."

"Here's our food. Let's just have a nice meal, and you ignore those two."

With all that's happened, I'm wound tight. "Not sure that will be possible."

The server places Ned's sandwich in front of him and my meatloaf in front of me. I should have ordered the fish sandwich, as it looks like a big fish steak deep fried to a golden brown. It has to be fresh. My meatloaf looks good but doesn't have the same appeal as Ned's fish. Ned takes a big bite, and the crunch confirms its goodness.

Ned speaks up with a mouthful of fish sandwich, "Why won't it be possible?"

"One of them is packing a gun in a shoulder holster."

"How do you know?"

"I caught a glimpse of it when he leaned over to talk to the other guy. His jacket slipped open."

"Okay, just keep cool. I'll handle it."

"Oops, the guy just got up, and he's coming over."

"As I said, stay cool."

"Easy for you," I say. No sooner are the words out of my mouth, than the big man arrives at our table. His bulk shuts out the light, and I feel as if an eclipse of the sun just happened.

"Can I help you?" Ned stares up at him.

"You can if you're Ned Tranes."

"I am. Who are you?"

"May I sit?"

"Help yourself." Ned gestures to a chair opposite me.

The big guy sits. "My name is David Kruse, and I work for the FBI."

"Excuse me, but could I see some ID?" Ned doesn't pause with his sandwich.

David doesn't seem to mind showing his ID, and the tension around our small table drops a few notches.

"Please, forgive us for continuing with our meal, but we've had a tough day. So, what can I do for you, David?"

"We've been instructed to help with the investigation of the killing of Assistant Prosecutor Herron. The justice department doesn't take kindly to the murder of its employees."

"I can imagine not." Ned nods and takes another bite. After swallowing, he says, "The killing happened within the city limits of Port Aransas and is under my jurisdiction."

"Notice I said *help* with the investigation. We know this is your case, and we just want to provide any additional assistance you may need."

"I appreciate the offer, but at this point, I don't know what you could do to assist."

"How about reviewing the evidence, as a starter?"

"You're welcome to do that. I already sent some stuff to your lab in Austin. Maybe you could get a rush order placed on it. You're more than welcome to look over everything we have."

"That's great. Thank you for your co-operation. Why don't we finish up here, and we'll meet you at the station."

"You know where it is?"

"Oh yeah. In fact, I was told to treat you and Mr. Cannon with the respect due national heroes. We certainly know a lot about what you've been doing and appreciate your service."

Ned turns red and thanks David. The agent gets up and goes back to his table.

Ned waves to the two agents and winces, which tells me that he still hurts. "What do you think?" he whispers.

"I don't know. You ought to check him out before we trust them."

"I thought the same thing. I already texted FBI ops with my security code and asked for a profile on our Mr. Kruze. They should get back any minute. Personally, I think it a little odd that he didn't introduce the other guy or even explain who he is."

"Would the FBI assign someone to a case without letting you know?"

"Yeah, it could happen. And there may be an e-mail on my secure computer explaining the whole thing. Let's not leave here until I get a text back with the information, though."

I nod in agreement and take the opportunity to look the two guys over in more detail. I have to admit, they look like FBI guys. They have on casual clothes, but their shoes are dress oxfords. Casual dress is always hard for those who need to wear a suit every day, and to think of pairing up the casual apparel with proper footwear is not high on the list. I can imagine that it would never make the list of a Federal agent. Ned looks at me with an expression that I can only interpret as asking for a status of what the two are doing. I tell him, "They're still looking our way. They seem to be finished with whatever they were eating. Now they're nursing coffee."

Ned finishes his sandwich and takes a long drink. Little waves in his glass of water accompany the vibration of his phone. "I just got the text. Let me check it out." I sit in silence while Ned looks down at his phone, which for some reason, he hides under the table. He has no expression on his face, and I have no clue what the message says. At last, he looks up at me and says, "They're legit. They're from the Austin bureau office, and under instructions to support our operation. Like I figured, I have an e-mail explaining the situation." He looks relieved to have the help. At least, his expression isn't one of consternation, although he doesn't go so far as to show actual pleasure.

"We can leave now. Let's go over and welcome our new support team to the case." Ned gets up and winces again, and then lets the server know we're ready to go. He walks over to the agents and extends his hand to the other man, and then waves me over. We all shake hands. The other guy's name is Rolf—a subordinate of David's. The server hands me the check, which I pay with a twenty, and I tell her to keep the change. A six dollar tip on top of a fourteen dollar tab causes her to twitter. I am not trying to act like a big spender; I just want to leave right away. Ned seems to share my feelings, and so we exit the café without much more conversation.

Chapter Eight

We get to the police station ahead of the agents. Ned tells the sergeant that the FBI agents will arrive soon, and to escort them to the conference room when they get here. We walk back to his office. "So, what do you think of them?" Ned says.

"Really not sure if they will help or hurt."

"What do you mean?"

"I just have a feeling these guys aren't too bright."

Ned sits at his computer, takes a moment to adjust to the pain, and taps a few strokes. He looks at the screen, frowns, and taps a few more times. "I'll be damned. These guys are heavyweights."

"Now I have to ask, what do you mean by heavyweights? You on the bureau site?"

"Yeah. I'm looking at their records. I have a supervisor's clearance, so if I'm on active duty, I can go hunting for new folks if I need to staff up. It looks like these guys have done some serious time in very dangerous situations."

"How serious?"

"Afghanistan, Kuwait, Iran—wow, even a stint in the Crimea."

"Both together?"

"Well, it looks like it. Let's just say, their tours of duty seem to overlap in what could be characterized as not random."

"Is that unusual?"

"You bet. It's obvious they weren't concerned about a covert operation since the bad guys would figure out a pair in an instant."

"What did they do?"

"By the looks, they were mostly involved in political organization."

"What the hell's that?"

"FBI-speak for establishing friendly government relations."

"I thought the CIA handled most of that stuff."

"It looks like these two *were* assigned to the CIA. Which could mean they handled some rough assignments. If something went wrong, the CIA would deny they even knew these two. As FBI personnel, our CIA brethren would throw them to the wolves. Obviously, nothing went wrong since they're still with us, and I don't see anything in the reports."

"Maybe they will be of use after all."

Almost on cue, the sergeant interrupts and tells Ned that the two FBI agents are in the conference room. Ned rises quickly, all but ignoring his pain, and we go next door. Ned walks in and gives a hail good brother kind of greeting. He asks if they need anything, and both decline. We all sit around the large table. Ned leans back in his chair and takes on the air of a college professor, ready to listen to his students present their oral exams. "So, where do we start?"

David turns to Rolf and raises an eyebrow, which I interpret as a confirmation of an early conclusion among the two of them that Ned and I are a couple of hicks, who are outclassed in the investigation. "Well," David says. "Why don't you tell us what you've found out so far?"

"That's going to be one short-ass discussion, seeing as about all we found out is Vincent Herron was blown up in his car, and the explosive of choice is C4."

"No idea who did it?"

"Oh, we have an idea who's behind it, but no evidence to prove it."

"Okay, then. Who do you think is behind it?"

"Do you know who Matt Jacobs is?"

"Yeah, who doesn't? He's a billionaire who controls a lot of oil."

"Anything else?"

"Not sure I'm at liberty to say."

Ned flares his nostrils. "What the fuck does that mean, agent Kruse?"

"Um. We've had Jacobs on our radar ever since the Annapolis Midshipmen episode."

"You know who screwed up his little caper?"

"Sure, it was John here."

"So why the hell do you say you're not sure you're at liberty to say?"

"The operation has been kept within the need-to-know level. My boss doesn't need to know. Do you have any idea how uncomfortable it is to go sneaking around your boss?"

"I can imagine it's not too comfortable. Why is your boss not on the need-to-know list?"

"It's real simple. We think someone in the Bureau has either knowingly or unknowingly tipped off Jacobs that we are watching him."

"How do you know?"

"We had special ops go in and bug the hell out of Jacobs' house, car, boat, and any other place we could find. For the last three weeks, he's said very little to anyone in all these places. We suspect that he knows the bugs are there and is being real careful. Of course, it's not natural not to talk with people who enter your home. He must be holding up signs or something."

"Do you think he has a special secure room?"

"We looked at all the blueprints on three of his places, and nothing showed up. When our boys went in, they didn't find a safe room anywhere."

I can't stay quiet anymore. "I'll bet he has a room in each place. It's not like him to be lax in security."

"I guess you know him quite well."

"Yeah, he keeps trying to kill me, so you might say we're real close."

Ned and Dave and I keep talking about Jacobs, but Rolf doesn't say a word. He sits paying attention, but not offering any information. To pull him into the conversation, I look at him and say, "Do you have any theories about the safe room?"

Rolf clears his throat and looks over toward Dave, who gives him a nod. "I think that this Jacobs fellow has enough money to buy anything he wants, and has the confidence that goes with it. Someone who knew about the placement tipped him off about the bugs. He's smart, not doing anything about the bugs. At the same time, I think he's dumb for not setting up some conversation scenarios to keep us from knowing he has knowledge of the devices. He's playing arrogant, and that's dangerous in this game."

I drum my fingers on the table. As soon as I notice, I stop. "Yes, he's arrogant, all right. And, yes, this conversation thing is unusual for him. He would be talking with people in his house. There could be something else."

Rolf raises his eyebrows. "Like what?"

"Maybe he just doesn't want to fool with setting up a charade. He's thumbing his nose at us." When I say the words, my anger rises.

Rolf smiles. "I thought that as well."

Ned speaks up, "So, what leads you to believe that someone in the FBI tipped him off?"

"We placed some super-secret listening devices in there, which couldn't have been discovered with conventional snooping equipment. R and D just developed these, and to my knowledge, there is no counter measure developed yet."

Ned sits forward. "So, even if Jacobs swept his places, his security wouldn't have picked up the bugs?"

Dave grows more animated. "We don't think he has enough money to get a counter measure this quickly. We do think that some asshole in the Bureau is on his payroll."

I think of the incident with Agent Ramon in the hotel in Washington. "I have a name which should be checked out."

Dave looks surprised and says, "Out of the blue, you have a name?"

Ned looks at me like I might be having a stroke. I say, "I was disappointed with this person's attention to detail while he was in charge of protecting Stephanie—er, Miss Savard and me." I go on to explain the phone story.

All three sit quietly, and finally, Rolf looks at Dave, who says, "Okay. I'll look into Agent Ramon as a possible risk. I have to admit, your story makes me uncomfortable. Also, we had thought that the mole was inside the FBI, not the Secret Service."

Ned speaks up, "If we have a Secret Service agent whom we think is on Jacob's payroll, how does that gel with your assumption that it's an FBI agent? What do you guys intend to do?"

Dave answers after a time of silence, in which he appears to mull over a few choices. "It could be that the Secret Service guy and the FBI guy are working together. One thing we could do is try and take advantage of the double agents, so to speak."

Ned leans back again. "Let's hear it."

"Well, we could plant some information with agent Ramon, and then wait to see how it plays out."

"You mean, lay a trap for Jacobs?"

"Yeah, I would say that describes it well enough."

I ask, "In order to capture him?"

"That would be one kind of trap. I'm thinking more of a trap where there is lawbreaking done, which won't be difficult to prove, and leaves no doubt that Jacobs is guilty."

I cannot hide my pleasure. "You're talking my kind of language."

Ned says, "That's a tall order. Do you have something in mind?"

"Not sure. I need to ask John a few questions before I commit myself to a plan."

"Okay, shoot," I say.

Dave pulls a piece of paper out of the folder he placed on the table. "Let me see. Oh yes, here it is. Do you think Jacobs would go for another attempt at destroying a national monument?"

I don't hesitate. "Hell, yes, he would."

"Do you think he would be dumb enough to actually visit the target?"

"He's not dumb, but I would say he'd want to see personally that all is in place. He's fed up with others making mistakes."

"That's good. What kind of target do you think he would be most interested in?"

I think for a second. "If he could take out something like the stock exchange or a major building on Wall Street, I think he would be in one hundred percent."

"Whoa, I never thought of those possibilities."

Ned shuffles and looks uneasy. "You guys better know what you're doing. What if something goes wrong and Jacobs actually accomplishes his goal?"

Dave furrows his brow. "You're right. This thing would have to be planned carefully and briefed at the highest level."

I have to add my two cents worth, "What makes you think you can influence Jacobs to choose a target we want?"

"Good question. If we know for sure whom the agent is on Jacob's payroll, we could pump some information through that would make the target irresistible. For instance, if we assign the FBI agent to act as a security liaison for an important person scheduled to open the stock market, it would be a natural incentive to do the job. Of course, we'd have to tie Agent Ramon to one of ours to make the ID possible."

Rolf's eyebrows look like they're about to hit the ceiling. Ned covers his mouth and chin with his hand and looks doubtful regarding the success of this plan. Dave waits for one of us to speak. I ask, "Who do you have in mind?"

"Oh, I don't know." Dave waves his hand. "How about George Bush?"

None of us says anything. Finally, Ned speaks up, "Yes, we can decide on the important person later. The plan will be tricky, to say the least. There are so many people involved in Wall Street who could get hurt. Can't a nice quiet museum be more the choice?"

"Well, we could think of MOMA or the Guggenheim. They're impressive and could be attractive as targets." Dave looks at Ned.

Ned shifts position again, and says, "What I'm saying is, the target has to be attractive and also one where we can handle any problems."

"Of course, we don't have to pick the target today. We can put a bunch of newbies on it, and they can do a proper risk analysis before we choose. In general, how does the misinformation-catch-Jacobs plot sound?"

"Pretty good," I say. "Although, I'm more than anxious to see Jacobs punished." I look at Ned, "How about you?"

"Well, you know I'm real conservative when it comes to this kind of operation, but for right now, it sounds okay."

Rolf, quiet until now, speaks up, "We'll give you a full overview of the plan before we execute anything."

Dave frowns. "I'm sure Ned would expect nothing else."

Rolf's face shows a blush, and he looks sorry he said anything at all. Being rebuked by his boss in front of us has to be mortifying. Dave doesn't pay any attention to Rolf's discomfort. "So, at this time, are you in?"

Ned thinks for another few seconds. "You can count on John and me for anything you need."

Ned can see that I'm willing to do anything to get Jacobs. I'm glad he spoke for me, as it looks like we're a team without even having to confer. I throw in a small statement of support anyway, "I agree."

Dave looks pleased. He smiles and says, "Good." Then he rises, and Rolf gets up too. "We'll be in touch to work out the details. Rolf and I want to go to the site of the explosion one more time." Dave sits again, as does Rolf. Dave continues, "We'll come back when we have something on the plan for you to review. Fair?"

Ned nods in the affirmative.

"In the meantime, we'll put an expedited request on the lab to see if we can come up with anything that might help to prosecute the case. I want to be clear with you; our interest is finding who killed Vincent, yet we also want to see if we can trap Jacobs. The bureau has warned me that we have nothing on him now except suspicion. I have personally read enough about this guy to be convinced he is guilty. I want to prove it."

Ned leans back in his chair, showing his discomfort. "I totally agree with you. Let's get this done."

Dave and Rolf get up again. We all shake hands, and they leave. I wait until I'm sure they've gone. Then I say, "You think these guys will come up with something?"

"They have the experience to deliver. My main concern is the agent on Jacobs' payroll. It might be hard to keep any plan private if they can't find the guy."

"I'm sure Ramon has something to do with all this. He was there when Stephanie got shot. He may even have allowed her to step out of that car knowing she would be shot."

"Well, if so, let's hope these two get the info to peg him."

Chapter Nine

I leave Ned and go home to take a swim. On Ned's insistence, a couple of officers go with me. They follow behind in a patrol car. On the way, I figure it's about time to start thinking about a new boat. I've had my eye on a sweet one, which should fill the bill. It's another Hatteras Sport Fisherman sixty-five footer. The only issue is that it's down in Ft Lauderdale. I'd like to take some time and go down there and look at it. Since Ned is nervous about me driving home without protection, I'd better ask him if he thinks it will cause a security issue if I go. I could do it in a couple of days max, so it shouldn't be a big deal.

At the house, I go in and change. Through the window, I see the patrol car in the driveway. The eighty-five degree Gulf temperature feels cool to the skin. I go under quickly to get used to the water, as usual. As I float on my back, it gives me a feeling of total relaxation. While floating, for some reason, the water brings me back to thoughts of Stephanie. A quick pro and con analysis leads me to plan to call Stephanie. Just the thought of doing so makes my stomach feel funny again—a tense feeling, which most describe as butterflies. It feels more like ice cubes to me.

Finished with my swim, I make my way to shore and try to tell myself that Stephanie will be glad to hear from me. Our previous call didn't seem all that warm, so I hope this is different. After I dry myself off and put on clean clothes, I pick up my phone. Seated on my bed, I pull up her number. Her phone rings twice, and I get an icy feeling that she won't answer since my caller ID tells her it's me. Almost like she could read my mind, she answers with, "Don't worry, John, I will always talk to you."

"How did you know I was afraid you wouldn't pick up?"

"If I were you, that's exactly what I'd be thinking right now."

"I'm glad you did pick up."

"Why's that?"

"I have to apologize for those pictures."

"Oh, I don't know. They were good pictures. I expect the camera was a nice one."

"I mean the subject matter."

"I know what you mean. I'm trying to keep it light."

"Stephanie, I'm really sorry."

"Sorry for what? Sorry that I was the recipient, or sorry to disappoint me?"

"Did I disappoint you?"

"We didn't have a committed relationship. I know how you think, and I know you wouldn't want me to be disappointed in you. I mention it because I'm sure it's on your mind. I must say, I was surprised. I thought you would be smart enough to understand that the Barsonne woman was not on your team."

"So, you *were* disappointed in me."

"I guess when it comes down to it. I felt sorry for you."

"Oh my God, that's worse."

"No, not really. You need to be accountable for your mistakes, but if I were disappointed in you, there would be no reason for us to continue this conversation."

"You think we have any chance?"

"Chance at what?"

"Yeah, I don't want to go there right now, seeing as I'm so embarrassed by what happened."

"Hmm. From what I saw, Sarah looked like a fun time."

"I'd hope, going forward, that we could be friends."

"I have too many friends now. I sure don't need any more."

"Sorry to hear that."

"Why?"

"I like you a lot."

"You've done nothing to make me want to be friends. Now, if you could think of something more, I might be in the market."

"You're kidding me."

"Think about it. You're a good man, and I'd like to get to know you better. What else can I say?"

"I've lost my train of thought."

"Yeah, gets you off the old guilt trip thing, doesn't it? I would like to see you, John."

"Oh man, you don't know how glad I am to hear that."

"So, when?"

"When?"

"God, you're making this more complex than necessary. Let me state it a different way. You book a flight, and I'll pick you up at the airport. You can book a flight can't you?"

"Damn, Stephanie. You're the best."

"Get off the phone and book it."

"I just thought about going to Ft Lauderdale to look at a new boat. Would you like to join me there?"

"I think I can get some time off. Yeah, sure, let's do it."

"Stephanie?"

"What?"

"You've made me real happy. I was so nervous about this call."

"I'm glad. Now, go and make some arrangements and let me know where and when to meet."

"All my treat, okay?"

"Will that make you feel better?"

"Yes."

"Okay then, big spender. I can be bought."

We ring off, and I have to lie on the bed for a minute. Stephanie's reaction has almost taken my breath. Obviously, I worried for no reason, and the old saying that ninety-nine percent of our worries never come true sure seems to fit this situation. I call Ned and let him know that Stephanie wants to see me. Also, I ask him what I need to do to take off for a few days. He says that I can't go off by myself and that he needs to check with the Secret Service for the protocol. Then he tells me to hold on while he makes a couple of calls. After a few minutes, he comes back.

"Sorry, John, but the Secret Service thinks you're a risk to the President, given the fact that you're a national hero. They think the trip is okay, as long as you have a couple of agents go with you."

"I just want to get away."

"Sure you do, but you need to think of others. What would happen if you got grabbed? The PR problem alone would be enough to cause the President nightmares. You don't need to put him through that."

"I understand. Okay, but we need some alone time."

"Yes, of course, you do. I'm not surprised Stephanie took you back, by the way."

"You're not?"

"Naw. You make a cute couple. You all hero-like, and she all military-like."

"I'm not sure where it will go."

"I would just relax and not try to push it."

"You're so right. Anyhow, I think we'll go to Ft Lauderdale to check out a new boat."

"Man, that sounds like fun. You want me to go and hold the door for you?"

"You're so funny. You have more important things to do than babysit me."

"I just want to make sure you treat the lady right."

"Don't worry. I will."

Ned says goodbye, and before he hangs up, tells me that the government will be flying Stephanie and me to Ft Lauderdale. I sit on the bed, amazed as to the amount of money spent to keep me from getting killed by Jacobs' people. I call Stephanie back and let her know that we'll be going to Ft Lauderdale by private plane. She doesn't seem surprised at all.

"It's the way the Secret Service feels more comfortable," she says. "Can you imagine someone getting a bunch of passengers involved in trying to get to you. It would be a nightmare."

"I just feel bad about the expense."

"Get over it. In the long run, it's cheaper this way. You take care and let me know the arrangements."

"Okay, thanks. I'll call when I have all the details."

Stephanie and I end the call. As I sit and think, my phone rings and causes me to jump.

"Hello?"

"Mr. Cannon?"

"Yes."

"This is special agent Samples from the Secret Service."

"Yes, Agent. What can I do for you?"

"I am in charge of setting up travel arrangements and need to know when you and Ms. Savard plan to travel to Ft Lauderdale."

"I haven't given it much thought, but I think two days from now would be great."

"Can you go today?"

"Today? What's the rush? Excuse me, special agent, but I need to get some verification of your credentials."

"We have reason to believe we need to move quickly in order to minimize the amount of information that might get leaked to those who don't need to know. If you will wait a moment, I will patch you into someone who can verify my identity."

The phone goes quiet for a moment. Someone knocks on my door. I get up from the bed and pull the door open. On my porch, stands Ned. "Come in," I say. "I'm on the phone with a guy who calls himself Special Agent Samples."

"Yeah, I know him. He makes the travel arrangements."

Agent Samples comes back. "I called Ned Tranes, and he should be there."

"Yes, he just got here."

"Let me speak to him, please."

I hand Ned the phone. "He wants to talk to you."

Ned takes the phone and nods a couple of times while looking at me. He smiles and then hands the phone back to me.

Ned says, "This guy's legit. Also, I'm proud of you for asking. I guess you are learning."

I hold up my hand and turn my attention to the agent. "I'm sorry, but I didn't hear you just then. Could you repeat what you said?"

"Yes, I asked again if you could leave today."

"Well, I'm good anytime. Have you talked to Ms. Savard?"

"I figured we would have a three-way now and ask her. Hold on."

I'm glad I get a lot of input with the government. After waiting for a moment, I give Ned an eye-roll, and then a ringing phone sounds. "Yes, hello?" Stephanie says.

"Ms. Savard, this is Special Agent Samples of the Secret Service, and I have Mr. Cannon on the line as well."

"Oh hi, John. Long time no hear." A lighthearted tone lifts her speech.

I say, "Agent Samples wants to know if you can go to Ft Lauderdale today."

"Well said, sir," says Samples.

"Today? Oh, my. Let me see. What have I to do to get ready? Hmmm, I don't think it will be too hard. A bathing suit and something to wear to dinner are about all I need. A couple of pairs of shoes, maybe." Stephanie pauses, and agent Samples and I stand by.

"Sure, I can go. What time?"

"A car is waiting out front of your place now. We will take you to LaGuardia, and then fly you to Texas to pick up Mr. Cannon."

"A car outside, you say? My goodness, you don't waste any time, do you?"

"Well, we can't afford to—"

"I understand, agent. I'm Navy, you know."

"Thank you, Ms. Savard."

Tension tightens the agent's voice. If we could see him, I'm sure he'd have sweat on his upper lip. I say, "Okay, so Stephanie is set. How long until you pick me up?"

"You will need to go to the Corpus Christi Naval Air Station. It is about twenty minutes by car. The flight time to Corpus Christi from New York is a little over three hours, and Ms. Savard will lift off in an hour. So, let's say, four hours from now."

"Okay, that makes it six o'clock Central time. How long to Ft Lauderdale?"

"Around two hours from liftoff."

"So, an eight o'clock arrival. That's not too bad. Okay, let's do it."

"Very well. Any questions, Ms. Savard?"

"No, I'm good. I see the car, and I packed while I talked. See you there, John."

"Bye, Stephanie." Since she's gone already, I'm not sure that she heard me. "Agent Samples?"

"Yes, I'm here."

"The car is in three hours?"

"Correct. You will have two agents accompany you."

"Okay, thank you. I don't have any more questions."

"Very well. I wish you a pleasant flight, then. Goodbye."

I don't have a chance to reply because, like Stephanie disappeared, he is gone. "Man, that was something."

Ned says, "What was something?"

"The whole last minute arrangement thing."

"You know how the gov' works. If it's inconvenient, it gets done."

"I didn't expect to get a private flight."

"There isn't another way that's as reasonable."

"I hope this doesn't turn out to be a mess like that trip to get a phone."

Ned sighs, then says, "You need to relax. The Secret Service knows what it's doing. If they say to fly private, they've thought it out. I'm glad they have Stephanie under their care as well. Remember, I mentioned she should be guarded as well.

With all that's happened, I didn't get around to it. I'm very glad I don't have to regret that delay."

"I'm so glad she's protected now, and that reminds me, did you get any word on the investigation of Agent Ramon?"

"No one has told me, but I get the feeling I don't have a need to know."

"It's funny that the two guys supposedly guarding me were so incompetent."

Ned thinks a minute. "If I know the service, those guys were operating under orders. Someone told them that loose supervision would be okay. All that has changed now. The supervision has to be as close as possible."

"I hope so. You want anything?"

"A beer would be nice. Don't get up. I know where it is." Ned turns and goes to the kitchen. He calls from there, "You want one too?"

"Sure, sounds good. Let's go on the back porch." I join Ned in the kitchen and take the beer, and then I go out the door and sit in one of the Adirondack chairs. He follows and takes the other. I take a drink and look out at the Gulf. "Sure is nice here."

"Yes, you have a nice view." After a sip of beer, he asks, "So, the Secret Service is picking you up here?"

"Yes. They're due in about three hours. Sorry, I should have let you in on the conversation."

"That's okay. Life moves fast these days."

"What are you going to do without me for the next two days?"

"Well. I hope I get some more info from the FBI lab that will help find out who blew Vincent away."

"Do you think you'll get anything that will help?"

Ned looks down at his beer. "I'm optimistic, but I also have to accept the fact that I might never get any information."

"I think it was a for hire situation, and the guys are long gone. Just like Jacobs likes it."

Ned seems a little distracted and, after a moment, turns to me and says, "You're probably right."

"What do you think will come out of that little plot the FBI boys are trying to hatch?"

"Ah, who knows? I don't have much faith." Ned takes a long drink of his beer and empties the bottle.

"Would you like another one?"

"Yeah. Maybe another six or so, but I do need to get back to the station. The call from that Samples guy surprised me. He made me a little nervous, in that I thought something was wrong."

"I can imagine. I don't know how you got here that quick."

"He called me a while ago. It must have been before he called you. Anyway, I'll see ya." Ned gets up and goes through the door. I thought he was gone, but he sticks his head back through the door. "The Secret Service guys are outside. Okay if they come in?"

"Sure. Tell them to make themselves comfortable."

Ned laughs as he leaves. He mumbles something to the two agents, and then I hear his SUV fire up. I suppose I should get up from here and be at least a marginally good host to my handlers. When I walk into the kitchen, I come face to face with two guys in suits.

"Mr. Cannon? I'm Agent Sieverts, and this is Agent Welles. We have been assigned to you for your safety."

"Nice meeting you. Do you have first names?"

"I'm Leroy, and this is Jesse."

"I'm John. Maybe we could call each other by first names if you're okay with that."

"Well, as long as the boss isn't close, we don't mind."

"Does Jesse have a voice?" The two look at each other and can't help but laugh.

Jesse says, "Yes, but Leroy is bigger."

We all have a laugh, which I think is good to relieve the tension. Leroy speaks up and explains that they will need to stay close, which I acknowledge as a good idea. Then I ask them if they have any relaxed clothes.

"Relaxed?" Leroy says.

"Yes. We're going to Florida, and you two will stand out like Penguins in a chicken yard."

"Chicken yard? I like that," Jesse says.

Leroy explains he and Jesse have clothes for the trip and will be changing once we reach Florida. I let them know they can change here if they wish. They seem a little undecided, and then Leroy tells Jesse to go and get the clothes.

"I'm sure you'll be more comfortable," I say.

Leroy nods and goes to the window. He watches Jesse open the rear hatch of the black Suburban in the driveway. He seems satisfied that no one is going to jump Jesse while he gets the suitcase. The hatch slams shut, and then Jesse comes through the front door. Leroy shuts the door and throws the deadbolt.

"Where can we change?" Jesse says.

"Right through that door is a guest room." I point down the hall.

Jesse smiles and carries the bag into the guest room. In a few minutes, he comes out and looks more casual in his khaki slacks, polo shirt, and deck shoes. Leroy takes his turn and comes back dressed and looking much the same as Jesse. "Are you packed?" Leroy says.

"I haven't even started."

"Do you need help?"

"No, I can handle it. I'll only need a few minutes. Would you guys like anything?"

"We're fine. Maybe water later," Leroy says.

"Just help yourself. There's plenty in the fridge. I'll go pack now."

Leroy nods, and I go to my room. I have to say, having two guys watch everything you do feels a little nerve wracking. It's like having guests come and camp out at your house. It's good that we're leaving here to go to a hotel; I'm not sure how I would entertain these two otherwise. I don't know the protocol for guards. Do I ask them to play a game of cards? How about when I sit down to dinner—do they join me? Where do they sleep? Good thing we're moving since this whole thing mystifies me.

I turn from worrying about my handlers to putting a bag together. My soft duffle-type bag will fit almost anything I need. With the private flight, I won't have to worry about checking bags, but I feel better without a big hard bag. I stick with casual wear and plan to carry a blazer. I can't imagine any place that I would need anything more formal. Just in case, I pack a tie and a dress shirt.

Chapter Ten

Finally, the time comes to go to the airport. We all climb into the SUV; the two agents up front, and me in the back seat. With the third row of seats folded down, our stuff fits behind me easily. Jesse and Leroy say little on the way to the naval air station. They do check in routinely to give whoever is in charge an update on our progress. We come to the guardhouse and Leroy presents his ID, and the guards wave us through. Must have called ahead, I think, as we come to another uniformed guard who directs us to pull onto the tarmac.

"We're here," Leroy says. He puts the SUV in park and turns off the motor. "We need to wait for the jet." Jesse turns around and gives me a smile. Do they know I've done this before? Still, I appreciate that Jesse is trying to assure me that all is normal.

"Here they come," Leroy says. He points off in the distance to a barely visible small plane, obviously on a flight path to land. We all watch as the aircraft grows and gets closer to the ground. In a flash, the pilot flares out and touches the rear wheels first, and allows the craft to touch the nose wheel to the ground in a smooth and gentle maneuver. In short order, the plane pulls off the active runway and onto the taxiway leading to our position.

The engines whine loudly while the plane approaches, and then after a quick turn, they wind down until silence settles. My heart pounds as I look forward to seeing Stephanie again. It seems like forever until the door of the plane makes its drop to the ground. The pilot descends the stairs and walks toward us. He carries a clipboard, and his uniform shows that he's a major in the Air Force. Leroy indicates that we should wait in the SUV. Then he opens the door and greets the major. The two talk, and then Leroy waves to Jesse and me to get our things. We get out as well and move to the back of the vehicle. Jesse raises the hatch, and I grab my bag. "Want me to get Leroy's as well?" Jesse shakes his head—probably used to carrying Leroy's luggage, and it seems to balance him. We move toward the plane.

The major grabs my duffle. "Welcome aboard, Mr. Cannon. I am Major Withers and will be flying Ms. Savard and you to Florida today."

"Nice meeting you, Major. I can get this bag."

"Please, sir. You are a guest of the Airforce, so I'll take it."

Guest of the Air Force. Sounds like this might be okay. "All right, Major, here you are."

"Thank you, sir. You can go right on board. I will put the bags in the luggage section."

I go up the stairway and turn into the cabin. Stephanie sits in the first forward-facing row. My smile could rip my face, it is so wide. She wears a big smile too.

"Pardon me, Miss, but is this seat taken?"

"It is now. Have a seat, Mr. Cannon."

"How have you been? My God, you're a sight for sore eyes."

"Oh, John. You know how to sweep a gal off her feet, don't you."

For a second, the smile jumps from my face, and I'm worried she's referring to Sarah. To cover, I smile wider. "Only some gals."

"Yes, so I've been told."

Uh oh. Am I sure she isn't smacking me for the Sarah thing?

"What's the matter, Mr. Cannon? Cat got your tongue?"

"I-It is so good to see you," I say in the hope that I can divert any negative thoughts should they be there.

"It's mighty good to see you, too. Okay, I'll admit, I want to punch you, but you are so damn cute I can't bring myself to do it."

I sit. "You have my permission to punch me if that's what you need to forgive me fully."

Stephanie chuckles. "I'll reserve that punch to be used any time I choose in the future. This should settle the grudge satisfactorily. Now, how have you been?"

"Did Ned give you any information?"

"He got shot, right? No, he and I haven't talked for a while. And the last time we did, I was well pissed at you."

"Yeah, he told me."

"Oh? What did he say?"

"That he would like to punch me in the nose."

"Goodness, well let's just keep the reserve punch as a warning not to repeat your bad boy behavior."

"On condition that we don't need to talk about this any more?"

"I can imagine, but one rule of your reserved punch option has to be a discussion about the punchable affair in between needs to be minimized."

Stephanie laughs hard. "Okay, you got it. Your seat belt fastened? Looks like we're about to leave."

"Thank you. With all the energy coming my way, I didn't even hear the door close or the engines start. Did the two agents get on?"

"They did. Right when you were stammering about how good it was to see me while trying to divert my attention from your bad boy status."

Stephanie makes me laugh, and I'm not sure if it's what she says or relief for being forgiven. "Yeah, you sure had me there."

"I love to see you sweat. You do so infrequently."

"Enough about me. How are you feeling? I understand you've made a full recovery, but I would like to hear it from you."

"Hold on. We're starting our takeoff roll, and it will be easier to talk once we leave this bumpy runway."

I give Stephanie a thumbs up and lean back in my seat. The takeoff is normal. The last time I flew with the Air Force, we had to perform anti-missile maneuvers and got slammed hard from side to side. In a few minutes, we're comfortable in the air, and Stephanie leans in closer.

"I feel excellent. There was a time when I had some double vision problems as a result of swelling. I can tell you, though, I wouldn't recommend being shot in the head to anyone."

"Do you mind talking about it?"

"No, not at all. I didn't feel anything when it happened. I woke up on the way to the hospital. One thing that hurt like hell was my wrist. I landed on it wrong when I fell."

"I couldn't get to you. The car pulled away and left you lying there with Ramon on top of you. I was frantic."

"I heard. It must have been heartbreaking for you."

"Not as bad as for you."

"I didn't know anything."

"Yeah, but having Ramon on top of you."

"You hush, John."

We both laugh, which is a good thing right now. Finally, that tense feeling in my stomach eases. The plane levels out, which means we've reached initial altitude. "You guys want something to drink?" Leroy says from the rear. "I have the bar back here. Soda, too, if you want one."

"Would you like something?" I undo my seatbelt and start to rise.

"A water would be nice."

"One water coming up." I move to the rear. "How's the water supply?"

"Got bottles in the fridge. How many?"

"Two, please. You guys having anything?"

"On duty. We'll have soda."

"Great, I like clean and sober. Thanks for the drinks. Oh, do you have a glass and napkin?"

"Sure enough. Here you go."

I go back to my seat, hand Stephanie the bottle of water and napkin, and then ask, "Glass?"

"Sure, now that you've brought it. Any lemon?"

I start to rise, and Stephanie stops me. "Just kidding. This is fine. So, what are we going to be doing in Ft Lauderdale?"

"I thought we would go to the hotel and check-in. Since it will be quite late, we might as well get some dinner, and then look at the boat tomorrow. How's that sound?"

"Great. How many rooms did you get?"

"Two, of course."

"Humm, Mr. Cannon. You are so provincial."

"Well, if you don't like yours, or if I don't like mine, we can switch."

"What if I don't like either?"

"Then maybe we can share."

"I like that option."

I've always loved Stephanie's direct approach to what could be considered touchy subjects. We sit in silence for a few moments, and then I say, "We could also take a little cruise to try the boat out."

"I like Florida. There're so many places to go. We could take the boat to the Keys and have lunch at one of those marina places. That sounds real romantic."

"From where I sit, with you, McDonalds would be romantic."

"You make me blush, John Cannon."

"Seriously, though, do you have any residual problems from the bullet wound?"

"None at all."

"That's great news." I don't go into the fact that Stephanie would never have been shot at had she not been with me. I couldn't figure out any way to say that it's my fault without sounding like I'm looking for sympathy. Had I said I'm glad there are no problems, it would sound like I'm trying to get off the hook. Better to keep my mouth shut.

Stephanie leans her head back and says, "I'm going to take a little nap. Don't think me rude, but I need a couple of minutes beauty sleep."

"No problem. I could use some snooze time myself."

"Great. If I snore, shake me."

I sit back in my seat. When I close my eyes, it brings a peaceful release to the day. I don't even remember falling asleep, but the major announcing our initial approach wakens me. I didn't catch the whole announcement. I look over to Stephanie, who seems to be wide awake already. "What airport are we going into?"

"Ft Lauderdale-Hollywood International."

"I would have thought we would land at a military field."

"Yeah, it used to be military, but was retired back in 1946 and given to the county here."

"You keep track of this stuff?"

Stephanie shrugs. "Sometimes the little pieces of information just stick. I don't know why."

We touch down, and Leroy comes to our seats. "You two sit tight until we unload the bags. I'll let you know when it's time to deplane."

"Okay," I say.

He moves to the front of the craft and takes up a position at the door. The plane continues to taxi and finally comes to a stop outside of a terminal that looks like it might be a charter hangar. The engines wind down slowly, and then Leroy deploys the door. The humid Florida air seeps into the cabin. Leroy goes down the stairs. Jesse moves forward and takes a position by the door. He looks to be a backup to Leroy. Out of the window, I see a dark SUV. It sits near the door, and I can't help but get a feeling in my stomach again. The episode with Stephanie has me a little gun shy. Jesse speaks up and lets us know that it's time to deplane. Stephanie gets up, and I follow.

We go down the steps and into the open door of the waiting SUV. Jesse follows and waves to the major. Then the door goes back into the fuselage, and the outboard engine makes its startup whine. Jesse jumps into the front seat. I turn around, and Leroy already sits in the back. He gives me a smile, which I return. So far so good. Jesse says something to the driver, and we pull away. As we cross the tarmac, we build up speed. Then, as the driver heads into a slow right turn toward a gate, a blinding flash rolls over the vehicle from the rear. Black residue from the blast obliterates the rear window. The driver hits the accelerator and swerves to the left, and we now travel parallel to the plane. A fireball blazes where the plane used to be. It's hard to tell, but the entire body seems to have blown away. In the back, Leroy hollers to the driver to pull further ahead and then stop on his command, as the rear end of the SUV is on fire. "Is there an extinguisher on board?" he yells.

The driver shouts back that the extinguisher is on the left side of the rear compartment. Leroy looks down over the back. "I see it." He jumps into the back and holds his arm between his face and the increasing heat. "We have jet fuel on the rear. Stop now." The driver hits the brakes, and we all jerk forward. My seat belt locks and digs into my collarbone and ribs. Leroy hits the rear seat hard.

"You okay?" I call.

He doesn't answer but jumps over the seat and says to me, "Open the door."

I pull the lever, and the door swings wide. The heat from the fire rushes forward. Leroy excuses himself, and I slide toward Stephanie, and then he jumps out the doorway. Jesse, with his weapon drawn, gets out as well. "Everyone out," Jesse shouts. "Move to the front of the vehicle and keep going."

Stephanie opens her door, and we both slide out her side. We move to the front, as Jesse ordered. Jesse and the driver stay back with Leroy. They have some trouble putting out the fire. Leroy sprays the rear of the SUV with the extinguisher, but the fire seems resistant. Sirens wail in the distance. When I look over at the fiery remains of the airplane, I see lights blinking off in the distance. I squeeze Stephanie's hand. "You okay?"

"Yes, but I think we should move a little further away. The guys aren't going to be able to put out that fire. Jet fuel is tough to extinguish."

"Those guys should do the same, shouldn't they?"

"I would say so. If that tank goes, they could be burned badly."

I let go of Stephanie's hand. "Stay put."

With a frown, she asks, "Where you going?"

"I need to warn the guys. I can't just stand here and do nothing."

"Don't be stupid. That's dangerous. The thing could go up any minute."

"Middle name."

"What?"

"Stupid. I'll be right back." I run past the SUV and yell at the three of them. "Y'all better get away. That tank could blow any second." Leroy looks at me, and then smiles. He waves the other two away and joins us."

"Mr. Cannon, you need to move away. We can't have you getting hurt on my watch."

"You coming?"

"Yes. I will follow you out of here."

We all hurry to where I left Stephanie. As we reach her, the gas tank ruptures, and a ball of fire lifts the rear of the SUV off the ground. "Well, that's it," Leroy says. "We're no longer in danger from the fire."

"What about those who caused it?" I say.

"Yeah, that's a horse of a different color. I need to get another car here. Jesse, you can put that gun away. If these guys had intended to follow-up with a ground attack, they would have done it already. I figure that was a missile of some kind. Don't know what else would make such an explosion from out of nowhere."

"You mean like a Patriot?"

"Something like that. We'll find out later, I hope. If your friends have access to remote weapons, this will be an interesting assignment."

114

Just when I was going to ask some more questions, Leroy turns away and gets into a discussion with someone on his cell. The fire trucks reach the plane and get busy pumping foam onto the burning hulk. Another truck screams to a stop by the SUV and does the same. I look at Stephanie, who looks calm. Her training as a naval aviator must have taught her to remain calm in times of danger. My cell phone rings, and when I pull it out of my pocket, I see there's no caller ID. This can't be good. Nervous, I answer, "Hello?" As calmly as possible, I look at Stephanie, and she gives me a look that begs the question, who?

"Hello, John." Immediately, I recognize Matt Jacobs' voice. I mouth "Jacobs" to Stephanie, but she doesn't get what I'm saying.

"What the hell do you want?"

"Nice friendly greeting, John. I thought you would be a little more cordial to someone who just spared your life."

"Spared my life? What are you talking about?"

"Don't tell me you don't see that inferno over on the tarmac?"

"Yeah, of course, I see it. Tell me you were behind this."

"Now, you know me better than that. I would never make such an obvious move to eliminate you."

"Then what do you mean, saved my life?"

"I said spared not saved. Spare means to set aside for possible use later. Oh, John, I didn't save your life. Your life will be mine to take when I choose. I spared it. I'm surprised you use words so casually."

"Listen, I'm in no mood to play word games with you. Tell me why you called."

"I simply want you to know that I haven't forgotten our little grudge and will look forward to settling it."

"Just give me a time and place, and I'll be there to kick your ass.'

"I can believe you will try. I don't want you to be too upset when I have the last laugh, so for now, let me just say the missile that hit that plane was a few minutes late per my instructions. I might even say you owe me one."

"Fuck you, Jacobs."

"I'm the one who should wish the same to you, John, even though your crude expression is not part of my personality. That broadcast you and your pals put together made me want to kill you so bad. I can also say, I am surprised you were able to pull it off."

"I suppose I should take that as a compliment."

"I have to respect your resourcefulness. You have outfoxed my team twice now. I wonder how long you can keep it up."

"For as long as it takes to see you in prison."

"Oh, that will never happen. I want you to sleep well, John. As well as a person can who knows I can eliminate you anytime I want."

"Why don't you then?"

"I have more in store for you than simple death. I want you to suffer deeply. Oh, by the way, I am sending you a little picture of a friend of yours. I hope you find it amusing. Goodbye, for now, Mr. Cannon. I'll be seeing you."

The phone goes dead.

Wide-eyed, Stephanie says, "My God, was that Jacobs?"

The notification tone of my phone sounds when a text arrives. "Yes, that was Jacobs. He said he was responsible for the missile."

Stephanie's hand goes to her mouth. "No way."

"I'm afraid so. He just sent me a text. I'm almost afraid to look at it."

"A text of what?"

"He said it was a friend of mine."

"You going to look?"

"I suppose I should, but I know it won't be something I want to see."

"Do you want me to look?"

"No, I'll do it." Leroy comes up just as I'm about to open the message. "Who called?"

"The guy who says he was responsible for the missile."

"No shit. Did you get his number?"

"Yeah, Leroy, he gave me his number and will be waiting for the authorities to pick him up."

Leroy looks sheepish. "Stupid question, right?"

"I guess we all do that. No harm."

"Thanks."

"He did send me a text."

"What's it say?"

"I don't know. I haven't read it yet."

"Don't you think you should?"

"Okay, here goes." I punch the message icon, and a picture pops up. It looks like Stephanie without any clothes, and then I realize that it's the still frame of a video. I push the play arrow, and the video is of Stephanie, poised naked over a man. It looks like she's getting ready to mount him. He says "wait" and takes the camera and points it at his face. It's Jacobs. He smiles and says "enjoy this" into the camera, and then turns it back to Stephanie. I click pause. I want to go to the grass and throw up. Instead, I hand the phone to Stephanie. "You should see this."

I feel weak and need to sit down. I can't see any place, so I just crumple to the ground. Leroy grabs my arm and tries, unsuccessfully, to break my fall. I hit the ground with a heavy thud, which knocks the air out of my lungs. I end up in a sitting position. I try to get my breath back and wish I had some oxygen to breathe. The more I try to catch my breath, the less I seem to be able to get any. Leroy tries to get me to my feet, but in my shock, I'm a dead weight. I don't want to get up and would be just as happy if I could die right here. How Jacobs got Stephanie to fuck him is beyond my ability to understand. He can't have anything on her since her brother is dead. I'm sure she has other relatives, but whom could Jacobs pick that would make her do such a vile thing. I had this kind of torture coming, but it doesn't make it any easier. First Sarah, and now Stephanie. To kill Jacobs with my bare hands would make me ecstatic. I make a vow to dedicate myself to bringing him to justice and, in addition, getting the opportunity to kill him. I flash on getting a gun.

As I think of the gun, Stephanie comes over and sits on the grass with me. "You okay?"

117

I pull up a fistful of grass. "Do I look okay?"

"No, I guess Leroy and I aren't thinking today."

"That's fine. You have a lot on your mind. You know, like what you'll say about that video."

"John, I—"

"It's okay. You and I weren't committed to each other. You're an adult woman. You can give your body to anyone you choose, even if he was the one who killed your brother."

"Oh my God. You need to listen to me."

"Why. What could you say that would make any difference in how disgusted I am right now? Oh, I know I had this coming because of Sarah. You could have picked anyone off the street, and I would have understood your desire to get back at me."

"John. I have no knowledge of this video."

"What kind of story is that?"

"I don't know this person or how this video was made."

"Okay, but how did you get yourself into a situation where you are climbing on someone's penis and letting him film the whole thing?"

Stephanie is crying and getting hysterical. Her words all run together. "I have no memory of this I remember waking up one morning with a strange feeling that I had been drugged I can't even remember where I was the night before." At last, she sucks in air. "Don't you understand how difficult it is to know that that motherfucker was inside me without my knowledge or approval?"

"Stephanie. I'm sorry. This now is making horrible sense. Jacobs somehow got to you and gave you something which wiped your memory and control of your actions." I take Stephanie in my arms, and she lets go with sobbing tears. She is such a strong person, and I feel sorry that I doubted her motives. Also, it is hurtful knowing such a strong person is near a breakdown. She continues to be wracked with sobs as I hold her close.

I murmur into her ear, "It will be all right. We will get this scum. Believe me, I will make him pay for this."

"I feel so helpless. I don't feel safe anywhere. This video is evidence that we're both vulnerable to whatever he wants to do." Her sobbing stops, but she continues to keep her face buried in my shoulder.

"We will overcome this." As I say this to her, I want to believe it myself.

Leroy comes up with Jesse. "We have some cars coming onto the tarmac. We need to get to the hotel."

"I understand," I say. "When they get here, we'll be ready."

The cars pull up. Two SUVs. After I help Stephanie to her feet, I take the cell phone from her limp hand. One SUV is full of armed people. Leroy explains, "They are Homeland Security Agents and will go with us to the hotel."

Stephanie and I get into the other vehicle. I keep her close and wrap my arm around her, and she puts her head on my shoulder.

"Armed guards aren't going to help," she says.

"Let's not worry about that now. We're alive, and that is all that counts."

"For now."

"Shush."

Stephanie lets out a little laugh, and I know it will be okay. Even though it's probably evidence, I delete the message from Jacobs. I never want to see it again.

Chapter Eleven

We arrive at the hotel and check in. I need to talk to Ned, but am afraid to use my cell phone. I encourage Stephanie to go ahead upstairs and clean up and maybe take a nap. Then I let Leroy know I need to talk to Ned but don't want to use my phone.

Leroy nods. "I understand." Then he offers his cell. When I think it through, I don't feel safe using his either. After all, Ramon is still the boss, and I can't be sure how much information we can keep from him. I don't trust that Leroy's phone is clean. I can imagine it being bugged by whomever in the Service is co-operating with Jacobs. While I ruminate, Jesse goes with Stephanie to the elevators.

Instead, I go to the gift shop, in the hope that they have cell phones. I ask the clerk, who says, "No, but there's a phone store right down the block."

"Thank you," I say, and then return to Leroy. "I need to get a phone." Even though he looks confused, he goes along.

While we head to the store, I say, "Please, don't tell anyone I'm getting a phone."

"Why would I do that?"

"I'm not sure how much you guys report, and this is a personal thing with me."

"Okay, but I don't see why you don't want to use my phone?"

"It's real simple. I don't trust anyone. Okay?"

We get to the store, and I buy a disposable. The clerk goes on about how the phone can be reloaded and asks me what seems like a hundred questions about plans. I ask her to give me the basic plan. I'm not sure the phone has enough charge to finish a call, so I decide to go to my hotel room to plug it in. In ideal circumstances, I would have preferred to make the call out in the open where I wouldn't be overheard, but I'll have to trust that the hotel room hasn't been compromised. I'll ask Jesse if he went into my room just to make sure.

We reach the hotel and take the elevator. I ask Leroy, "Do you think Jesse checked my room?"

"I don't think so. He won't have a key."

"Can't he just get one with his ID at the desk?"

"Yeah, I suppose, but normally, since I'm with you, I'd do the checking like he did with Ms. Savard."

"Can you find out?"

He gives me a piercing stare. "There's more to your question. What the hell is going on?"

"Did you not see the plane go up like a Roman candle?"

"Yeah, but how's that connected with not trusting the people assigned to protect you?"

"How does Jacobs always know where I am? No matter how secure the information?"

"You think someone inside is leaking?"

"You said it, not me."

"Shit. That would be a problem."

"A big fucking problem." When we reach the room, I say, "You want to check it out?"

Defensive, Leroy says, "Of course, that's what we do. Stay here."

"No, I'm coming with you."

"Yes, right, we don't want me to plant a bug without you knowing, do we?"

"If I knew who it was, I would tell you. For now, I'm not trusting anyone."

Leroy gives me a frown, but I think he understands. He moves around the room, checking in the closet and bathroom, too. I stay so close to him that he almost runs me over when he turns to leave.

"Excuse me. I think it is clear."

"Thanks, Leroy. I know you think me crazy, but I need to do my own thing for a while."

"That's okay. Just don't leave without calling me. I'll be close in case you need anything. My room is right next door. You going to do dinner?"

"We could go down in about thirty minutes. I'll let Stephanie know if you tell Jesse."

"Done. See you later." Leroy pulls the door shut behind him.

Once I'm alone, I pull the phone out of its packaging and plug it in, and then I look up Ned's number on my other phone. Ned's phone rings, and he answers immediately. "This is Ned."

"Ned, this is John."

"John, for shit's sake, what was all that at the airport. Whose phone is this?"

"I bought a disposable. I don't want to take any chances. Is your phone secure?"

"Let me call you right back." The phone goes dead.

The ring startles me, as I've never heard it before. "Yes, Ned."

"I'm on a more secure line. The other one is my personal, and who knows how many times it's been hacked since this mess has started. So tell me, what's going on?"

"I got a call from Jacobs a few seconds after a missile took out the airplane Stephanie and I were on to Ft Lauderdale."

"You're kidding me."

"No, I wish I were. Jacobs also sent a disgusting video of Stephanie to my phone and let me know he was going to torture me as much as he could."

"You and Stephanie need to get out of Ft Lauderdale as soon as possible."

"What about these Secret Service guys? They any help?"

"We need to engage more force. This is getting out of hand. Those guys are limited. I'm gonna get another SEAL team activated. We need to make sure you're not either kidnaped or worse."

"I certainly appreciate that, and hopefully, we can set some kind of trap for Jacobs."

"He seems to stay one step ahead of us. It would be nice to get him."

"Have you heard anything from Dave and Rolf?"

"Not a thing. They were on my list to call tomorrow. I think they've had enough time to investigate Ramon. I'll be interested in what they say."

"How do we get out of here?"

"Give me a few minutes. I need to call the team lead and get some people to join you there. I also have to get someone at the Secret Service who can get another plane down there."

"Agent Samples?"

"I don't think he works twenty-four-seven, but there has to be somebody on duty."

"What should I do?"

"Get you and Stephanie in the same place and wait for my call."

"We can do that."

"Okay, kid, I'll call you back shortly."

The phone goes dead again. I feel a little better now that I've talked to Ned. I look at my watch—almost nine o'clock. My stomach feels like it's eating itself. I give Leroy a call and suggest we get some room service. He asks about my call to Ned. I don't tell him much, seeing as he will get instructions soon, but I do let him know Stephanie should be in the same place as me. He thinks it makes sense and says he will have Jesse bring her here. I tell him that when Jesse and Stephanie get here, I'll order. He rings off.

A few minutes go by while I try to think about our next flight. Should we go to Port Aransas or somewhere else? Well, it won't be my choice if the government teams get involved. The call from Jacobs shook my confidence. I haven't made up my mind what to do about Stephanie. She's been taken advantage of in the worst way, and I can hardly hold it against her. I feel so sorry for her, realizing she had no knowledge of Jacobs' perversion. When did he have the opportunity to grab Stephanie and film her having sex with him? I must shake off these thoughts. Unfortunately, I still have the vision of Stephanie on top of Jacobs in my mind. When I shake my head, it doesn't help. A knock sounds at the door, which does manage to chase the vision from my mind's eye.

I look through the peephole. Jesse and Stephanie stand on the other side. After I open the door, I wave them in. "We should have dinner in the room. Why don't you look at the room service menu, and we can order."

Stephanie looks at me but seems far away.

"You okay?" I say.

She glances at Jesse, and it's clear she doesn't want to say anything in front of him. "Jesse, could you excuse Stephanie and me for a moment?"

"Oh, certainly. I need to go and see what Leroy is up to anyhow. Don't answer the door for anyone but Leroy or me."

"Thank you. We won't." He leaves. I put my hands on Stephanie's shoulders. "Tell me what's wrong."

"That video."

"You need to get that behind you. It wasn't your fault. Obviously, that bastard drugged you."

"It doesn't change the fact that I've been violated and feel dirty."

I take Stephanie in my arms. "I'm sorry for this and my poor choice of words, but like you, I feel violated as well."

With a sniffle, Stephanie nods. "We need to work this out, and I'm not sure we can do it alone."

"We'll get whatever help we need. You and I can get over this and look forward to better times."

"I'm not so sure about that. The fact that you saw me on top of Jacobs makes me want to be sick. I'm not sure I can get over that."

"But, if we can't get by this, Jacobs will have won. He will have come between us and destroyed what could have been a beautiful thing."

"Keep talking." Stephanie gives me a watery smile. "You're helping."

"I just think that you and I are so much better than Jacobs. To have a snake like that destroy our future is just wrong."

"Can you get the vision out of your head?"

"Right now, it's gone. Does it come back? Of course, but it can be told to disappear."

"How do you do it?"

"I just shake my head, and it goes. And, I admit, it's easier for me because I want it to disappear so that I can go on with you."

"That's so nice. Oh, John, I'm so humiliated, I could scream."

"You're innocent. Please, believe me."

"Can you imagine what it feels like to know that that monster molested me, and I didn't even know it until I saw the video?"

I rest my chin on her head. "It has to be mortifying, but you need to fight that thought. You had nothing to do with it. Sure, he used you, but he never got to your mind, so you're still free."

"Thanks. I will try and let it go. Can you bear with me while I try to get over this?"

I release Stephanie and turn her to face me, and then I look her in the eyes. "I'll give you any help I can."

She smiles. "Okay, when I get weird, just let me talk it out, okay?"

With a warm smile, I say, "You got it."

Jesse comes back and knocks on the door. When I open it to him, he asks, "Do you two need more time?"

"We're good," I say, and Stephanie nods her agreement.

Jesse says, "Leroy is on the phone, getting instructions. Looks like we're about to have company."

I tense up. "What kind of company?"

"Some heavyweight SEAL team."

"You guys are off the case?"

"No, they told us to stay put 'til they get here."

"How long will that be?"

"Leroy said about thirty minutes. We'd better plan on leaving."

"Yeah, I get that." I don't mention that I've talked to Ned about this already. "We should get some dinner before we head out. Stephanie, what would you like?"

"I'm not hungry. Salad will be enough."

"Okay." I look at Jesse. "How about you?"

"I'll just have a burger and fries. Leroy will have the same."

I dial room service and place the order, and decide to have the burger as well. Before hanging up, I order water, as I don't think anyone is in the mood for much more.

"They'll be up in about twenty minutes," I say, and then turn to Stephanie. "Why don't you lie on the bed a minute."

"I think I will. Please, excuse me."

Stephanie goes over to one of the queen-sized beds and drops onto the mattress. Jesse leaves to check with Leroy. I sink into the chair near the window; I feel so tired. There's nothing more exhausting than fighting for your life. Stephanie asks me what is so funny, and I guess I must've had a goofy expression on my face. I explain about the thought about fighting for life, and she gives me a smile.

"Pretty funny, huh?"

"I'm smiling because I think you're the dearest person right now."

"Damn, you'll make me blush."

"Please, come over here and sit on the bed with me."

When I get up, I can't help but feel a hundred years old. I sit on the bed and put my arm across her shoulder. "How's this?"

"Couldn't feel safer. Where are we going, do you think?"

"I figure we'll go back to either Washington or Port Aransas."

"Why Washington?"

"These guys will think it's easier to protect us there."

"But won't it be possible for Jacobs to attack us in Washington as well?"

"Yes. That's why I think it's also possible that Port Aransas might be the destination."

"Or, how about some remote place in the Midwest somewhere?"

"Yeah, that too." A knock comes at the door, and I go to the viewing port. A room service waiter stands there. Jesse also comes into view. Once more, I open the door. Then I wave the room service clerk into the room. He asks, "Where would you like the food?"

I tell him, "Just leave the cart, and we'll work it out." Then I take the check and sign it. "We're good for now."

Leroy comes into the room, almost like the smell of food lured him there. I get the salad for Stephanie, and she sits up so I can set the plate on her lap. Then I place a bottle of water on the end table next to the bed. She seems interested in the salad, which is a good thing. Jesse and Leroy have already dug into their burgers.

Hungry, I get my burger, and then sit on the edge of the bed with Stephanie. I take a bite and almost want to inhale the rest, I am so famished. Instead, I take it slow, and after swallowing a mouthful, I ask, "So, is everything set?"

My question catches Leroy with a mouthful, and he holds up a finger. Once he clears the food, he says, "Yes, it looks like a SEAL squad will be here within the hour. Once they are here, we will go back to the airport, where a plane should be waiting."

"Where will we go?"

"I don't know. I'm not sure they have set a destination yet. I think this caught someone with their pants down. Oh, sorry, Ms. Savard."

Stephanie stifles a laugh and waves her hand in a gesture of "think nothing of it."

"So, we probably won't know until we're in the air?"

"That's my guess. My boss told me to stay with you both until we reach the destination." He shrugs. "Strange order."

I sit up straight, food forgotten. "How so?"

"We're normally cut loose when the military steps in for protection. My boss was adamant about staying with you."

"Ramon, you mean?"

"Yeah. You know him?"

"Yes, we both know him. He guarded us in Washington."

"Oh yes, he was the one who was in charge when Ms. Savard got shot."

"Yes, he was." Suddenly, the room goes quiet. I think Leroy now feels he's said too much. It seems that Ramon wants him and Jesse to stay with us so that they can report our destination, and then he can report it to Jacobs. I need to place another call to Ned. In a hurry, I finish my burger, and then go into the hall to give my friend a call.

"Yes, John?" Ned answers on the first ring.

"Did you know the Secret Service has been asked to stay with us until we get to our location?"

"Yes. We've started to set the trap for Jacobs. You'll have to go with the punches on this. Also, you didn't say anything bad about Ramon to his boys did you?"

"No."

"Good. I don't have to remind you not to say anything."

"Not me. I'll keep any comments to myself."

"Good man. Talk to you later."

Ned rings off, and I don't know too much more than before I rang. His advice is good, and I will just have to grin and bear it, after all. Back in the room, Leroy tells us that he's been in contact with the SEAL squad, and they should be with us in about five minutes. With a nod, I go into the bathroom and splash some water on my face. I can't shake the weariness—I thought eating would help, but it hasn't. Exhausted, I dry my face—all I want to do is to lie down. It will be impossible, so I'll have to rally somehow. A few deep breaths make me light-headed but seem to do the trick. I rejoin the group.

Leroy gets up to answer the door. He looks through the port and swings the door wide open. Five troopers stand waiting to come inside. One, who appears to be the leader, moves into the room. "Mr. Cannon and Ms. Savard," he says. "I'm Lieutenant Wilson. We are here to escort you to the airfield. Please, come with us."

Stephanie gets off the bed, and she and I go into the hallway. We follow the lieutenant to the elevators. The rest of the squad escorts Leroy and Jesse. Two of the SEALs take a position between Stephanie and me and the agents. Almost as if they don't trust the agents to be with us without being watched.

We take the elevator to the lobby, and then go to the curbside. Three Humvees sit lined up in front of the hotel. "Looks like we get a military ride," I say. Stephanie gives my arm a squeeze, which I believe tells me not to get separated from her. I smile and pat her hand in response. There is no way I will allow her to go anywhere without me.

Lieutenant Wilson directs us into one of the Humvees, and the rest get into the other two. Wilson gets in the front seat and turns to us. "Hope you don't mind a little bit of a rough ride. We didn't have time to get more comfortable vehicles."

"I'm sure it will be fine," I say.

The lieutenant orders the team to deploy, and we pull away from the hotel. As we start moving, I remember I haven't paid for the rooms. "Lieutenant?" He doesn't hear me, so I speak up, and he turns around.

"Yes, Mr. Cannon?"

"I didn't pay for the rooms. We need to go back."

"That's okay. I'll give them a call and leave the rooms on your card. Okay?"

"That would be swell. Thanks."

I can't hear much of the conversation due to the noise in the Humvee, but it sounds like he connected with the hotel and asked them to send a receipt to my home. He gives me a thumbs up, and I say "thank you," which I'm sure he could make out. "I guess no worries now."

Stephanie smiles and nods. "You can relax. It's all taken care of for the time being."

I can't help but feel that Stephanie is giving me a little jab about the fact that I would, indeed, be bothered if I couldn't take care of the rooms, despite all the more important stuff going on. I'd worry about the impact on my credit score if I ran out on a hotel room, not to mention feeling guilty for the dishonesty. Of course, they always had my credit card number, so it would be nigh impossible for me to skip. We were supposed to stay two nights so, at least, the lieutenant's call canceled the second night. I'm almost tempted to ask him if it was clear we were checking out early. I catch myself before I make a fool of myself. The curse of OCD.

Stephanie puts her head on my shoulder and closes her eyes. She's had a rough few hours here in Florida. I feel so sorry that I just handed her the phone without thinking it through. I should, at least, have waited for a better time. Of course, when is a better time to face something like that? With the hope that it will work out, I glance at her and feel some relief at the peaceful look on her face.

In what seems like a few minutes, we get to the airport. We pull up to a rather large airplane, which looks like it will seat more than ten. Probably the military equivalent of the Boeing 737. The lieutenant tells us to wait and gets out. At the other Humvees, he gives the orders needed to make a coordinated move to the airplane.

He comes back and opens the door on Stephanie's side and asks her to step out. He leans in and tells me to wait until Stephanie is on board. Four SEALs surround Stephanie as she goes up the stairs. They return for me, and I enter the cabin to find what could be a commercial airliner. There must be seats for eighty. Stephanie sits about midway down the aisle. I go to her, and she slides over to the window and nods to the aisle seat. Grateful, I flop into it. "Some plane, huh?"

"Yeah, this is the C40 Clipper, which is the military version of the 737."

"You ever flown one of these?"

"I sure have. I don't have enough hours to be safe, but I could fill in as a co-pilot."

"Well, let's hope we don't need to call upon you."

Stephanie smiles and, looking ahead, I can see the rest of the team getting on. Leroy and Jesse take seats up front. A couple of SEALs go past us and take up a position behind. The door closes, and it looks like we're on our way. Stephanie takes my hand, and I give hers a squeeze.

"I guess we're off."

Chapter Twelve

"I think I'll go ask the lieutenant where we're headed." I get up. Stephanie doesn't hear me; she is sound asleep. I don't blame her. At almost eleven o'clock, I'm pretty much dead on my feet as well. I manage to slide out without waking her and head to where the lieutenant sits.

"Hey, Lieutenant." He is dozing as well, and I startle him. "I'm sorry for that. I just want to know where we're going."

"That's okay, Mr. Cannon. I was just catching a few winks. Yeah, I wish I knew where we were going, too. I don't have a need to know, though, so I'm along for the ride the same as you."

"The captain knows. Would he be able to tell us?"

"Sure, but, unfortunately, he's in the cabin and the door is locked. He's not allowed to open it for anyone once we're airborne."

"I guess I'll have to wait and be surprised."

"Yes, sir, I guess we will all be surprised."

I just wasted both of our time. With a nod, I thank the lieutenant and head back to my seat. When I slide back in, I'm pleased I don't wake Stephanie.

"You find out anything?" Stephanie says.

"Damn, I hoped I hadn't awakened you, but I see I did.'

"It wasn't you. I just had a bad dream, and waking was a good way to get out of it."

"Not about the video, I hope."

"Oh yeah, about the video. That will stick with me for a long time."

"Well, I didn't find anything out. It seems our lieutenant has no idea where we're headed either. We'll have to wait until we get there."

"This is typical for this kind of operation."

"Well, then we might as well try to rest until we get to wherever we're going."

"Well said. I'm going to close my eyes now. You should do the same."

I lean back and make myself a little more comfortable. With the seat reclined, I close my eyes and figure I'll catch a few winks. To my surprise, the captain comes on the intercom and gives us the military equivalent of a welcome aboard announcement. He tells us we will be cruising at thirty-five thousand feet, and our destination is Greenbrier, West Virginia, which we should reach in two hours.

"I'll be damned," I say.

"What? What's the problem?"

"Oh, nothing. Greenbrier was my destination when I got drugged, and the aircrew flew me to San Francisco instead."

"Oh yes. They were working for Jacobs, right? You were headed to Greenbrier since it was a good location where you could be guarded better."

"Yes, that's right. I hope we make it this time."

"I'm sure we will. How long did the Captain say the flight is?"

"Two hours."

"Enough time to still get a nap. I'm going to try."

I smile at Stephanie and go back to relaxing. I fall asleep quickly and wake up to the slight turbulence as we start our approach into the Lewisburg airport area. Stephanie wakes, and I let her know we are on an initial approach.

She puts her seat upright and looks out the window. "Not much to see in the dark."

I nod. "I'll bet."

"You know, Greenbrier resort was a safe house for the President in case of emergency."

"Yeah, I did some reading about it and think it's a great place to hide out. This may even be better than Ft Lauderdale."

Stephanie raises her eyebrows. "What about looking at a boat?"

"I think that'll have to wait a while."

After the captain asks us to buckle up, we fall silent. The approach and landing go smoothly enough, and a contingent of SUVs meets us. They have the look of government all over them. We deplane and get into the vehicles for the ride to the resort.

It being so dark, we see almost nothing on the way. I came here one time a few years ago to attend a legal conference, and I remember the countryside to be lush and green with a mountainous topography. However, looking out the window doesn't give me any clue if things have changed or not.

We reach the front of the hotel, and the lieutenant asks us to remain in the car. He goes into the hotel. Does he have a reservation? The thought brings a chuckle, and Stephanie asks me about it. I tell her, and it brings a smile. At one-thirty in the morning, it's the best I can do.

The lieutenant comes back and gets in the car. "We're going to the bungalow area where we've set up secure accommodations."

The car pulls away and takes a secluded road around to a set of one-story log cottages, arranged in a semi-circle. With the roughhewn outside appearance, they remind me of Boy Scout camp.

"We will use all five of the buildings," the lieutenant says. "You and Ms. Savard are in the middle two, and my team will take up the others." The SUV pulls up to the middle ones. "Follow me," the lieutenant says.

We get out and trail him. He goes to the cottage with a three on the door. When he opens it, he says, "This is your room, Ms. Savard. I ask that you don't leave without an escort."

"What about clothes and things?" she asks.

"The room holds most of what you need. You can arrange to pick up some other things at the hotel shop. It has quite a selection." He steps out of the way, and Stephanie says goodnight to me and goes in. We go to the next cottage, which is number four. The lieutenant repeats his instructions. When he's done, I step into the room and turn on the lights. The décor impresses me.

The room has two beds and a huge sitting area. It also boasts an efficiency kitchen and adjoining bath. The colors remind me of those you'd find in Miami Beach. In fact, the room looks like it was decorated to be more near the ocean rather than the middle of West Virginia.

In the bathroom, I see a selection of shampoo, soap, conditioner, and even shaving cream and razor. These items make me want to take a shower to get some of the grime off. Two Terry-cloth robes hang on a hanger on a hook on the wall. The room looks like a double. I waste no time, take off my clothes, and start the shower. After I step in, the tension leaves my body. The shower will be short since I feel exhausted.

Once I get out and towel off, I skip the shave and climb into bed. Before I can even think about falling asleep, my phone rings.

"This is John."

"This is Ned."

"Oh hi, Ned. How's it going?"

"Boy, you sound tired."

"Well, it's almost two in the morning, and I just now got into bed."

"I wanted to let you know that you guys will be kept at the Greenbrier for a while. No other place is as secure, short of locking you up in jail."

"Yeah, well, this isn't exactly roughing it."

"You'll be able to walk around and maybe try to enjoy some of the things to do there. It has a lovely pool and nice golf course."

"I don't play golf. The weather looks like it is changing here. I couldn't tell, but I think fall is coming. Seems cool."

"The pool is heated. Anyway, just try to relax, and we should have Jacobs where we want him shortly."

"So, Stephanie and I are the bait?"

"Such a harsh term, John."

"But yes."

"Yes."

"I hope you guys know what you're doing. Jacobs is clever and will be hard to trap. Is Winther still in custody?"

"Oh yes. We have him in solitary confinement with chains and cuffs twenty-four-seven."

"That's good. If Jacobs can spring him, all will be lost."

"Why so?"

"If he can get Winther out, we'll have no way to hold onto him."

"I see your point."

"I'm tired, Ned. Anything else?"

"That's it."

"Oh, wait, I forgot to ask about Ramon."

"We will see. If anyone finds out about where you are, it has to come from Ramon through his guys. They haven't been involved from the get-go, so we don't think they're involved in giving Jacobs information. To be sure, we're monitoring their calls. They'll report your location to Ramon as a matter of standard operating procedure."

"So, if he *is* dirty, we should get a visit. Is there any other way Jacobs could find us?"

"We don't think so. The Feds swept the plane clean before you took off. We also had the pilot fly blind with no identification or flight plan filed so that there would be no way to track."

"Okay, I guess we'll be good to go, then. Looks like all the bases are covered. Am I going to hear from you anymore?"

"We should set up a call time each day. How's two o'clock Central time sound?"

"You call me, or I call you?"

"Why don't you call me? If you miss the time, then I'll know something's up. Don't forget."

"I won't forget. Thanks, Ned."

I put the phone on the side table and switch off the light. Before I know it, I've fallen asleep.

*

A noise outside reminds me of a leaf blower working around the cottages. How inconsiderate for workers to blow leaves so early. When I look at my watch, I'm shocked to see it's after eleven. I've been asleep for over nine hours. After stretching, I get out of bed and go to the window. Sure enough, it looks like midday out there. Workmen bustle around the grounds. Silently, I apologize for thinking them rude.

I'm not sure how to proceed today. I need to call Ned but have to wonder what to do about clothes. I decide I'll put on my dirty stuff and go knock on Stephanie's room to see if she wants something to eat, and maybe go to the hotel shop and see what's there. I should shave, and I find it easier to take another shower. I finish and feel better having shaved. At least, I won't look as dirty as I feel in yesterday's clothes, grimed by the smoke and debris. I can still smell the smoke on the shirt.

When I step through the doorway, the sight of an armed SEAL standing there with his back to the door and looking off to the woods shocks me. "Have you seen Ms. Savard this morning?" I ask.

He turns and gives me a shake of the head. Another stands outside Stephanie's door. I ask him the same question and get the same response. With a gentle knock on the door, I hope I'm not waking her. She calls, "Just a minute."

I don't have long to wait, and the door opens. "Come in."

I follow her into the room. "Did you sleep well?"

"Boy, I sure did. How about you?"

"Wonderful. I thought I'd stop by and see if you've had anything to eat today?"

"No, I was going to call room service since I don't like to eat alone in the restaurant."

"Why don't we go down to one of the eateries and live like human beings?"

"Absolutely great idea. Hold on. I'll get my jacket." As she walks away, I can't help but feel Stephanie seems to be in a much-improved frame of mind today. This is a good thing since I'm somewhat responsible for her problems. If Jacobs is trying to hurt me through her, it's not something I can just brush off. Like it or not, it's my responsibility. Stephanie acting more normal takes some of the burden from me. She comes back to the door. "You ready?" she says.

"More than ready. Let's go."

I let Stephanie go through the door first. I barely think about my chivalry. Then Stephanie says, "Nice guy, letting me walk into the ambush first."

It takes a second to understand, but then I get it and say, "Mrs. Cannon didn't raise an idiot. I know when to let a lady go first. Saved my butt many a time."

We both laugh, which feels good. I go up to the SEAL and let him know we're going to the restaurant. He nods and holds up his finger for us to wait. Then he talks with someone and signs off with a, "Yes, sir." Most likely, he just spoke with the lieutenant. I ask, "What's the protocol here?"

"The lieutenant asks that you remain with me for a few minutes until agents Sieverts and Welles arrive to escort you."

"Sieverts and Welles? Oh yeah, Leroy and Jesse. Okay, we can do that."

"Appreciate that, sir."

I smile at the SEAL. I should ask his name, but from experience, these guys like to remain as anonymous as possible. If he wants me to call him by name, he'll let me know what it is. I'm sure glad he's on our side. I wouldn't want this guy as an enemy. The SEAL turns and walks down the path to give us some privacy.

"What is going on?" Stephanie says.

"It probably wouldn't be good for business to have a couple of SEALs walk us into the restaurant, so we're waiting on Leroy and Jesse."

She grins. "That would be a sight."

"It would, right? How about, after lunch, we go to the store? I sure could use something else to wear besides what I've had on for two days."

"That would be great. I'd like to tour the facility as well. We're in one of the greatest resorts in the country, and I want to see some of it."

"You're a person after my own heart. This is shaping up to be a great day."

Stephanie laughs easily as Leroy comes down the path. Jesse follows close behind him. Leroy walks by Stephanie and me and talks to the SEAL. They look like they have all their signals straight, and Leroy comes back to us. "So, you guys want some food, huh?"

"Yes, is that allowed?"

Leroy laughs. "We will go with you. Is there anything else on your agenda today?"

"Yes, we need to get some clothes, and then would like to take a look around."

"Can do." Leroy nods. Then he asks Jesse to take the point position, which he does. Jesse starts up the path, and I assume he knows where he's going.

"Where did you guys get the new threads?"

"We went to the store earlier. They have a nice selection, and we found what we needed fast."

"I almost don't want to ask the price."

"Not that bad. Certainly not your bargain basement, but reasonable."

"So why the jackets? It's not that cold."

"You probably know the answer better than I do."

My prying showed me that Leroy wouldn't give up any secrets. He and Jesse need the jackets to cover all the equipment they have packed in and on their body. I imagine they're both packing automatic weapons plus all the communications gear. I nod to Leroy. "Just trying to get your goat," I say.

Leroy lets out a big deep laugh. Before long, we reach the hotel. A wide driveway rises to the left. Jesse suggests that we go in the door, which is on this level, rather than hike up the drive to the front door. It won't be as beautiful, but will be shorter. "Next time, we'll take a golf cart," Leroy says. "We will be able to drive up in style."

We go through the door, which puts us on a lower level with a few shops. The stores sell art, jewelry, real estate, and golf supplies. I look at Leroy. "I don't see a clothing store."

"It's on the next level. You'll find an escalator right over there."

We take the escalator up and come out in an exquisite lobby area. A huge reception desk forms the heart of the hotel. It has places to book tours and arrange reservations for dinner. New arrivals fill the check-in area. The whole room seems as if it's located in a large city. The energy feels amazing. Fresh flowers everywhere, as well as nice quiet furniture groupings, which can be used for private discussions and a cup of tea if you wish, all add to the special atmosphere. Leroy guides us over to one side of the lobby, where a wide hall has a bar on one side and a restaurant on the other.

In the restaurant, the hostess asks if there are four of us. Leroy says, "Only two eating, but Jesse and I will have coffee."

The hostess takes this oddity in stride and shows us to a table for four, where she sets our menus on one corner. I thank her and ask Stephanie where she wants to sit. Stephanie takes a chair facing the room, and I take the one next to her. Jesse and Leroy take the other two. "Keep your eyes peeled," Leroy says to Jesse. "You have the only other seat facing the room."

"Oh, I'm sorry." Stephanie moves to get up, but Leroy gives her a sign to stay seated.

"Don't worry, Ms. Savard. I don't think we'll need to have us both watching. You stay where you are."

Stephanie hands us each a menu. I glance around the restaurant. A large bank of windows off to the right overlooks a vast, rolling lawn. Several paved paths cut through the grass, and it looks like people use them to stroll around the grounds. Bright colors decorate the interior of the restaurant, reminiscent of a floral garden. Stephanie and Leroy seem engrossed in the menus, and Jesse—as Leroy asked him to—looks the room over with care.

"Hello. I'm Renee, and I will be your server today. Can I start you with something to drink?"

Stephanie says, "I see you have custom ice teas. I will have the peach mango ice tea."

Since I haven't looked, I ask for the same. Leroy asks for coffee for both him and Jesse.

When the server leaves for the drinks, we all go into the menu reading trance. I'm not sure how much conversation will go on with Leroy and Jesse sitting here. I don't want to discuss much with them, even though they might tell me what's going to happen now we're cooped up in this beautiful place. They may not know, let alone want to share anything with me.

The server returns with the drinks and we all order. After she leaves, I decide to see what I can find out, and just for grins, ask. "So, where are we going from here?"

Leroy had just taken a sip of coffee. He sets down his cup and gives me a "you should know better" look. "Well, I think you know as well as I do that we're not privileged to any information beyond the current assignment."

"Yes, I know. I just wondered how long we'll be here."

"I'm just as curious as you, but unfortunately, I have no information about that."

"Okay. Thought I would ask is all." Oh well, he was one step ahead of me. Of course, you don't become a member of the Secret Service by being stupid. I turn to Stephanie. "We still on for a tour after lunch?"

"You bet. The store's on my list as well."

"I haven't forgotten." I look at Leroy. "They have a good selection of clothes?"

"You can find what you need. I'm not an expert on women's clothes, though."

The server comes back with our lunch. We spend the time talking small stuff like how good the decorating is and how sunny it looks outside. We don't cover anything of substance, and Stephanie and I don't say too much to each other. Two relative strangers being here makes it difficult to chat. I hope we can have a different arrangement for dinner. It would be nice to have a decent conversation without extraneous ears listening.

We finish, and Leroy gets the bill. We are officially on the government tab. Does this extend to new clothes as well? Not wanting to push it, I refrain from asking. Leroy leads the way to the store. Upon looking around and checking a few things, I find that Leroy was correct. I should do quite well here. Across the aisle, Stephanie wears a frown. I go over. "How's it going?"

"I'll be able to find something. I just hate to pay these prices, though."

"Yeah, I know what you mean. Would you consider a gift from me?"

"No. I just have to suck it up and get what I need."

I let her know I understand and, if she changes her mind, my offer stands. Then I leave her and go back to the slacks, where I pick up a pair of cotton khaki pants and a polo shirt. A couple of pairs of boxers will hold me. Since I want to hit the pool, I buy a pair of board shorts. They will be good to wear even if I'm not in the pool. My last choice is a lightweight jacket, which has the name Greenbrier stitched on the right side. I pick the color black, even though the official Greenbrier color is forest green.

Stephanie has made her choices as well. We meet up at the register. The sales clerk doesn't show any sign that she finds the quantities of our purchases to be in any way out of the ordinary. I hand the assistant my card and say, "Put all of this on my card."

Stephanie protests, but I hold my ground. Finally, she gives up and says, "You didn't have to buy my clothes, but thank you kindly."

All done, we leave the store, and I suggest we go back to the room and change so we can be comfortable. Stephanie thinks the idea a good one, so we head back. The SEALs still guard the rooms. Once inside, we take a few minutes to change.

When I emerge from my room, Stephanie already stands in front of my cabin.

"My, you look relaxed in those shorts," I say.

"Don't think they're too casual, do you?"

"Too casual would be your underwear. You're fine."

We share a laugh and start on the path to the hotel. Leroy and Jesse take their usual positions. The day turns out to be in the low eighties with the barest of breezes. A few broken clouds add a postcard feel to the sky. I glance at Stephanie. "What would you like to see first?"

"I read in the brochure that they have horses and a trail to ride. I'd love to go to the stables and see what they have."

"Do you ride?"

"Oh, yes. I used to compete in the English jumping event. Actually, I had my own horse."

"Compete? What was that like?"

"Thrilling. I competed in the five meter and Grand Prix events."

"Five meter is high, isn't it?"

"I guess. Once you get used to the height, it's about the same as one meter in style and form. It's just a longer trip up and further to fall. Do you ride?"

"I *have* ridden, but nothing like you describe. I did mostly western trail rides."

"Oh, they can be fun. Where did you ride?"

"California has a number of places. Mostly out in the sticks. We used to go to the Marin Headlands and trail ride there. I went to Colorado one time. Aspin—ten thousand feet in the air and scary as hell. The group and the horses walked on these little ledges, and it was snowing, in July."

Stephanie smiles and nods. "I've heard about those mountain trips. Always wanted to do it, but never got the chance."

Leroy says, "If you want to go to the stables, we need to get a golf cart. Let's go in and get one reserved."

We follow Leroy into the lobby, and he goes to the activity desk. Stephanie and I continue to talk and don't notice Leroy's return until he says, "All set."

By the front door, a guy waits with a golf cart with enough seats for four. "You want to drive?" Leroy says.

With a shrug, I say, "I don't know my way around. You can drive if you want."

Leroy goes to the driver's side, and Jesse gets in next to him. They give us a wave, and Stephanie and I climb aboard. This is the same kind of golf cart they use at the beach back in Port Aransas. One of the key components is the sound system, which most tourists play way too loud. I ask Leroy to tune into a good station, and he does. Sounds like he picked up an oldies station since the song in progress is Peaceful Easy Feeling by the Eagles. We pull away from the hotel, and Leroy follows the path, which winds around the hotel, past the cottages, and into the pines. When we pass the cottages, we can see the SEALs are still on duty. I have to admit, the sight of those guys is comforting.

We come out of the pines. The barn stands about a hundred yards ahead. It looks massive from here and keeps growing as we get closer. Leroy slows the golf cart and looks up at the sky. "What's the matter?" I ask. He turns and shakes his head but doesn't say anything. Silent and wearing a frown, he stops the vehicle and steps out.

"I thought I heard an airplane, or maybe even a chopper."

"I didn't hear anything." I look at Stephanie, and she gives me a sign to confirm she didn't hear anything either. The only sound comes from Sweet Home Alabama on the radio. Leroy reaches over and turns it off. Jesse gets out of the golf cart and has his ear cocked in the direction of the barn.

"Hear that?" Leroy says.

I still don't hear anything but do feel a slight thumping like a song with the bass turned up too loud.

"Shit," Leroy says. "Get in, Jesse." Leroy jumps back in the cart and turns the key. The vehicle jumps when Leroy stomps the accelerator. He yanks the wheel hard to the right. The cart sets off at a crawl, and then picks up speed while Leroy takes us in the direction from which we came. Jesse runs beside us and, finally, grabs the sissy bar and swings in.

"What's the problem?" I yell above the whine of the small engine.

"Chopper. Coming in low. No reason for one in this part of the resort. I gotta assume it's not one of ours."

"Where are we going?"

"I'm trying to make those pines again. They can't fly in there."

Jesse looks over his shoulder with concern on his face. Calm, he says, "They're here."

Just as Jesse announces the arrival of the chopper, the grass beside the cart erupts in two wild stitches that look like two gophers having an underground race. The stitches cross the path ahead of us and tear up the asphalt. Chunks of grass and asphalt hit the windshield. Leroy swerves to the left and runs off the path. "Fifty-caliber machine guns," he shouts. "We gotta get into the woods before he comes back." The helicopter roars past us overhead. Alarmed, I look at Stephanie, who appears to be remarkably calm. I take her hand and give her a smile that I hope says, "Don't worry. We're in good hands." She says nothing but smiles back. I'm more worried than her. The huge helicopter passes close. On its belly, I can almost see the rivets in the skin of the craft. Just when it looks like it's going to leave, the pilot executes a complete one-hundred-and-eighty-degree turn. He intends to go for another pass. Two crew members sit in the front of what appears to be a Blackhawk. A machine capable of so much more than bullets. They have two rocket pods and two twenty-millimeter cannons. If they're intent on killing us, they won't have much trouble.

"Hold on," Leroy yells. When we close in on the trees, we lose sight of the Blackhawk for a moment. The wash of the rotor blows up sand, twigs, and leaves, and it feels like we're driving into a tornado. The chopper once again goes over the top of us but doesn't fire any shots. I turn to look back. The pilot maneuvers to make another run from the opposite direction. We reach the pines, and the helicopter heads into its turn. Leroy tries to avoid the trees and has difficulty keeping up speed. He stops the cart and yells for all of us to get out and run. I jump out, dart around the back, and grab Stephanie's hand. We sprint deeper into the woods. Hopefully, we can find a ditch or hole to jump into. If that chopper lets fly with those rockets, we do *not* want to get caught above ground level.

While running, I feel like I have a large target on my back and imagine the red laser tracking to the bull's eye. A big explosion pushes me forward, and I toss Stephanie to the ground. After the shockwave, a roar sounds, and the heat of something massive washes over me. The trees around us sway as if a large wind passed through. I have Stephanie covered and try to get my arm over my head. The sound and fury are much bigger than a canister of rockets.

Just as suddenly as the noise and heat blast over us, the quiet comes. I look up carefully. The Blackhawk burns furiously at the edge of the tree line. It looks like it blew up and then cartwheeled into the ground. While I try to make sense of what's going on, the SEAL lieutenant kneels next to us and asks if we're okay.

"We're good. What the hell happened?"

"Those guys tried to kill you." He nods toward the burning Blackhawk.

"Leroy and Jesse?"

"Both all right."

"How'd you bring it down?"

"A shoulder mount missile. Does the trick."

"How did you guys get here so fast?"

"We got an alert from Homeland when these guys took off without a transponder. They were only a few miles away, so they must have trucked the craft in. We hot-footed it here as soon as we realized they were coming to get you. We're looking for the truck now. Can't be too many flatbeds in the mountains of West Virginia. Hold on." The lieutenant cups his hand over an earpiece, acknowledges the message, and ends with, "Yes, sir."

"News?"

"Looks like the search team has the truck. As I suspected, it's a sizeable flatbed. More like the kind that moves houses. Those guys trucked the Blackhawk into these hills and then took off from the truck. No one's there right now. I suspect the two in the chopper were the only ones involved."

"Damn, this is getting to be a bit tedious." Stephanie chews her bottom lip. "How did they know where we were?"

"I have no idea, ma'am. We need to follow up on that. In the meantime, I have orders to get you both to the airport."

"Not again?" I say. "We need to move again?"

"Yes, sir. Those are my orders."

"I feel like a criminal on the run."

"Yes, sir. I understand. Shall we get going?"

Rattled, I help Stephanie to her feet. We each brush the dirt from our clothes. Leroy comes up and waves us toward the golf cart. I can't imagine how it survived the blast, but it seems untouched. Jesse sits behind the wheel, and we get in.

"Leroy?" I say. "You been in touch with Ramon?" Just as I say it, I realize that, in the excitement, I haven't called Ned. I should have called at two o'clock, and it is now half past three. I reach into my pocket and get my phone. Here in the woods, I can't get any service and will have to wait until I get to my room. Jesse pulls away, and two SEALs in another golf cart follow us.

"Yes, we have been in touch with Agent Ramon." Leroy nods. "He was stunned by the report."

"Yeah, I'll bet he was."

"What do you mean?"

"Oh, nothing. Will we have time to clean up?"

"We need to be at the airport by four o'clock, so there isn't much time, but yes, you can clean up if you're quick."

I look at Stephanie, and she gives me a weak smile and a look that says, "We need to do what we need to do."

Chapter Thirteen

We get back to the cottages, and I rush into the room and pull out my phone. I hit the redial button and wait. Ned picks up on the third ring. "Well, hello, junior. I gave you up for dead."

"Hi, Ned." I couldn't keep the frustration out of my voice. "I'm getting tired of this shit."

"I'm sure you are. You need to hang on a little longer. We got a few interesting hits on our Ramon track."

"You what?"

"We've called the trap we set 'the Ramon track.' We assume Ramon is in direct communication with Jacobs, and we got a couple of hits on our surveillance that look suspicious."

"Oh yeah. Like what?"

"Not for the phone. Let me say that Ramon won't be easy to get information on to prove his alliance with Jacobs. He's a seasoned professional and knows ways to keep communications private. Lucky for us, we're just a bit better. I see the SEALs saved your ass again."

"Yes, they did. They were marvelous. You help 'em?"

"You betcha. I've been watching the airwaves and the airspace all around you. That truck trick with the Blackhawk was savvy. Almost didn't catch that."

"Well, I'm glad you did. Where are we going now?"

"No reason you can't come back to Port Aransas. It will be easier to watch you, and I've convinced the authorities you and I should be in the same town. While Ramon is in charge, Jacobs will know where you are, no matter what we do."

"Why not get rid of Ramon?"

"Yeah, good question. If we do, then we lose the ability to manipulate him to lay the trap for Jacobs."

"Why do I feel like bait?"

"Oh, my boy, you may have hit the nail on the head."

"Thanks, Ned. You're enjoying my angst, aren't you?"

"Just pulling your leg, which I must say, is fun. I'll be seeing you in a couple of hours. I'll be at the airport to get you and Stephanie. From there, you'll go to the Naval Air Station again."

"I'll look forward to getting home. See you then."

"Bye, kid."

When I look at my watch, I see I have only ten minutes to shower and dress. I throw all my spare and dirty clothes into a cleaning bag, which I found in the closet, and jump in the shower. Washing up is quick, and dressing is just throwing the clothes on. All done, I grab the bag and move out of the door. The SUV waits in front of the cottages. With my hair still wet, the afternoon air feels chilly. The small shiver that prickles goosebumps up my arms, I rationalize as a reaction to the cold and not fear. Am I kidding myself? When I see Stephanie, it takes my focus from me. She looks like she's going on a date. Evidently, she managed to shower as well. When she gets closer, the aroma of fresh soap and shampoo wafts over me. Stephanie gives me a hug, and the heat of her body radiates and surrounds me with a comforting feeling, which makes me forget how close we came to being history.

After a final squeeze, she asks, "You okay?"

"So much better now. You ready to go to Port Aransas?"

"You're kidding? Isn't that dangerous?"

"Ned seems to feel it will be safer. Not sure how, but he's convinced the authorities."

"I believe we might be the goat staked out to draw in the lion."

John W Howell

Perturbed, I give Stephanie a sign to say no more, and then point to Leroy and Jesse while I imitate Mickey Mouse ears with my hands. She gets it and can't help but laugh. Leroy turns around and almost catches me looking ridiculous. He gives me a look that you would get from a teacher who thinks you've passed a note but can't prove it. This forces Stephanie to fake a cough or get caught laughing out loud. Leroy looks disgusted and gives us a wave to get into the SUV. We climb in and keep our things with us. Leroy and Jesse get in front. Another SUV pulls up behind us with the SEALs inside. We all head out and away from the hotel.

"Those guys were sure on it," I say to Stephanie.

Leroy turns and nods. "Man, you can say that again. They saved our lunch today."

"What did your boss have to say about it?"

"He didn't say much. He seemed surprised to hear from me. I guess he didn't think they would try something in this locale."

More like Ramon was surprised because he didn't expect us to survive, but I don't want to engage Leroy in any more conversation about his boss, so say nothing more.

"So, where will I stay in Port Aransas?" Stephanie asks.

"We have rooms for everybody including John," Leroy says.

I chuckle. "Gee, I was just going to invite Stephanie to my house."

"Yeah, well, just call me the Grinch that stole romance."

Stephanie gives my arm a squeeze. "That would have been nice."

Stephanie's comment causes me to blush since I knew I was a little out of line with my comment. "Yeah. Maybe this will be over soon, and I'll just say you have an invitation anytime."

"Thank you, I hope it won't be too long."

The look in Stephanie's eyes makes something flutter inside me. She has me locked in a spell, which I don't want to break, so I keep looking into her eyes and think I just might pass out. She looks away, and I feel like I've been dropped on the floor.

"That is some look," I say. Nervous, I check in the front, and Leroy and Jesse seem preoccupied.

"You intrigue me."

I keep my voice low, "What do you mean?"

She looks back, and I purposely avoid her eyes. "I've met a lot of men in my time, but you're someone with a decent heart. I find that attractive if you must know."

Now I do look at her. "You know I'm attracted to you as well."

"I certainly hope so."

We both laugh, and I say, "I want us to become more than friends, but it'll take a while. We should take it slowly, so we're both sure."

"Sure of what?"

"Of our feelings for each other."

"I can vote for that. How long do you think you need?"

"Me? I'm talking about you."

"Why don't you let me talk for myself? I'm a big girl. I fly fighter jets, for heaven's sake. Not much bigger girl pants than that."

"I just don't want you to be hurt."

"What are you going to do? Find another girl to have sex with and send me the photos?"

"Whoa, that was low."

"Well, you have to get a grip. Either you want us to hang out together or not. All this crap about being sure is just that, crap."

Leroy turns at the word crap to see if we are getting out of hand. Stephanie and I give him a butt out stare, and he flushes. "We took care of him," I say.

Stephanie nods. "Looks like the first output of a fine relationship."

We laugh again and reach the airport, where we pull onto the tarmac to a waiting Gulfstream.

"Here we are," Leroy says.

"Looks that way," Stephanie says. Not catching the sarcasm, Leroy gets out, and then Jesse follows. Stephanie and I leave the SUV last. Leroy directs us up the stairway and into the plane. We go where directed. Once inside, we take seats across the aisle from each other. The SEALs, Leroy, and Jesse file past us and take other seats. The co-pilot raises the ladder and shuts the door. The engines whine to life.

The pilot comes on the intercom and lets us know we will be flying to Corpus Christi Naval Air Station. It will be about three hours in the air. He then indicates that if we need a snack to help ourselves. He makes a joke about budget cuts on the flight attendant, asks us to fasten our seat belts, and then clicks off the mic.

The force of the engines builds when we start the takeoff roll, and in no time, we shoot into the air.

"Well, goodbye Greenbrier. Didn't get much chance to relax, did we?"

Stephanie shakes her head. "That will change."

I blush and realize that Stephanie is someone who can take care of herself, which means I can remove her from my worry list. I want to get close to her, and I guess, she'll just have to take care of herself in the process. It feels good to be able to be myself and go for what I want.

"I love this part of the country," Stephanie says. "The mountains are beautiful. Did you notice the pilot reduced the power after we lifted off?"

"I was thinking of something else and didn't notice."

"He got enough altitude to maneuver around the mountains but not to go above them. The view is lovely. We're winding through the mountains now. Take a look."

I glance out the window and see beautiful hills. The other side has the same view, so we must be flying through a valley. "Wow, I wouldn't want to do this in the fog."

Stephanie laughs. "I wouldn't do that either."

"I don't know why. I thought you could do almost anything."

"Flying without being able to see is not one of them."

The nose of the plane lifts, and the engine power increases. I look toward Stephanie.

"We've cleared the mountains and will now go to the cruising altitude."

"Oh, good. I thought for a moment the pilot was going to try to get over the mountain tops. This makes sense."

"Stick with me, and all the mysteries of life will be exposed." Her expression is so serious that I can't help breaking up, and she follows. We laugh for way too long. Finally, getting composed, I suggest we grab a drink. I offer to go back and fetch something. She asks for water. Just as I rise, I see the seatbelt light is still on, so I sit back down.

"Looks like a few more minutes," Stephanie says.

"I guess we can wait that long." I smile at her and pick up a magazine from the pocket in the fuselage. Not surprisingly, it's a magazine on flying. It holds numerous stories about different types of aircraft—almost like a boating magazine—with stats on takeoff speeds, operating costs, weight, and altitude ceilings. "Hey, Stephanie," I say.

"Yes, John?" I pause for a second, realizing I have no nickname for Stephanie, and her response with my name was to my more formal use of her name.

"Do you read these kinds of mags? I read a lot about boating and wondered if you do the same about flying."

"Yep. You'd be amazed how interesting some of those articles are. There'll be a section on causes of air mishaps that's fascinating."

"Yeah, I'll bet. Not sure I want to look at those while I'm miles high."

"Well, any good pilot should understand the causes of accidents and how to prevent them."

"I can see that. Can you tell how high we are by looking out the window?"

"That's random. Why do you ask?"

"I just wonder how long it will be until we reach cruising altitude so I can get a drink."

Stephanie takes a look. "The light will go off in three seconds."

"Yeah, right." Of course, the light goes out just when Stephanie said it would. I jump up and go to the back. Leroy, Jesse, and the SEALs are asleep, so I go by them quietly and open the refrigerator. Then I reach in and grab a couple of waters. As I pull them out, I hear what sounds like a crunch followed by a lurch that drops me to my knees. It sounds and feels like we just hit something. Impossible in mid-air, though, right? Stephanie looks back at me, and then the oxygen masks fall from the ceiling. She reaches up, pulls down a mask, and then waves to me to come back to the front. I glance at Leroy and Jesse, and they look frantic at being awakened by the falling masks. They grab them and put them on, as do the two SEALs. The bottle of water lost, I get off my knees and go back to Stephanie. She hands me a mask and tells me through hers to put it on.

I don't delay and take a few breaths. Stephanie comes close to me and pulls her mask off.

"I think there's some kind of problem in the cockpit. Obviously, we're on autopilot. I need to go up there and find out what's wrong. You should stay here with your seatbelt on. Understand?"

I nod, and Stephanie takes a deep breath and then goes to the cockpit door. She reads something by the handle, and then comes rushing back to me.

"The door's locked, and the crew key is back in the galley. I'll be right back." She takes another deep breath from the mask, and goes to the rear. In what seems like an hour, she comes back to our seats and grabs her mask. After a few well-deserved breaths, she's ready. "Okay, I've got the key, and I'm gonna try and open the door. You need to stay here and keep your belt in place. I told the rest of them to stay in place until I call for them."

When I mumble my understanding, Stephanie takes another big breath and moves to the cockpit door. She unlocks and opens the door a couple of inches, and air rushes toward her from the main cabin. The door won't open far enough for her to get through. Stephanie lets the door slam shut and comes back to her seat. She grabs the oxygen mask and takes a deep breath. Then she removes it and looks at me.

"The cockpit windows have been compromised. We need to get in there and get control of this airplane. If we don't, we'll run out of oxygen, or worse, the plane could disintegrate. The only thing stopping that now is the substantial cockpit door that seems to be airtight. Here's what we need to do. You help me with the door. Once inside the cockpit, we need to take this baby below ten thousand feet. I'm not sure of the condition of the pilots." Her take-charge attitude reassures me. "When we get in there, grab the copilot's oxygen, and I'll get the pilot's. It didn't look like they had time to put them on. If that's the case, they'll not be needing them anymore. You got all this?" She takes a couple of deep breaths, and then shouts back to the SEALs and Leroy and Jesse to keep their masks in place until she tells them it's okay. They wave their understanding.

Stephanie looks at me. "You got this?" I nod. She holds up her hand with three fingers and counts down to one, and then we rush the door. I grab the door handle and pull the door open a fraction. Stephanie reaches through the crack and holds the door until I can grip my hands below hers. We both pull as hard as we can, and the door opens. "I'm not sure how long we can do this," I yell. The noise of air rushing out of the cabin through the cockpit window is earsplitting, and flying objects hit the bulkhead behind us.

Stephanie yells, "I have my foot in the door. Come around behind me, and both of us can push against it." I let go of the door and do as she says. We both struggle but manage to get the door open far enough to squeeze inside. Once in, I let the door slam shut, glad to get my fingers out of the way just in time. "Grab that oxygen mask above the co-pilot's seat," Stephanie yells. The noise from the rushing air has calmed down, and Stephanie flinches with surprise that her voice sounds so loud. I grab the mask and put it on, but when I take a deep breath, I can't feel any air. I'm also light-headed. Stephanie reaches across the co-pilot and throws a switch. My knees go limp, and I grab hold of the pilot's seat.

"Take a deep breath," Stephanie says.

Glorious air hits my lungs, and I gulp it in and then let it out slowly. Now I feel more secure standing. Stephanie leans over the unconscious (or dead) pilot and makes changes in the flight controls. The plane slows and makes a gradual descent. Then she reaches for the microphone and calls a mayday. "Permission to descend."

The controller responds with, "Unidentified craft, please, give your tail number."

Wide-eyed, Stephanie says, "I can't read the number on the firewall."

The controller says, "Okay. Please, confirm your transponder setting."

Stephanie gives the four digit code. The controller confirms the tail number and approves a descent to 10,000 feet. Stephanie asks for the nearest military base and the radio setting for approach control. When she makes a writing sign, I grab a clipboard from the center control console. The controller gives us the most practical landing site as Langly Air Force Base in Virginia and the radio setting. While I write them down, Stephanie asks for routing instructions. The controller requests a slight turn and a heading of ninety-two degrees. Stephanie makes the adjustment.

Once she's double-checked our heading, she says to me, "We were at twenty-five thousand feet and, with a standard thousand feet per minute descent, we should be at ten thousand feet in about thirteen minutes. We'll be able to take off these masks and get these two into the main cabin."

"What do you think happened?"

"I can't tell but, by the looks of the burns on the windshield, I think a missile exploded in proximity to the cockpit. The concussion knocked out the pilots. Check the co-pilot. The pilot is definitely dead."

When I check for a pulse on the co-pilot's neck, I feel nothing. "Dead as well."

"Damn. This has to be the work of our pal Jacobs. I'm going to engage the autopilot again and see if I can move the pilot out of his seat. I can't control this thing if I can't reach the ailerons, which the foot pedals control."

"Can I help?"

"Yes. Grab his arm as I roll him over. Then try to drag him out of the seat."

I pull as hard as I can, and the body slips out of the seat. One of the pilot's shoes drops off, and I manage to get him the whole way out of the seat. "Perfect," Stephanie says. "Now, pull him back as far as you can."

Although not easy, I manage to get him into the space between the seats and the door. The glass fragments have cut the pilot's face up, but I don't think he would've felt much before he lost consciousness.

"See if you can do the same with the co-pilot." Stephanie takes the pilot's position at the controls and puts on headphones with a microphone attached, and then switches to intercom.

It is somewhat easier to roll the co-pilot out of his seat, as he's a smaller man. I drag his body behind the seat and manage to pile him on top of the pilot. Poor treatment for a human being. With no space, and not wanting to risk breaking the seal on the airtight door, I don't have much choice. So, I shake off the thought and drop into the co-pilot's chair, where I don the headphones. "You there, Stephanie?"

"Yes," she says into her microphone. "Better put on glasses. This wind will tear you up if you get caught sideways. I've slowed us considerably, but can't afford to lose any more speed. We need the momentum to keep in the air."

"Yeah, not flying at this point would be a mistake." I pull my glasses out of their case and put them on. Only now do I realize that I'd been squinting a great deal, and with the glasses, I can see clearly. The wind still pulls at my cheeks and sends my hair all over the place, but at least my vision is better.

Stephanie looks at the altimeter. "We're almost at eighteen thousand feet. About eight minutes to go. It looks like all the controls are working normally, so that's a break."

I nod and give a relieved smile. "Looks like you are officially in control, Captain."

Stephanie's smile looks strained, but it's something.

Stephanie calls the controller once again and gives our position. "We have lost our windshield on both the pilot and co-pilot sides and will need a slow approach."

The controller acknowledges the transmission. "USAF 141, be advised. Two F18s have been scrambled to escort you to the base, Military Center."

Stephanie thanks him and confirms, "Military Center, understood USAF 141."

The controller says, "USAF 114, stay on the current frequency so that the F18s can communicate with you." Then he gives his final instruction, "Please, wait until I ask you to switch to the airfield frequency, Military Center."

Stephanie acknowledges with a, "Roger. Out, USAF 141."

"He must think you're nothing but a pretty face," I say.

Stephanie laughs deeply. "He's following protocol. Wants to make sure I'm not doing my nails while I'm flying. Actually, he wants to make sure we can land safely while I'm doing my nails if I'm so inclined. Gotta love those guys."

"You sure you can do this? The wind looks like it's giving you some trouble?"

"It's rough, but I've got it. Sixteen thousand. Six thousand more and we can take off the oxygen masks."

"Roger that," I say. Stephanie looks at me and smiles at my use of the communication lingo. She shakes her head, and I feel good for being at the center of her humor.

Chapter Fourteen

"**USAF 141,** this is Flight Leader Foxtrot."

"Roger, Foxtrot. We are copying you, USAF 141."

"We have you on camera. We should be closing in about two minutes. Foxtrot."

"Roger, Foxtrot. USAF 141." Stephanie looks at me. "Keep an eye out for those two birds. If they do what I would do, one will come up on your side and one on mine. I need to keep this plane on the glide path, so I don't have much time to glance around."

"Got it." I look to my right. The wind gives me pain in my ear, so I cover it with my hand.

"USAF 141, Military Center."

"Go ahead, Military Center."

"Your F18s are about a mile to your stern."

"We have had radio contact. Roger one mile to the stern, USAF 141."

"USAF 141, please, turn to ninety-two degrees."

"Ninety-two degrees, USAF 141."

"USAF 141, Foxtrot."

"Go, Foxtrot."

"We are closing and will come beside you. Your current heading is ninety-two degrees. Please confirm."

"Confirmed ninety-two degrees, USAF 141."

"I think I see one of them over here. Yes, it's him. He's giving me the thumbs up."

"Give him one back. That'll let him know you see him. Look over here as well."

"Yes, there's one on your side too." Without looking, Stephanie raises her thumb, too worried to take her eyes off the instruments. I ask, "Is there a problem?"

"The vacuum gauge on the port engine is acting weird. Maybe nothing, but I'm keeping my eye on it."

"You seem transfixed."

"I know. It's so hard with this wind. I don't want to look away for fear I can't look back."

"Do the F18s know where we're heading?"

"I suspect it's their home base. So, yes, I would imagine."

"USAF 141, Foxtrot."

"Foxtrot, go."

"I see a trail out of your port engine. It could be fuel or smoke. I can't quite tell at this point. Foxtrot."

"Roger that, Foxtrot. I'm getting a bad reading on the vacuum gauge. Could be smoke since the fuel readings are all stable. USAF 141."

"We will stand by, Foxtrot out."

"What the hell?" I say.

"Don't worry. This baby will still fly on one engine. The port engine temp is on the rise. I'm going to shut it down, so we don't have a fire on our hands."

"I'm glad you know what you're doing."

"You think?"

"Don't joke with me. You do know what you're doing? Right?"

"Yeah, I do. We're at twelve thousand feet. Another two to go."

Stephanie makes a couple of adjustments, and the auto warning system goes nuts. She overrides the system alarm to enable us to think and shuts down the port engine. A noticeable drag pulls at the plane after the engine goes dead. Stephanie struggles with the yoke and says, "I'm working the trim to get this beast into a better flyable position. The windshield and the dead engine aren't helping the aerodynamics one bit."

The yolk stops its fight and Stephanie looks pleased. She glances at the instruments, and I take it that all is normal. At least, as normal as can be with only one engine and nothing between the rushing air and us.

Stephanie relaxes and pulls off her mask. "Okay, we've reached ten thousand feet. You can take off your oxygen now. If you would, can you drag those guys into the main cabin and check on Leroy, Jesse, and the SEALs. They should be okay, but let's make sure."

I get up, not looking forward to pulling these guys out into the aisle. Upon opening the door, I see Leroy and Jesse sitting calmly with their masks on. I shout to them that they can take them off, and would they please help with lugging the two corpses to the rear. Leroy and Jesse come forward and grab the wrists and ankles of the co-pilot and take him aft of the galley. The SEALs take the pilot. I let the door shut and follow them.

Leroy and Jesse and the SEALs look at me for an explanation. I tell them, "Looks like a missile hit the front. These two got knocked out and then oxygen starved. We're flying on one engine, and a couple of F18s are giving us an escort to a Military base. The windshield got blown out completely, and we don't know what else is damaged. Any questions?"

The SEALs don't say a word.

Leroy and Jesse look at each other. Leroy says, "We're fortunate to be alive."

I nod. "Yeah, I'd say."

"Ms. Savard flying this thing?"

"Yup. She is."

"Well, I guess we're lucky to have her on board."

"I would say so. If nothing else, I need to get back up front. You guys should buckle up and get ready for landing. Not sure how nice it will be, but we're about ten minutes out."

The four look at me like I know what I'm talking about. In fact, I kind of do. I turn and leave them there. Back in the cockpit, Stephanie concentrates on the instrument panel. "We still okay?" I ask, taking my seat and glancing over to Stephanie.

"I don't like the look of the other vacuum gauge." Stress clips her voice.

"USAF 141, Foxtrot."

"Foxtrot, go."

"Sorry to report another trail out of the starboard engine. Foxtrot."

"Roger, Foxtrot. We may have some more trouble here. USAF 141."

"USAF 141, what is the trouble? Foxtrot."

"Same as before, Foxtrot. Vacuum gauge isn't looking right. Temp is still fine, but I expect another flame out."

"Roger that, USAF 141. If you can hold for another five minutes, you will be able to glide her in. Foxtrot."

"Roger that, Foxtrot. Not sure I can but will try. USAF 141."

"My God. What're the odds of being able to hold it?"

"Not sure. I shut the other engine down as a preventative—starting it up again will be on the cards if the temp rises on two. I'll reduce power a little to take the strain off."

Stephanie makes a small adjustment in the throttle, and the engine responds. The cockpit grows quiet. Then she scans the instruments and looks satisfied with what she sees. "I pulled that off nicely," she says. "Now, the only possible issue I see is that our rate of descent has picked up a little. I don't think it's a problem since the temp is holding. I can adjust to the increased speed and maybe bleed off a little."

"You're the boss. I have no idea what you are talking about, but I'll just take your word all's good."

"Good is relative. Right now, we're in reasonable shape. We're descending through eight thousand feet, and we should prepare this thing for a landing. You see that binder in the console? Would you get it out, please, and we'll go through the initial checks."

I look around and put my hands on a binder that has a bunch of laminated cards on plastic rings. "Which one is it?"

"Go to the one labeled emergency landing."

"Okay, here it is. What do you want to know?"

"We'll start with the first item on the list and go through the entire sequence. After you read the item, I'll confirm the activity has been accomplished by saying 'check.'"

"Okay, got it. The first item is to maintain aircraft control."

"Yeah, check. We have one engine, and it's looking shaky. Two pilots dead, and we're still flying."

"The second is to analyze the situation and take the proper action."

"Check. We need to make a landing with one engine."

"The third is to land as soon as conditions permit."

"Check, we're on a heading to do that. Now, go to the specifics."

"Let me see, there are a few instructions. How about engine failure during flight?"

"Yeah, that's good, give me that one."

"Okay. FAILED ENGINE CONDITION LEVER— FEATHER & FUEL SHUT-OFF."

"Check."

"Operative engine power lever—ADVANCE as required."

"Check, lever in place."

"Gear up."

"Check."

"Flaps up."

"Check."

"Maintain minimum single-engine speed or above."

"Check."

"Stores—JETTISON as required."

"Check. We're not throwing anything out."

"The next is to attempt air starts."

"I think we'll hold right there, as we can do an air start if engine two heats up. Okay, we need to contact ATC and tell them we're ready for a one-engine landing. If we need to, we can restate later. Keep that checklist handy. Military ATC, USAF 141."

"Go ahead, USAF 141, Military ATC."

"We are with you at six thousand feet and have completed the emergency checklist for engine out, and request initial landing instructions. We do not have the airport information."

"Roger, USAF 141. Continue on a heading of ninety-two degrees and descend to twenty-five hundred feet mercury, and then contact the tower on one-six-one-dot-niner. Military ATC."

"Ninety-two degrees, twenty-five hundred one-six-one-dot-niner, USAF 141."

When the exchange finishes, I ask, "Everything okay?"

"Yes, we're cleared to the tower. We'll need to use the emergency landing checklist. It should be there below the engine failure one."

"I have it here. There isn't much to do until we reach a place called High Key."

"Yeah, that's at twenty-five hundred feet.

"We're supposed to be doing a hundred and thirty KIAS until there."

"We are. The checklist says gear and flaps up, right?"

"Yes."

"Oh, well now. This is not good. The temp is rising too fast. I'm not sure it will stay out of the red for enough time to get us the landing. We better try a restart of the other engine. Worst case, I can shut this one down as well. Get that restart list."

"Yes, ma'am, I got it."

"Read 'em all to me. I don't have time to check them off."

"Condition lever—FUEL SHUT-OFF, Power lever—Halfway between FLIGHT IDLE and MILITARY, AIR START—ON, Condition lever—NORMAL FLIGHT AT TEN PERCENT RPM, AIR START—AUTO."

"Okay, I got it. I couldn't remember the condition lever setting. Here goes nothing."

Stephanie goes through the list, and the other engine kicks in. I smile at her, but she's too busy to acknowledge. With her brows furrowed in concentration, Stephanie mutters encouragement to the engine. Gradually, the RPMs rise on the port engine. When she adjusts the levers, I can feel more power under us.

"I'm worried about the other one now. It will take some time for the heat to get to the port engine. We'll be in trouble on the starboard. I'll keep it running but will slow it to almost idle. Just like working a boat one engine at a time."

Stephanie makes the adjustment. I remind her that we're approaching twenty-five hundred feet. She adjusts the radio and informs the tower of our condition. The ATC give us clearance to land. Stephanie turns back to me. "Grab the checklist again."

I go over the list, and now we have nothing to do but wait. A tiny image of the airport comes into view, which seems a lifetime away. We continue to descend, and Stephanie deploys the flaps and landing gear. She says, "Three in the green." The gear locks in place. Red lights blink on the control panel. I point to them, and Stephanie says, "I'm driving the engines beyond their safe operating capabilities, seeing as both are overheating right as we begin the final approach. Get on the intercom and tell those guys in the back to prepare for a rough landing and to get the hell off the plane as soon as it stops."

It takes a few seconds for me to figure out how to work the intercom, but I get it finally. I make the announcement and look up to see the runway filling my vision. A shrieking sound erupts from somewhere under the control panel. Two bright red lights blink and have the word "Fire" on them.

Stephanie says, "Hold on, we have two fires. Pull that lever over there marked 'Fire.' I got the one on my side."

I pull the lever, but the shrieking doesn't stop. Worried, I look over at Stephanie. She seems calm and continues to maneuver the airplane. I remember the first lesson the instructor taught me when I thought I wanted to be a pilot. *Fly the airplane.* The nose rises and the warning alarm screeches on. Stephanie fights to keep the craft under control. At last, at long last, the

165

main wheels touch down on the runway, and Stephanie works to get the nose wheel to touch the tarmac gently. When she pushes the yoke forward, the wheel makes contact, and the plane eases down on three wheels. Then she pulls the power control levers into a neutral position and deploys the reverse thrusters. Lastly, she applies the brakes. "Son of a bitch," she says. "The engines just quit. The thrusters are worthless. This is going to one hell of a roll. Hang on."

The end of the runway comes up fast. Stephanie keeps us on the centerline. The brakes protest with a high-pitched sound that reminds me of metal rubbing on metal. Finally, we come to a stop. A lot of smoke billows up and into the cockpit, and I can smell burning rubber and fuel. "Let's get outa here," Stephanie yells to me.

"After you, Captain."

"Smart ass."

"Okay, I'm going." I get up and open the cockpit door. Smoke fills the passenger cabin. One of the guys has deployed the stairs. Leroy, Jesse, and the SEALs wait for us to leave. I look back to make sure Stephanie is out of her seat. She comes by me, and we both head for the stairs. I follow her down the steps with the guys right behind us. On the tarmac, Stephanie encourages us to get away as far as possible. The crash crews pull up to the fuselage and pump foam everywhere.

"We have to stop meeting like this," I say.

"No kidding." Stephanie grins. "This running away from burning planes is getting old."

"Not to mention losing all our clothes each time."

Stephanie throws her head back and laughs hard. I have to join her, if nothing else, to relieve the tension. Leroy and Jesse stare at us as if we're crazy. The SEALs look like this is all perfectly normal.

The emergency crews contain the fire, and it seems as though there might only be a little damage to the main body of the airplane. "Our clothes may be okay, after all," I say.

"Yeah, if you're a smoker." Stephanie laughs.

"I suppose that fuel smoke isn't something that'll come out easily."

"Think greasy smoke."

"Oh well. Easy come easy go."

With a shrug and a grin, I move over to Leroy and Jesse and ask what the next steps will be. Already, Leroy has called in the problem to his boss, which I assume is Ramon, although Leroy didn't mention his name specifically.

I push for more information, "What did he say?"

"To sit tight, and a car will be here shortly."

"Okay. Sounds good. I'll bet you didn't know your job was going to be this complex, did you?"

"I have to say, Mr. Cannon, I never thought I would be guarding a person who has such a powerful enemy. At least, one who wants to keep trying to kill him. That attempt on the plane took some real coordination."

"I wish someone would go after the source. Matt Jacobs is trying to kill me, and he doesn't care a jot who goes with me."

"Yeah, I wish I could help. I'm getting tired of being in the line of fire."

I don't know what to say to that, and while I try to think of something good, my phone rings. "This is John."

"John. Thank heavens," Ned says. "You okay?"

"Yes, all of us are fine."

"Man, that's a good thing. What the hell happened? I'm getting the info off the accident notice."

"After we climbed to our cruising altitude, a missile hit us. It blew out the windshield and, unfortunately, killed the crew."

"Oh, my good God. I can't believe it."

"Let me ask. Who knew we were on that particular plane?"

"That's the interesting part. No one knew the exact plane. On purpose, I put that information on a need to know basis, and I didn't think anyone needed to know."

"Hold on, Ned. Let me walk away for some privacy." I move away until I'm sure none of the others can hear me. "Okay, I'm back. Is there any chance Leroy or Jesse gave the information to Ramon? They could have given the tail number to Ramon before takeoff. These guys are always on the phone with someone, so I wouldn't have noticed."

"Could be possible. We're still checking the cell tower information back at Greenbrier to see what transmissions we pick up. We're close to springing the trap on Ramon. I can't believe Jacobs appears to know exactly where you are at all times."

"Getting a little tense, Ned. Is there a way to hurry the hell up?"

"Yeah. I think we'll do it when you get back here."

"Do ya think Jacobs will try another rocket or missile or whatever that was?"

"Not going to take a chance. You and Stephanie will be packed into an F18 and shuttled here at Mach speed. The fighters will detect any missile and avoid it."

"What about the Secret Service? Leroy and Jesse, that is."

"They'll go on another plane. They'll be okay. They won't know how you're getting home, and we'll plant the information that you and Stephanie will be taking a G4 to Corpus. We'll order them to put you on the plane and proceed back to Washington. That will allow them a chance to report the tail number if that's what they're gonna do. The G4 will take off and wait until those two are on another plane before returning to base. From there, you'll get a super ride. How's that sound?"

"Again, a lot of trouble, but I won't fight it. I'm tired of trying to avoid getting killed."

"Okay, so—needless to say—you don't need to do anything. Just go with the flow."

"Needless, but I'm glad you mentioned it. I'll cool it."

"Good boy. See ya." Ned is gone. Should I say anything to Stephanie? Perhaps it's best to keep her in the dark, as she might act differently if she knew. Most likely, she'll get angry later, but in the meantime, she'll have some peace of mind, not having to worry about everything working. The plan feels somewhat open-ended. If Leroy and Jesse report the tail number of the plane they think we're on, and Ramon reports it to Jacobs, there's a strong possibility that Jacobs will make another attempt.

If he does, then Ramon is caught. If not, then we'll be in the same place we are now, not knowing if Ramon is guilty or not. Oh well, the main objective is to get Stephanie and me to Corpus and not necessarily to catch Ramon.

"What's going on?" Stephanie comes up behind me, and I jump at her words.

"Not too much. Ned just told me that another plane will take us to Corpus. A G4. They're recalling Leroy and Jesse to Washington. Looks like we'll be on our own."

"I can't say that they were of much help in fighting off missiles, helicopters, and rockets anyway."

"I have to laugh at that, but you're right. I don't think that Jacobs has a hand-to-hand elimination plan in mind. He's looking for a total wipe out. We should be okay."

Stephanie entwines her fingers in mine and leans on my shoulder. "I guess, if we're together, we'll be safe. We make an awesome warrior couple."

"You mean, you make a warrior couple. I feel helpless most of the time. You were so good in that cockpit. I don't think anyone could have done a better job."

"Oh poo, John. We worked together and got it done. Nothing more needs to be said." She rubs her eyes. "I feel wiped out."

"I know what you mean. Once the adrenaline stops, all that's left is a wilted body. We should get some rest on the plane."

"You promise? I sure hope no one shoots it down. That would put a real crimp in the rest program."

"Okay." I dip my head and glance at my feet. "I have to let you know the plan." I drop to a whisper. "We're going to take a couple of F18s after we pretend to get on the G4."

"No shit. Damn, I wonder if the pilot will let me fly it."

"That's your only comment?"

"Yeah. What else would you expect me to say?"

"Oh, I don't know. Maybe some complaint about no rest."

"Believe me, this trumps the rest."

Chapter Fifteen

An SUV arrives and picks us all up. We'd gotten so lost in watching the emergency crews put out the fire that the car might have been there waiting for a while. When the driver taps on Leroy's shoulder, his presence startles us.

We get into the vehicle, and the driver takes us to a hangar on the other side of the base. A G4 sits inside. A young officer comes up to us and explains that we should get on the Gulfstream. He turns to Leroy and Jesse. "Your plane is another car ride away, in the next hangar."

Stephanie and I climb the stairs, leaving the two agents, and enter the cabin of the plane. We drop into the first set of seats we come to.

"Man, I'm tired." I lean back and sigh.

"Tell me about it." Stephanie slumps into her chair. "You say we're just going to taxi, take off, and then return?"

"That's what Ned said."

"You think these guys will send the tail number?"

"I think that's part of their regular operating procedure. What isn't normal, is if someone like Ramon sends the information to Jacobs."

"Yeah, I get that."

The young officer comes to us. "Excuse me. It is my understanding that we will do a go around and come back to base. I ask that you buckle up and make yourself comfortable for this short flight. I'm sorry there won't be time for any beverage service. Would you like anything before takeoff?"

Stephanie and I both decline. The officer goes into the cockpit and closes the door.

"That was nice," I say.

Stephanie frowns. "I hope he didn't let the Secret Service know."

"Good point. I'm sure they briefed him not to say anything."

"We'd be wise to ask on the way out."

"I'll do it. Thanks."

The engines give their usual whine in complaint at having to go to work and, before long, we roll out of the hangar. I look out the window and cannot see Leroy or Jesse anywhere. I can't see the SUV either, so I assume they're headed to their plane, and may have taken off already. While we taxi, the captain comes on the intercom and says, "We are number two for takeoff." The plane with Jesse and Leroy will take off before us. The pilot chuckles, and then says, "The co-pilot and I were too slow for the other captain, and he wants to go in front of us."

Stephanie and I smile at the poetic justice here. The captain further explains, "We will take off according to plan. There is no telling who may be watching. I plan to call an emergency once we're airborne, so we will be required to go around. If anyone *is* watching, they will think we have left the area. Please, check your seatbelts, as we are ready to roll."

I grin at Stephanie. "That answers the question about the co-pilot saying anything. Looks like these guys are fully checked out."

"This kind of close co-ordination always makes me nervous."

"How so?"

"Almost anything can go wrong."

"Well, check that seatbelt—we're rolling."

We start down the runway, and in what seems like seconds, we are airborne. We climb for a few minutes. Stephanie looks through the window and confirms that we've reached about three thousand feet. The engines slow, and the plane enters a slow turn to bring us back in the opposite direction. Another few minutes pass and the landing gear deploys.

Stephanie says, "We're at twenty-five percent flaps. Looks like we're cleared to land."

We sit in silence as the various noises of landing prepare us for a touchdown. The tires squeal, and then a bump comes when both wheels connect with the runway. The nose settles toward the ground, and now all three wheels run on a firm footing. The captain deploys the reverse thrusters, and the plane slows dramatically. We taxi to another hangar and go right inside. The pilot breaks hard and kills the engines.

The co-pilot comes out of the cockpit and gives a thumbs up. We undo the seatbelts and move to the door. The stairs descend, and we go down. We stand in the company of a number of people. A Navy Commander comes out of the crowd and extends his hand to Stephanie and me.

"Commander Hanlin," he says. "Let me introduce you to a few folks here."

"Thank you, Commander. That would be great."

"First up are your two pilots. This is Lieutenant Weems, who will take Ms. Savard to Corpus, and Lieutenant Henly, who will take you."

We shake hands and express our thanks for the ride. They are both gracious and let us know it is their pleasure. I believe them.

"Next, you should meet the intelligence officer, Captain Weber."

We shake her hand as well. She and Stephanie have met before, so they have a little reunion.

The commander cuts the chat short. "Two FA-18F Super Hornets will transport you to the Corpus Christi Naval Air Station. The second seat is usually occupied by the fire control officer, but since we don't intend to do any shooting, we think you will be okay back there."

Stephanie and I laugh, and the commander grins. "The rest of the folks here are flight crew personnel. They will get you suited up and into the cockpit. Ms. Savard, we understand you are a combat pilot and a full commander."

Stephanie blushes. "Yes, that is correct."

"You checked out in the 18F?"

"Yes, sir, I have over ten thousand hours in the 18E, including two tours over Iraq and Afghanistan."

The entire room holds its breath, and then air rushes over lips in a collective gasp. They're all impressed. "Well, then, if Lieutenant Weems approves, maybe he will let you take the controls for a bit." Lieutenant Weems speaks up and says loudly, "She is more than welcome to fly the mission." Hearty laughter meets that statement. Weems adds, "Besides, she outranks me, and I never argue with a superior officer." This brings more laughter and a feeling of comradeship between the pilots and crew.

"Okay then," the major says. "Let's head out to the line. The vehicle is right outside."

Stephanie shakes hands with the intelligence officer, and her aircrew surrounds her. More than impressed that this innocent looking person is a rock star in the air combat world. All kinds of smiles blossom.

My crew also surrounds me, and although we don't have the same electricity, they seem pleased to have me aboard. They lead the way out to a four-by-four, which has enough seats in the back for all of us. We climb in, and the aircrew throws in equipment, including helmets and flight suits, and climbs in as well. A jeep waits in front of us, with a large sign that says follow me. The jeep sets off, and the four-by-four follows, as ordered.

We pull out onto what appears to be an active runway. I ask one of the crew, "Is it dangerous?"

He shakes his head and says, "There are no flights scheduled, but if there were, we would take a different course."

"Thanks." How different a military airfield is from civilian. Maybe five minutes later, we arrive to find six beautiful fighters lined up. Our vehicle stops, and the crews jump down. I do likewise and look back to see Stephanie's pilot holding out his hand to help her. A nice gesture. My blood rises in my face. I should have been the one to help her. My problem is, she would have declined my help but freely accepts Weems' assistance. Am I jealous? A little voice inside me says, "You think?"

We separate, and the commander points to two of the planes. Stephanie's crew takes her to the one furthest away. My crew leads me to another. The crew chief comes over with some equipment.

"Here is your flight suit. You can put it on over your street clothes."

I take the suit and need to sit to put it on. Once I've removed my shoes, the crew chief takes me over to the four-by-four, where I sit on the running board and pull on the tight-fitting suit. At the end of the row, Stephanie has managed to get her suit on by using her crew chief's shoulder for balance. Our pilots have started the ground check already. They each walk around, feeling the wings and inspecting various places. Now that the suit is on, I feel quite warm. Drops of perspiration bead on my upper lip.

Next, the chief gives me a hand with the parachute. He explains, "The emergency chute is on the front, and the main one will be under you for the trip. In the case of an emergency, the pilot will instruct how to leave the airplane. Don't jump out before he gives you some advice. There is a way to release from the plane that will become apparent should you need it. I don't want you cut in two by the stabilizer." He walks over to the pilot, and they share an inside joke, and when they look over at me, they're chuckling. Most likely, he thinks he scared me with the bailout brief and the comment about getting cut in two. I'm glad I managed to keep up my poker face.

Finally, the word comes for us to man our planes. The chief takes me to the rear of the wing and instructs me to climb to the rear and use the little ladder there to get inside. "I'll meet you up there," he says. Climbing on the wing isn't as easy as it looks. Without sneakers, my soles slip on the slick skin. At last, I manage to get up and reach the ladder, and then I climb into the cockpit. I hold onto the sides and lower myself into the seat. To avoid hitting the side of the open canopy, I crab into place. My first impression is how small the space is. Each side gives me almost no room to move my arms. The chief appears over me and helps adjust the lap and shoulder harness. "This needs to be tight." Then he yanks something and pulls the whole thing snug. "Here is your belt release lever. Pull this when you land in Corpus and you can get out. Do not pull it until you are clear of the airplane should you have to eject. You are now one piece with your seat."

"Thank you, chief. I hope I won't need to remember what you just told me."

"Here is your helmet. It has a communication module built in so you and Lieutenant Henley will be able to communicate. You will also be able to hear the communications with the ground and with Ms. Savard's plane. Here, let me help you with it."

The chef fits the helmet on my head and then hooks up the electronics. He also pulls an oxygen face mask inside and tells me to put it on. The mask connects to the helmet via snaps, which the chief helps me find. "Your mic is inside the mask. You'll need to go on oxygen for take-off since you will climb to your cruising altitude quickly. Where you guys are going, there is no air to breathe. We don't want to lose you."

"I appreciate that." The chief then shows me how to lower and raise the visor on the helmet. "Leave it down for the trip. You'll avoid the glare of the sun," he says. Finally, he gives my helmet a slap and disappears, after wishing us God's speed.

It feels funny being bolted into this plane—as if I'm wearing it rather than riding in it. With a glance around, I recognize a couple of instruments from my flying lessons in a Cessna 172. The artificial horizon sits directly in front of me. I can pick out the attitude indicator and the directional finder. There is an altimeter, but the rest of the screens look like an expensive video game. The guy who normally rides back here must be brilliant, as it's my understanding that he's the one in charge of getting to the target and unloading whatever needs unloading. A red button, with the letters JETT in the center, catches my attention. It must be the final button to push for ejection out of here. Maybe I should forget that button for a while. In fact, I'd best keep my hands to myself unless instructed to do something.

Lieutenant Henley slides into the front seat. The crew chief gives him the same help, minus the pep talk. After the required helmet slap, the chief drops out of sight. "Mr. Cannon, Lieutenant Henley here. How's the intercom working?"

"I hear you. Can you hear me?"

"Yessir, just fine. We are going to get underway. I will close the canopy now and start the engines. Look to your right. See the cabin temp dial?"

"I sure do."

"Go ahead and adjust it if you get cold. We will be close to fifty thousand feet, so the temp outside will be in the minus thirty to fifty range. You just might need some heat. Your temp setting is just above the knob."

"Yes, I see it. Seventy-two degrees."

"Good. Are you ready?"

"All set. You will give me any instructions if I need to do anything, won't you?"

"I hope all you have to do is look around and enjoy the ride. This flight will last a little over two hours, and should be routine."

"Maybe routine for you, but for me, this is exciting stuff."

"I can imagine. I remember when I had my first solo in the F18. I thought I was going to throw up, I was so nervous."

"You're kidding?"

"No. I mean it. I was shaking the plane apart."

"Well, lucky for both of us, I won't be flying this baby."

"Okay, stand by. I need to call the tower." The lieutenant clears his throat. "Military ATC. Flight leader Maddog is ready to enter the active runway."

Stephanie's pilot speaks on the comms, 'Military ATC. Ripper ready to enter the active runway.'

"Roger, Maddog and Ripper, you are cleared to the active runway. Depart on one-five-left. You may start your engines, and when in place, contact flight control on one-three-eight-dot-seven."

"One-five-left. One-three-eight-dot-seven. Roger, Maddog. Ripper, you got that?"

"Rog, Maddog, one-five-left. One-three-eight-dot-seven. Ripper, out."

"Okay, Mr. Cannon. We will get underway. If you need to talk to me, just touch the intercom button on the panel to your right. Otherwise, everything you say will be heard by Ripper and Ms. Savard since we will be on an open frequency."

"I got it. Thanks."

The lieutenant works switches, and then an engine turns over. It catches, and the second follows. The lieutenant releases his brakes, and we move to the taxiway. We pass Ripper's and Stephanie's plane. We taxi past the hangars and make a turn. Ripper takes position beside us. It looks like we'll take off in tandem. I've never seen this so up close, and my heart pounds in my chest. The lieutenant calls flight control, who give us the authorization to take off.

The plane strains against the brakes, and the nose moves closer to the runway, as the lieutenant raises the power level. He releases the brakes, and the plane jumps forward. I've been in fast cars before but nothing like this. We roar down the runway. The force presses against the seat, and my skin feels stretched across my face. Suddenly, the nose lifts off, followed by the rest of the plane. We are airborne. And then, just as fast, it feels like we're standing on the tail of the craft. I look over at Ripper's plane, and which seems no more than six inches away. "Ripper, come to two-four-oh on my mark. Maddog."

"Two-four-oh on your mark. Ripper."

"Mark."

We enter a gradual turn to the west. Ripper's plane looks like an invisible wire attaches it to our craft. In formation, we continue to climb, and I'm not sure how fast we're going. I look at the airspeed indicator—nearing five hundred miles an hour. The altimeter looks like a clock that has gone haywire due to the velocity of our ascent. Above, I see the perfectly blue sky with

John W Howell

not a cloud in sight, and at this speed, it feels like we could go to Mars.

Chapter Sixteen

The flight to Corpus Christi takes two hours. We descend into the airspace, and control clears us to land. The two planes taxi together and follow orders to head inside the hangar. Once in, the engines stop, and the canopies raise. In the other plane, Stephanie shakes her hair free, and it falls on her shoulders when she takes off her helmet. She looks like a kid who's just had a roller coaster ride. Obviously, she had a great time flying the F18.

A crewman comes up and helps me with the helmet and harness release. I say "thank you," and he looks pleased to be part of the team. It seems a little easier getting out of the plane than getting in. Once on the ground, I realize I feel weak in the knees.

"Perfectly normal," the lieutenant says. "The speed and G-forces tend to make you a bit wobbly. Drink some water; it should pass soon."

"Thanks." I feel like I just got off a boat but manage to walk over to Stephanie.

"How did you like that ride?" She wears a huge grin.

"I loved it. It was way cool to see the darkness beyond us, above the atmosphere. I don't think I'll forget that very soon."

"That always gets to me, as well."

"You fly that thing?"

"Sure did. It was great. Makes me miss going up. I'm still not cleared for flight. Hope it will be soon."

"For your sake, I hope so too." That was my outside voice. My inside voice wanted to tell her, I hope you don't get cleared for a while since I know, when you do, you'll be gone. Who can think of getting serious with a guy who can't fly a damned sophisticated jet fighter? Certainly not some female jet jockey used to landing on aircraft carriers.

"Hey, kid." Ned's voice.

I turn around, and there he stands with a big smile. I grab his hand. "Hey! How you doing?"

"Not a question of how I'm doing. How are *you* doing?"

"Just fine. Hey, Stephanie, look who's here."

Stephanie is all smiles while she shakes Ned's hand. Ned asks her, "How you feeling?"

"Great. How about you?"

"Well, now I know you two are okay, I'm just fine."

I ask, "So, what's the drill?"

"We're gonna get out of here and motor back to Port Aransas. Then we'll grab some dinner, and I'll give you a briefing on what we found out about Ramon."

"You going to make me wait until after dinner for that?"

"You won't like it."

"What do you mean?"

"We found nothing, that's what."

"Nothing? How is that possible? He was the only one who knew that Stephanie and I were on that plane."

"Come on, let's get in the car. We can continue this talk on the way back."

Ned takes the lead, and we go to his Police SUV. While walking, I can't help but feel that someone must have overlooked something if he thinks Ramon is innocent. There can be no other explanation for the missile attack. Someone knew where we were. We get into Ned's vehicle. "So, what makes you think Ramon isn't giving information to Jacobs?" I ask.

Ned starts the vehicle and pulls out before he says anything. A Humvee follows behind us, and I have to assume the SEALs have returned to guard duty.

Ned speaks with care, "John, we've monitored hours and hours of conversations involving Ramon. He hasn't contacted anyone who could be considered remotely connected with Jacobs. We've tailed him, put bugs in his house, car, and office. His timeline is covered end to end, and all his activities check out."

"Couldn't he use phones that you don't have covered?"

"I don't think so. If he made a call on, let's say, a disposable phone under observation, and we didn't have a corresponding recording, we'd know he'd used another phone. There have been no other phones."

"Could you observe him twenty-four-seven?"

"I suppose he could somehow sneak away, but the important thing is, he was never out of our contact. We either had him on video or sound wire. Every moment is accounted for."

"How about when he was asleep?"

"The microphones picked up his breathing. And our infrared picked up the heat of his body. I'm telling you, he did not do anything suspicious."

"Okay, I guess I'll have to take your word. I'm just not pleased since I looked forward to eliminating the leak to Jacobs and thought Ramon was it."

"Yeah, well, sorry about that one myself. I would love to pin it on someone and have it end."

"So, where we going?"

"Your house is as good as any. It's remote enough that we don't have to involve your neighbors. Also, it's in a nice spot on the beach and gives us a great three-hundred-and-sixty-degree view, which will be easy to defend."

"Defend?"

Ned laughs. "Don't worry, junior. If Jacobs tries anything, we'll be ready. Wait until you see what we've arranged."

"Arranged?" I sound like a parrot.

"You'll be impressed. If Jacobs does decide to do anything funny, we have plenty of coverage. We set up a field defensive post around your house."

"I wish I could tell you this is entertaining, but I don't like putting Stephanie at any risk."

She looks at me like I walked out of a cave somewhere. "Speak for yourself, John Cannon. I can certainly handle anything that comes up."

"That came out wrong. I just meant that maybe we should go somewhere else. We can't conduct a major battle in my neighborhood."

Ned says, "I don't think there'll be a major battle. I *do* think Jacobs will try something, though. You know, like kidnaping one of you, or something like that. This is all we want to prevent."

"Okay. I just don't want any innocent people to get hurt because of me."

"For sure."

We ride along in silence. Finally, I ask Stephanie to tell me about her ride in the F18. Her eyes light up, and she recounts how great she felt to be in control of the plane.

I ask, "Did you fly it the whole way?"

With a nod and a grin, she says, "I even landed."

Not thinking too much of myself, I say, "I'm delighted that you got the chance."

At last, we pull into my driveway, and Ned asks us to keep our seats while he talks to the guys in the Humvee. He gets out and goes back to them. I turn around to watch him through the rear window. Ned stands talking to a couple of guys in uniform. After making wide gestures with his arms, he returns to our car and opens the door. "Okay, y'all can go inside."

Stephanie and I get out and walk toward the front door. The men spread out around the house, probably to take up positions on all sides. I count six of them, so they should have all four corners covered with a couple of extra. Walking along, I see what looks like rocket launchers leaning against the house. "What are those things?"

"Ah, those. We decided to have a couple of shoulder-mounted Stingers around just in case Jacobs repeats the missile thing."

"You said there wouldn't be a major battle. This looks like something out of Afghanistan."

"Yeah, I have to admit, it does look a little hairy, but believe me, we want to be careful."

"I can just see one of these Stingers taking out a plane or missile, and the damn thing crashes into the neighbor's house."

"Not going to happen, John. It's just, we need to be prepared in case. We think any attack will come from the Gulf side, and we'll have enough warning to scramble a jet or two. These are just in case something gets through."

"Okay, I'm through trying to be the voice of worry here. I just hope you guys know what you're doing."

"Now you're hurting my feelings." I look at Ned, and his smile shows that he's totally putting me on. He could care less what I think or say. He has a job to do and, like always, he will do it well.

I take Stephanie's arm and guide her through the front entrance. "Welcome to my humble abode."

"Oh, this is lovely. I like the furniture."

"It's brand new. I rented this place furnished, and Jacobs' thugs made mincemeat out of everything in the house."

"Why did they do that?"

"We thought they were looking for evidence of Jacobs and I being together—he'd given me one of his cards. They didn't know it, but the card went to the bottom of the sea when they blew up my boat."

"So they didn't find it?"

"No, but they did plant some tracking devices in my shoes. The destruction turned out to be a mere ruse to cover the fact that they could now find me anytime they wanted."

"Clever."

"You want to freshen up?"

"Sounds good right about now."

"Follow me. Here is the spare room, and it has a bathroom inside. Please, make yourself comfortable."

"Okay then. I'll take a shower if that's okay."

"Yeah, anything. There should be towels and stuff in there. Why don't you check? Also, we need to find you a change of clothes, but first things first."

"I'll be right back."

While Stephanie goes to make sure she has what she needs, I try to think of anything I have that she could wear. I have a pair of board shorts and a t-shirt that are too small. Maybe she could put a belt on the shorts and wear the t-shirt on the outside. That would, at least, be something clean until we can get her more.

"All looks good. Oh, sorry, I didn't mean to startle you."

When she spoke, I jumped, lost in thought. "Oh no, that's okay. I was just thinking about suitable clothes. Wait here."

I go down the hall to the master bedroom and pull open a drawer. The shorts and t-shirt lie among a few other items. After grabbing both, I head back to Stephanie. "Here. This t-shirt is too small for me, so maybe you can wear it outside the shorts, which will be too big for you."

"Oh, thank you. Let me see if these work. You wouldn't have a spare pair of panties would you?"

Blushing to the maximum, I barely sputter out an answer. Stephanie laughs deeply and closes the door. When I return to the living room, Ned meets me.

"We need to get some clothes for Stephanie."

"Yeah, already taken care of. We have someone getting her some basics right now."

"How do they know her size?"

"I'll call my guy once she's told me. Where is the lady?"

"In the shower. I gave her some shorts and a t-shirt."

"Okay, when she comes out, we'll sort it. I'd like to talk to you about the investigation into the killing of Vincent Herron."

"You guys know who did it?"

"We think, the same guy who ambushed us in front of your house and built the bomb. We did some lab work on his clothes and found traces of C4 on his pants. It looks like he had some of the explosives on his hands and wiped them on his pants."

"Yes, but that guy died in the ambush long before they blew up Vincent."

"True. I reckon that he built the bomb, and someone else detonated it."

"Any clue?"

"We do have the cell phone records, and we picked up three possible signals that occurred at around the same time as the explosion."

"You're saying you can find those numbers?"

"We've accounted for two of the three. It seems the third number was a throwaway. So all we know for certain is that a phone detonated the bomb. We don't know who belongs to the number."

"What's next?"

"We've sent officers to the local dump to see if we can find it. Whoever used it, most likely turned it off and threw it away, seeing as that number isn't active anywhere in this area."

"How you going to find it in a dump?"

Ned looks skyward before answering, "We know where the trash from that particular pickup is located. And we can use careful search techniques to try and locate the phone."

"It'll be like the old needle in a haystack."

"We know. If we can find the phone, we might find prints or something. That would help us track it back to the retailer. Who knows? It's the only evidence that we have that hasn't been blown to bits."

"Better than nothing, all right."

"We also confirmed that the guy who shot me was a hired hand. He went by the name Tombstone and was a gun for hire. He had no ID, but we picked him up through a facial recognition scan. Regular Army with a boat load of ribbons all the way back to Viet Nam. He was an explosive expert and an Airborne Ranger to boot. One tough SOB."

"Who killed him, do you think?"

"I'd guess, another hired gun. I'm not so sure this guy was ever supposed to live. The way he placed those four bullets, he was a good shot. I still don't know why he didn't shoot to kill. We may never know."

"Not until we catch Jacobs."

"I wouldn't hold your breath. Jacobs is a tough one too."

Stephanie walks into the room; hair still damp from her shower. "What's up?"

Ned shrugs. "Nothin' much right now. John's stuff looks good on you."

Stephanie gives us a cat-walk twirl. It's hard for that woman to look bad in anything. I nod in approval and say, "The chief wants your measurements so he can send them to his guy, who's shopping for clothes."

She grins and wags a finger. "You be careful with that tape measure."

Ned blushes a deep shade of red. "Just give me your sizes, and I'll write them down."

We all laugh at Ned's embarrassment, and then Stephanie does as asked. Ned writes them in a small book and then steps away to make his call. It takes a few minutes, and in the meantime, I ask Stephanie what she would like to do this afternoon. "Mmm, I'd like to take a tour of the Port Aransas area. Do you suppose it's okay to go out?"

"We'd better check with Ned." Just as I say his name, he returns. "Stephanie and I wondered about taking a tour of the town. What do you think?"

"I don't like it. You two ought to stay put for a while. If you go wandering off, Jacobs' job will be much easier. Why not watch a movie or something."

"Gee, Dad. That sounds like no fun at all, but you're probably right." I catch Stephanie's gaze. "What do you think?"

With a shrug, she says, "Ned makes a good point. Why don't we think of what to have for dinner, and then we can just relax here."

Ned says, "Now, here's someone with sense. Your clothes should get here a bit later. A person named Sally will deliver them. She's a Marine but seems to know something about style."

"I'm sure the clothes will be fine." Stephanie offers a warm smile Ned's way, and then turns to me. "What goodies you got in the freezer?"

"Let's look and see." We head into the kitchen to check out the food situation. "Well, I've got a nice packet of chicken breasts. They won't take long to thaw. And I see some mixed veggies."

"That all sounds good. Can you handle the cooking?"

"Yeah. I'll do the chicken on the grill and the veggies in the microwave. We've got ice cream, too, and I know I have some fudge in a jar, which we can heat."

"Mmm. Now I'm real interested."

"Great. I'll put the breasts in cold water. Ned, you staying for dinner?"

"Sure would like to, junior, but I have some things to do. I'll take a rain check if you don't mind. Okay, you two. I'm leaving now. Don't go anywhere."

I nod. "We got it."

"And, if you go outside for any reason, let one of the squad members escort you around."

"Okay. When you coming back?"

"I'll give you a call."

"See you later."

Ned leaves, and Stephanie and I go to the living room. I tell her, "I have streaming Netflix, so if you want to watch a movie, we can."

She smiles. "Thanks, but I'm happy to sit and relax. "You have some interesting magazines here. It'll be nice just looking at something mindless for a while."

Stephanie sits on the couch and picks up a copy of GQ magazine. As she flips through the pages, I move to the sound system. On the remote, I hit the power button, and then the shuffle button—I have a number of different styles racked up, and I hope it will be a nice selection. Stephanie smiles, so hopefully that means she likes it. I check the volume and keep it on the lower end of the range.

"Would you care for something to drink?"

Stephanie glances up from the mag. "Do you have any ice tea? If not, water will do."

At the refrigerator, I call back that I think I have some bottled ice tea.

"That would be great."

I return with the beverage. "Green tea with lemon, and I put it over ice."

"Sounds refreshing. Thank you."

Stephanie takes the glass and asks for a coaster. Since the coffee table is made of rattan, I tell her a coaster won't be necessary. I give her a napkin instead, and make a mental note to get some coasters so that she won't feel uncomfortable the next time. Always hoping there will be a next time. She sips her tea and raises her eyes in pleasure. I smile and take a gulp of mine. Then I pick up a magazine, stretch out on the other couch, and leaf through Coastal Living. The homes pictured in this magazine always surprise me. They all look like nobody lives there. The paint and furniture seem perfect, and there is never anything out of place. I'd like to see how the house looks with people inside. But then, who can afford these kinds of homes? Some of them must cost several million. With a shrug, I turn another page.

Stephanie startles me when she asks, "You ever think about that night we made love?"

"Yes, I do. It's one of my nicest memories."

"Mine too. Do you think we'll ever get back to that kind of relationship?"

"If you mean having sex, I would hope so."

"No, it's not the sex. I'm talking about the trust we had then."

"I didn't even think about trust. I thought you liked me, and I liked you, and we made love."

"Yes, well, this may be my feminine side talking, but I had a feeling we could be close."

"I had the same feeling."

"You did? It wasn't just a one-night stand for you?"

"No. I hoped we could see more of each other."

"What happened with you and Sarah?"

Damn. There it is. I've been worried about this conversation, and now it's upon me. "Jacobs forced Sarah to have sex with me so that the pictures would drive us apart."

"I understand why Sarah acted the way she did. I just don't understand how you could have sex with someone without thinking through the consequences."

"I recall that you and I had sex without thinking through the consequences."

"Yes, we did, and I don't know why this particular situation bothers me, but it does. I tried hard to ignore it, and then when I'm alone with you, it all comes back as a promise broken."

"Broken? By who?"

"I'm somewhat foolish, I know, yet I still feel betrayed by the whole thing."

"I understand. I'm not proud of what happened, and I would like to get it behind us if we can."

"Maybe it'll just take time. It would be nice to make love and again, but that thought feels wrong."

"Until you trust me, that kind of intimacy is out of the question."

Stephanie sits in quiet contemplation but does offer a nod.

"You'll learn to trust me. It'll just take time. In the meantime, you ready to start dinner?"

"Boy, you know how to change a subject."

"This one is a little embarrassing, and I want to drop it for now. I do appreciate you being honest with me and sharing your feelings."

"I hope I don't hurt them. Your feelings, I mean."

"If anyone has a hurt anything, I believe it's you. So, don't worry about me."

Chapter Seventeen

Stephanie and I manage to put a decent chicken dinner on the table. When we've eaten, I suggest we go out on the porch to take advantage of the cooler weather that's descended on the Gulf. At least, the nights have cooled off. September is a great time on the coast. The daytime temperatures are in the nineties, but then the night drifts down to the high seventies. We take our wine with us and move to head outside. "Excuse me, sir." One of the SEALs steps up to me. "You should stay inside."

"Come on, will a couple of minutes watching the waves hurt?"

"As long as you're okay with me standing here, I don't see a problem."

I nod. "You're more than welcome to. There won't be any juicy conversation, I'm afraid."

"That suits me fine, sir."

Seated in the chairs on the porch, Stephanie and I enjoy looking at the Gulf while the sun sets behind us. A few clouds drift through the sky, and the setting sun casts a beautiful pink hue to the East over the Gulf.

"Wow," Stephanie says. "Gorgeous."

"Most evenings end like this, and I wanted you to see it."

We sit in silence, and I think over our earlier conversation. Hopefully, we can get past the Sarah thing. I made a mistake, but not on purpose. If those pictures had never been taken and sent to Stephanie, we'd have no problems.

Noise from behind catches my attention. The SEAL lieutenant stands in the doorway.

"Mr. Cannon, we have visitors. You and Ms. Savard need to step inside."

I look at Stephanie and motion for her to get up and go in.

"What kind of visitors?" I ask as I walk into the house.

"Not sure, sir. We've picked up a low-flying plane coming from the East."

"Over the Gulf?"

"Yes, sir. We're not sure what kind but it seems to be traveling at high speed. We've tried every frequency, but it hasn't responded. We have to assume it isn't friendly."

"Can you shoot it down?"

"Yeah, we can use our shoulder mounts once they get within range."

Apprehensive, I glance out of the window. "How soon?"

"A few minutes. You and Ms. Savard should take cover on the beach. I'll assign a man to you. Better get moving." The lieutenant waves one of the SEALs over and gives him instructions. He looks at Stephanie and nods. The second SEAL motions us out. He follows, and then says, "Go over the boardwalk to the beach."

I grab Stephanie's hand, and we head for the sand. Once there, the SEAL tells us to move closer to the dune and try and make ourselves comfortable. The SEALs want us to have a dune between the house and us in case of an explosion in or around the house. The SEAL then takes a position facing the Gulf, with Stephnie and me between him and the dune. Grim-faced, he raises his weapon and aims it out over the water.

The SEAL listens to something, then says, "Yes, sir, roger that." He turns to us, "Mr. Cannon, the lieutenant says the plane is about ten miles out and moving at over five hundred knots. It'll reach us in about a minute. You and Ms. Savard need to keep your heads down and cover up as best as you can. We have two guys with stingers, which they will let go in twenty seconds. With any luck, the explosion will make a nice display over the water. If he gets through, we think he'll drop incendiaries on the house. Either way, you need to stay down."

I don't hear the bullet, but the SEAL's head disintegrates in a blur of red. Shock freezes me in place. The power of the shot drives the SEAL to the sand. Since she is looking away from the water, Stephanie has no idea that something isn't right. Finally, I get my limbs to move and shout for her to run.

Stephanie looks around, and her eyes go wide. A dark circle spreads from under his head. She freezes, so I grab her arm and yank her to her feet. "We need to get out of here." Just as I finish speaking, four trails of orange flame come out of the darkness over the water. The rockets hit the house, and the force of the explosion knocks us both to our knees. Evidently, the stinger missiles missed the incoming aircraft. A dark shape roars over the top of us. The heat from the jet blast indicates that he must be real close to the ground. I don't hear any weapons firing from the direction of the burning building. Not a good sign. I look up, and the plane makes a slow turn. In the dark and smoke, I lose sight of him. There is no doubt in my mind that he will come back for another run. Adrenaline pumping, I grab Stephanie and force her to run down the beach. I want to get as far away as I can.

Winded, we ease to a stop. "We need to keep moving." I'm so out of breath that I barely get the words out.

Stephanie gasps for air. "Just let me catch my breath."

Up ahead, headlights come into view. For once, I'm glad Texas allows driving on the beach. "I'll wave down this driver and see if he'll give us a lift."

Stephanie shakes her head. "He's going the wrong way. We'll end up going back by the house."

With an eye roll, I tell her, "I'll get him to turn around."

Another explosion erupts. The firelight shows the silhouette of the returning plane, which banks for another pass. Thank goodness we made it out of there. I turn back to the headlights and wave my arms. It doesn't occur to me that Jacobs' men might be in the vehicle.

The driver of the black SUV lowers his window. "Mr. Cannon. Please, get in."

Startled, I take a step back. "Who're you?"

"Agent Mead of the Secret Service."

"Do you have ID?"

"Of course." He reaches into his jacket breast pocket. "Here, take a look. I would like to vacate the vicinity, sir. So, if you could examine my credentials inside the vehicle?"

Another two guys occupy the back of the SUV. They each climb out and hold a door.

I move further away. "Just a minute." I hold the ID portfolio out to Stephanie. "How do these look to you?"

"Legit."

I glance at the driver. "What's your date of birth?"

"It says right there."

"I want you to tell me."

From behind, someone grabs me around the arms and shoves a black bag over my head. It feels like two people hold me, and struggling produces nothing. I shout out to Stephanie, but she doesn't answer. Then a sharp pain stings in my right bicep. My brain tries to catch up to what is happening, and the realization finally hits. Hypodermic shot: they've drugged me.

The world slows dramatically. My mouth feels like someone has stuffed it with cotton and I have a hard time forming my words. I try to call for help but sound like I'm talking underwater. Desperately trying to remain conscious, I struggle more. At least, I think I'm struggling, but can't be sure. Oh God, Stephanie has to be all right. I hate that I can't protect her right now. These thugs must work for Jacobs. It irks me no end that this looks like another Jacobs kidnap. I'm getting tired of being grabbed. Damn tired.

*

Slowly, I inhale. My fuzzy mind believes that what I thought was someone grabbing me was, in reality, a nightmare. Unfortunately, my relief is short-lived as the idea gives way to the truth of the situation. With a bag over my head, I'm lying on my back. I try to move, but restraints across my chest keep me in place. My arms, pinned beside me, likewise feel bound at the wrist. I won't be moving until someone decides I should.

I strain to listen for any clues as to where I am. No sounds reach me. For a moment, I think I may have lost my hearing, but clearing my throat gets rid of that notion. Wherever they have me, it's quiet as a tomb. They must have soundproofed this place. Why would they go to the trouble of soundproofing a room? The easy answer makes me flinch. No one will hear my screams. Just thinking about the prospect of torture brings shivers. The trouble is, I don't know much that would warrant using torture, but they're unlikely to believe that. Hell, I'll tell them whatever they want to hear. All they have to do is let me know what.

What happened to Stephanie? I never heard her cry out, and nor did she answer my warning. Also, how did the SEALs get decommissioned so effectively? That must have taken some excellent planning. The image of the SEAL taking a shot to the head won't leave me anytime soon. The shooter could have been the same guy that took out Ned's attacker. I'm not sure I'll get any answers, but I can't help thinking that there will be no good news on either question.

The bag over my head feels stuffy and uncomfortable, and every time I exhale, the heat of my breath makes it feel like a small sauna. I'm hot and struggling to get enough air. The fact that I can't see a thing, makes me feel more vulnerable. The heavy material must be a tight weave. I have to fight my looming panic and keep my wits about me. If I hyperventilate, it won't help the situation at all. With my eyes closed, I concentrate on slowing my breathing to a point where I feel in control again. Slowly, I pull in each breath and hold it for a few seconds. Then I exhale just as slowly until I have a rhythm that I can sustain. With each exhale, the bag puffs up, which takes my mind from my breathing, and I turn to the consideration of what comes next.

A door opens. If I know Jacobs, this will all run to a script, and on cue, I'll find out what the hell is going on.

"Mr. Cannon." A voice I don't recognize. "I want to welcome you, once again, to our little compound."

"Once again?"

"Yes, you've been here before. Not that I'd expect you to remember."

"So tell me. Where am I?"

"The headquarters of Taft International."

"Matt Jacobs' company." I sigh in frustration.

"The very same. Although the last time you were here, we provided a comfortable room. Unfortunately, Mr. Jacobs has decided you need to be accorded all the hospitality one would afford a mortal enemy."

"I'm sorry, but I missed your name."

"I don't believe I gave you my name, but if you're that interested, it's Gregory."

"Nice to meet you. What's your specialty in the Taft organization?"

"Not that it's any of your business, but I clean for Mr. Jacobs."

"Clean?"

"Yes. I clean up certain unfortunate mistakes that could be an embarrassment to Mr. Jacobs or the firm."

"You kill people."

"Oh, my goodness, Mr. Cannon. You certainly are a smart one, aren't you?"

"You were the guy who put the bullet into Stephanie's head in Washington?"

"You embarrass me, Mr. Cannon. To be more correct, I'm the guy behind the rifle that missed killing Ms. Savard due to a small miscalculation of the wind speed."

"If you give me two more guesses, I'll bet you're also the guy who took out that shooter who wounded Ned Tranes, not to mention the brave SEAL on the beach."

"You flatter me. I'll admit, I am the one."

"You're here for what reason?"

"You sure get to the point quickly, don't you?"

"You know, after dealing with Jacobs all this time, information doesn't get any more pleasant."

"Yeah, I can appreciate that. To your question, I'm here to take you to Mr. Jacobs, and then, when he is through with you, to—as you might say—eliminate you."

"You have a way with words. What happened to Ms. Savard?"

"That's none of my business. Although, it would have given me a whole lot of pleasure being with her in her final moments."

I suck in a breath. "She's dead?" I try to keep my roiling emotions out of my voice. Clearly, this guy is certifiable. I'm not too successful, as my voice comes out a little too high.

After a pause, Gregory says, "I don't know anything about where she is. Now, let's cut the talk and I'll take you to Mr. Jacobs."

I refrain from saying anything else, and he pulls the bag off my head. The new air rushes to my face. I inhale deeply and can't remember when air felt so fresh and clean. The light in the room looks too bright for a few seconds. I blink a few times. Gregory works over me and loosens the straps across my chest and thighs. Once he removes the wrist constraints, I bring my arms up to my face. It feels good to be able to move freely.

"Okay, Cannon," he says. "Sit up slowly. You might feel light-headed. Also, if you make any sudden moves, I'll have to pop you in the knee with my little friend here."

He waves a large revolver back and forth. As he suggested, I ease up and feel like throwing up. The drugs they used have made me nauseous. Also, I need to use the bathroom with some urgency, or I may have an accident. I glare up at Gregory. "I need a toilet."

"Not surprised. You've been out for almost twenty hours. I'm amazed you haven't pissed your pants by now."

"Nice thought." I nod at his gun. "What kind of weapon is that?"

"I'm proud of this baby. It is a .357 magnum."

"Bit big, isn't it?"

He shrugs and smiles. "You ready for the bathroom?"

"Lead the way."

"Ah, no. After you. I need to keep an eye on you."

I slide from the hard surface, and now see that it looks like an operating table. My glance around brings an operating room into focus. This must be some kind of medical facility. Gregory grabs my left arm and walks me to the door, which has large handles that can be pushed with the arm. "Is this a hospital?"

"Well, it's sort of a hospital," Gregory says. "Not many patients, though. Go through the doors, and then we will cross the hall to the bathroom. Unfortunately, I need to go in with you. Not my favorite activity, but I need to watch you carefully."

The bathroom surprises me—I'd expected a small room, but this looks like a large locker room. It holds stalls, and a few lockers line the wall. I go into a stall, not in the mood for putting up any resistance. After a few minutes, I come back out and go to one of the sinks to wash my hands. Done, I throw some water on my face. The mirror shows me that I don't look so good. Don't feel that good, either.

"Okay, champ. Let's get going. You can admire yourself later."

I straighten up and turn toward the door. "Mind telling me which way to go once we hit the hall again?"

"No problem, chief. We'll make a left and then take a little walk down the hall until we need to make another left. I'll try to give you plenty of warning."

Always love a smart ass—I just wanted to know which way. At the door, I pull it open. Should I take off running? I have a rough idea of the route, so maybe I could beat this guy and somehow lose him.

"Turn right." Gregory gives me a nudge.

"You said left."

"Yeah, it's the old fake-you-out-incase-you-think-of-running trick."

"Well, it worked."

"I'd counted on it. Go right."

Gregory annoys me. His warped sense of humor seems mostly at my expense. With Gregory right behind me, I take the right and walk down the hall. All too well, I can imagine him with his hand on that giant firearm. We reach another set of doors, and Gregory tells me to go through. We enter what looks like a waiting area with people passing through, going to different places. Gregory nudges me over to a reception desk. "Mr. Cannon to see Mr. Jacobs," he says. The young woman behind the counter picks up a receiver and repeats his message to whoever is at the other end.

Without putting the receiver back, she says, "Mr. Jacobs will be with you in a minute. Please, have a seat and I will call you when he is ready." Gregory nods toward a settee to the left. We go over and sit. "Would you shoot me right here in the lobby with all these folks around?"

"Please, make my day and try something."

"I guess that's a yes."

"That would be a definite yes."

"What if someone turned you in?"

"They won't."

There will be no more information forthcoming from Gregory. I shut up and reach for the Forbes magazine on the low table. Matt Jacobs' face fills the cover. The headline for the story reads, *Self-Made and Proud*. Inside, a lot of pages look to be devoted to Matt and the Taft Corporation. I scan the article quickly and determine that the article favors him strongly. My eye falls on a heading that begins with the Taft-Avery lawsuit. Sure enough, my name is there as the opposing counsel. The footnote at the bottom details the fact that I'm considered a hero who was supposed to get an award from the President. There is also a note to read more in the June issue. The article does say that the defeat of Taft caused the exposure of Matt Jacobs as not being American born, even though his official bio states he was a natural American citizen. It appears Matt was successful in explaining away the lie on his bio.

A lot of information covers how the IRS and the Nationalization service conducted extensive investigations only to clear Matt of wrongdoing. "He made a mistake and fudged his resume," was how the justice department summed up the investigation.

Damn. How did he pull that off? He must have paid someone. How else could a Palestinian national, found to have played a frat-boy joke on the business world by passing himself off as American born, be received so casually? Even his name would lead you to believe he was born here. What's his real name? How did he manage to wipe his background so completely clean?

The article summarizes the opportunities at Taft as being extremely optimistic. It cites examples of many new products and services in the pipeline, as well as dominant market positions in the telecommunications sector. A chart gives a one year view of the stock price and earnings profile. All the figures are in green, and the basic recommendation is to view the stock as a long-term investment, which will provide favorable returns.

I'm sorry I picked up the magazine. Now I have a knot in my stomach. It will prove almost impossible to bring Matt Jacobs to justice. This guy is not only a cold-blooded killer but also has enough money to keep himself above any involvement in any of his dirty deeds. The fact that he is the head of a large international corporation will keep him insulated from the crap that he hires done. When I look at Gregory, I see him as an example of just how low Jacobs will stoop. Having a scumbag like this on his payroll is typical.

"Gentlemen, Mr. Jacobs will see you now."

Gregory gets up and motions me to go through the archway behind the reception desk. I feel as if I have sandbags on my legs. I rise and head in the direction Gregory points. Dread fills me at the thought of seeing Jacobs again. He's had me drugged, beaten, and shot at, and the memories make me break into a cold sweat. The man has threatened and hurt people I love, and he continues to take perverse pleasure in meeting me in person. If I were him, I would've killed me a long time ago. No, Jacobs wants to sit and gloat and savor that delicious coffee of his while he gets his rocks off.

We reach another reception desk manned by a tough looking guy. He rises when we approach and comes around the table, holding a wand. Huh, even Gregory isn't to be trusted. The guy does the usual with the wand and asks Gregory to remove his weapon with two fingers. Gregory looks embarrassed as he complies. The guy whistles when he sees the size of the gun. You don't see one of those every day. He takes the weapon and places it in an envelope, and then hands Gregory a receipt. "You can have it back when you leave."

Gregory looks at his receipt like he just swapped it for his firstborn. I don't feel sorry for him. He must not know what it's like to work for Jacobs. I'll be real surprised to see him leave this place alive. He did his job and is no longer needed—any fool could be assigned to kill me. Not wishing to add insult to injury, I say nothing. The big guy opens a door for us, and I go through, with Gregory bringing up the rear. We enter an immense office with a huge desk at the far end. A substantial conference table pulls my gaze. At least ten chairs surround it. Four other people occupy the office. They look like security detail. They all have the dark-suit-white-shirt look, and I'll bet they talk to their cuffs as well. Jacobs isn't here yet. Two of the suited men approach, and one tells us to have a seat. Apparently, Jacobs is in the men's room and will be out shortly.

I take a seat, and Gregory does the same. No sooner have we taken a chair than Jacobs enters, wiping his hands on a paper towel. He throws it into a wastebasket by his desk and walks over.

"John Cannon," he says. "Once again, it is my honor to welcome you to my office."

"Matt Jacobs," I say. "We have to stop meeting like this."

Jacobs throws his head back and laughs—a little too hard in my opinion. "You always have a quick word, don't you, John?"

"Well, you know, being a lawyer and all."

"Oh yes, I forgot. Do you have plans to go back to your law firm?" He pulls up a chair.

"I haven't had a chance to check with them yet, but I was thinking of taking another six months of leave."

"That will be special. You getting another boat?"

He has me confused. Jacobs is carrying on a discussion like we're old friends or something. What's he up to? As always, I get the impression he thinks that a recorder might be running and is careful of what he says. I shrug. "Not sure about the boat. I haven't heard from the insurance company yet."

"I'm sure they will give you the full value of … uh, what was the boat's name, again?"

"My GRL, spelled with no i."

"Ah, yes, a delightful name. Nice play on all consonants, too. I see you have met Gregory."

"Yep. Nice fellow. Says he's going to kill me after you've done whatever you're going to do."

"Oh, I'm sure you misunderstood him. Am I right, Gregory?"

"Yes, sir. I never said I'd kill him."

"He said he would eliminate me when you've done what you are going to do."

"Well, that does sound ominous, doesn't it?" Jacobs keeps his face blank.

"I thought so," I say.

"I'm sure we don't have to go that far, but this is a discussion for a later time. Would you like some coffee?"

"I would never turn down a cup of your special blend. Before we get to the pleasantries, though, where's Stephanie?"

"Yes, we do have the love of coffee as a common trait. I can assure you, Stephanie is quite safe."

"The coffee's the only thing we have in common. What do you mean by safe?"

Jacobs gives one of his deep laughs, and then turns to one of the guys standing around and asks for coffee. The guy gives what could be interpreted as a Nazi click of the heels and leaves the room crisply.

"Well trained." I raise fix Jacobs with a stare. "I asked how safe is Stephanie?"

Jacobs ignores my comment and sits looking at me to the point where it becomes uncomfortable. I refuse to give in or look away, and so we both sit in a stare off like a couple of cats. "While my man prepares the coffee, why don't I give you an idea of why I sent for you."

"Sent for me? You mean manhandled, drugged, tied up, and strapped down. Not to mention killing innocent people."

"If you must be literal, yes. I had wanted to keep our conversation at a more civil level. I imagine, if I had sent word that I would like to see you, you would have accommodated that request. Am I right?"

"I see what you mean. I wouldn't have taken two steps toward you."

"As I thought, so that is why I needed someone to fetch you to me."

"Okay, so now what?"

"Patience, my friend. You must have patience. We will get there soon enough."

"Get where?"

"To the reason. In fact, let me begin."

"Okay, I'll be quiet."

"As you will recall, John, I have been trying to make a statement with Americans on behalf of my homeland Palestine."

"Oh, I recall your attempts to destroy the Annapolis Midshipmen and to launch that ridiculous story using me as the spokesperson."

"Please, let me finish, won't you?"

"Sure."

"Thank you. No matter what you think of my methods, I am committed to making a statement, which will hopefully disrupt the infidels as much as possible. I believe I have found a way to get to the heart of what I want to accomplish."

"To the hearts of innocents, I suppose."

"John, you and I have had a discussion about innocence before. There are no innocent members of the Western world. All of the citizens in the West have allowed the perpetuation of the destruction of my country and, more importantly, my culture. Let's not go down this path again. I will not be able to convince you of the rightness of my cause, and you will not convince me of the goodness of your culture."

"I'll never accept your cause as just. You have mental problems and have allowed your money to get in the way of your moral compass. All I have to do is remember what you did to Stephanie. Drug her and violate her? A real man does shit like that?"

"Spoken by a true liberal, and a jealous one, at that."

"Killing innocent people isn't just, and raping drugged women wholly immoral."

"Exactly my point, John. Your people have been killing and raping mine for centuries. How just is that?"

"And your point? Get on with explaining why you had me kidnaped and brought to you."

"Yes, I'm trying to get there. Oh, here comes coffee."

Jacobs motions to the guy to set the tray down between us. As usual, his coffee smells delicious. "Mind if I pour?" Jacobs says.

I nod, and he picks up a silver pot and fills two cups. After passing mine to me, he sets the pot back on the tray. I'm surprised when he fails to offer Gregory any. This confirms my belief that Gregory will not make it out of here. Jacobs probably doesn't want to waste his good coffee on someone who will be dead shortly. A shiver goes up my spine. I get the feeling that whatever Jacobs is thinking, it will somehow include me getting put into a compromised position. On one hand, he tries to kill me and then does this kidnap thing. On the other, he didn't jump at my bait about Stephanie, so must have something bigger in mind and doesn't want to get bogged in the sordid details, the son of a bitch. The knot in my stomach reminds me that this is no ordinary man. Jacobs is dangerous, and this coffee and chat thing will, no doubt, turn ugly soon. In the meantime, I'll have to wait it out to see where he goes. With a show of nonchalance, I reach for the cream, Splenda, and a spoon.

Chapter Eighteen

I take a sip of the coffee and look at Jacobs. Obviously, he wants a reaction to this wonderful elixir. I contemplate telling him that the beans seem a little burned but decide to keep him in good humor.

"Fabulous coffee."

His broad smile tells me I did the right thing. He now believes there has been some common ground established between us. This may be the way to get more information. When Jacobs gets pissed, he cuts the conversation, and I find myself in a dark room somewhere.

My nemesis sits back and sips his coffee, contemplating his next words, and I manage to refrain from trying to rush him along. Since he hasn't answered my question about Stephanie's safety, I don't mention it again. I'll just have to hope he'll give me more information later. We watch each other while we enjoy the wonderful taste. Finally, he puts his cup on the saucer, entwines his fingers, and sits forward with his elbows on the table. "So, let's get back to why I brought you here. As you know, I have been interested in having your co-operation in my endeavor. I see some great value in having you as a spokesperson for my cause. You are a national hero, and I could use you to my advantage."

"Well, you know from my past action that my helping you isn't going to happen."

"I know you won't do it on your own volition. However, if you had some incentive, you might be convinced to help me."

I take another sip of coffee. "I can't imagine what would incent me to help you. You've tried to kill me and those I love, not to mention taking me against my will."

"John." He steeples his fingers at his chin. "As you can see, you are still alive. All those attempts were to drive you to a point where you would discuss my side of the story. I could have had you killed at any time. Those pitiful strikes served only to get you to this point here, now. Before I make a plea for your cooperation, let me describe my next mission, which will give you a good idea why your help will be key."

"I hope if you tell me, you won't have to kill me."

Jacobs looks surprised and then breaks into a wide smile. "John, there is only one way you are going to stay alive, and that is to align yourself with me."

"I was afraid of that."

"You are priceless. I wish you had been born into my family. I would love to have you as a brother."

"I'm sure we would never get along."

"If we had the same blood, I'm sure we would. Besides, you would keep me laughing at your humorous quips."

I shake my head. "I'm not so sure."

"Well, anyway, what I intend to do is have a private meeting with the President and then take him out."

"Take him out? You mean, assassinate the President?"

"I prefer to describe it as bringing the leader of the Western world to justice."

"You are absolutely out of your mind. You'll never get away with it."

"Oh, I think I will. I am almost positive the President will not be able to resist having a meeting with a fairly big contributor to his party. Also, don't forget that I am a big business leader. How can he refuse?"

"Why would you need me in this scheme?"

"I figure the President still owes you a personal presentation of a medal from your last heroic action, and if you worked for me as a personal assistant, all this crap about me being behind terrorist activities would go away. You can see that, can't you?"

"Me work for you? That's not gonna happen."

"This is the reason I will have to give you a little incentive."

"I shudder to think what you would consider an incentive."

"Don't worry, it does not include any harm to you. I know from past experience, you do not respond to personal threats."

"I wish you would just leave the rest of the world out of this and torture me. Who knows, maybe I'll break and do whatever it is you want me to do."

"No. Once the pain stops, you will be right back in your stubborn, uncooperative profile. No, that won't work. We need to have your undivided loyalty. The only way to get that is to threaten someone you care about."

Immediately, my thoughts go to Stephanie. These guys have her somewhere and intend to threaten me with harm to her.

Jacobs says, "Take a look at the monitor on the wall, and I'll see if I still know how to work this remote. Ah, there, I think I have it."

The large screen TV on the opposite wall comes to life. A person sits on a chair, and although the picture is in color, the scene is one of gray tones—much like you would see in a prison. A black hood covers the person's head and shackles circle the ankles. With their arms behind the chair, I assume the wrists are shackled as well.

"Yes, now this is a person we have borrowed from his home." Matt leans toward a panel on his desk, pushes a button, and speaks. "Would the technician in the studio remove the hood so that Mr. Cannon can appreciate who we have here?"

An arm comes into the picture, and the hand grabs the top of the hood and yanks it off. Ned Tranes blinks at the bright lights. He looks rather ruffled, and his hair stands up straight from the static electricity. He continues to blink and has what looks like silver duct tape over his mouth. After a few moments, he struggles against his restraints but, finally, slumps in defeat.

I sit speechless. Not only did these guys manage to kidnap me with six Navy Seals present, but they also grabbed the Chief of Police. Now I have a big problem. Ned would not want me to give in to Jacobs' threats and would understand if I didn't. This guarantees that Ned will have a rough time, as I cannot think of giving Jacobs what he wants.

Jacobs leans toward me. "Do I need to tell you what will happen to Mr. Tranes if you decide not to co-operate?"

"I get the picture. Do you see any way you and I can make a deal?"

"Like the last time when you went back on your word and screwed me royally?"

"No. I mean, is there any way I can appeal to you to give up this quest of yours and let Ned go. You can kill me if you want, but I just don't see how hurting or killing him will help anything."

"So, you won't help me, even though it could cost the life of your friend?"

"I don't see how I can."

"Well, let me add a little more to the mix. Here is another shot, which you should be interested in. Damn this remote. Oh, there it is."

The screen flashes in a channel change, and a similar scene to Ned Tranes comes up—another hooded person bound in a chair. A hand lifts the hood, and Stephanie blinks in the glare. She, too, has duct tape over her mouth. Her eyelids narrow to defiant slits—she's telling me to resist.

"How about now?" Jacobs' calm tones fuel my fury.

"You know, Matt, you're a real son of a bitch. How in the hell can I help you when you have people I care about held captive?" I take a slow breath and swallow, trying to control my anger, as it will only work to Jacobs' advantage.

"At least, they are live captives."

I glare at the man. "Yeah, and they would gladly give their lives to see you brought to justice."

"The sad part is that they will give their lives only because you will it to happen. It is on your back."

"Don't try to twist this around. You're insane, and I can do nothing about that. You're forcing me to deny you and your group with my success on the blood of people I care for."

Jacobs' eyebrows lift. "You still refuse?"

"When you put it that way, yes."

"Mmm. Yes, we need to go to another channel. You might like this one as well."

The screen changes again, and the same scene comes into view, only with two hooded and bound subjects this time. A hand does the reveal. My parents. Tears well in my eyes and I blink them back. My mother and father look so frightened. They have a deer-in-the-headlights look, and I'm certain they don't understand what's happening. They know they're in trouble but not why.

"What do you think, John? Any change of mind on this?"

"Just when I think you can't possibly get any lower, Matt, you surprise me by exceeding the depth of sleaze."

"Yeah, John. Sometimes I surprise myself at what I will do for my cause. So, what do you think about helping me?"

Jacobs has the upper hand. Damn him. Can I live with myself for sacrificing the lives of my parents, Stephanie, and Ned?—But helping him take the life of the President is out of the question. I have to think of a way to pretend to go along with Matt, and then (somehow) turn things around. Where is he keeping them? It could be here or in some other city. Maybe I should work on trying to discover their locations.

"Can I think about it for a while?"

"How much time do you need?"

"How about until tomorrow?"

"How about tonight. I would like your answer at dinner. Oh yes, I want you to be my guest at a quiet dinner tonight. There will be just three of us."

"Sarah going to be there?"

"Why yes. How did you guess?"

"Just lucky."

"Okay then." He catches Gregory's attention, "Take Mr. Cannon to his quarters. We will meet at six for cocktails." He nods at me. "We will come to your place."

"Sure you will." I feel completely drained. The lack of food for God knows how long and the fact that I have no idea what to do to stop this madman, only add to my extreme fatigue. Gregory takes my arm, and I get up. My legs feel like rubber, but I don't want Jacobs to know I'm shaky, so I stiffen my legs and move on my own. We exit the room, leaving Jacobs sitting at the table playing with his remote.

A short hallway brings us to a dead end with three doors available—at the twelve, three, and nine o'clock positions. Gregory opens the door at nine o'clock and, passing through, I see a small brass plaque on the wall marked Guest Suites. The door leads to a lounge area with additional doors, all as spokes of a wheel off the center.

"Here is your room." Gregory opens the door and waves me inside. He follows me in and points out the bathroom and sitting area. "You don't have TV or room service," Gregory says. "You'll find clothes in the closet. The dress for tonight is coat and tie. I'm sure you will find what you need in the closet and bathroom. I'll come back to pick you up at about five-forty-five." He looks at his watch. "That's about an hour from now." He turns and goes back to the door. "This will be locked, and the room has no window." He leaves, and a second later, the lock turns.

Normally, I would spend some time trying to figure out how to escape. Since this is about the fourth time that I've been a guest of Jacobs, I know escape will not be possible. Instead, I will have to content myself with trying to figure something out after I get more information and a better idea of where I am. Ha, I don't even know what country or city I'm in. I could assume California, seeing as San Francisco is the Taft corporate headquarters, but I can't be sure enough to base the lives of my loved ones on it.

After wandering around the room, I check the closet. A suit and sports coat hang from the rail. Experience tells me that they will fit fine. Next, I go to the chest of drawers and confirm that I also have underwear, socks, and a pair of pajamas. Back in the closet, I pull the door out fully and see two pairs of shoes. One is Oxfords and the other Loafers. This must be a thing with Jacobs. He must get a kick out of selecting clothes for his victims. He's done it for me each time he's taken me.

The clothes remind me of his plan to assassinate the President. Somehow, a guy who would even think of such a horrible thing also thinks of dressing his pawns in the latest attire. Jacobs is truly a sick man. I turn to wondering if I could pretend to go along with his plan, and then at the last minute, expose the plot. Of course, doing that will cost the lives of Stephanie, my parents, and Ned. Not to do it will cost the life of the President. There has to be a way to even out this *damned-if-I-do-damned-if-I-don't* conundrum. If I had some information on where he's holding the hostages, I could (maybe) try to warn someone, and they could be rescued. I made a deal with Jacobs before, which worked out for me. I asked for phones and managed to warn the hostages away from danger. Will he fall for a similar ruse a second time? No, he won't be that dumb. He has me between the proverbial rock and hard place.

The bathroom contains the usual array of shampoo, conditioner, deodorant, and soap. In addition, Jacobs' people have provided toothpaste, toothbrush, comb, and hairbrush. Looks as if I'll be here for a few days. A nice hot shower will be just the thing, so I drop my clothes and get in. The water feels great, and I feel normal again.

Afterward, I put on the suit, along with a white shirt I found in the chest of drawers. In my reflection in the mirror, I look about as normal as I always have. I may be a little tired looking, but other than that, pretty fit.

A knock sounds at the door, and the lock turns. Gregory opens it and comes in. "You ready?"

"As I'll ever be. He's going to kill you; I hope you know."

"How are you so sure?"

"For one thing, he discussed his plans in front of you. He never does that with people not in his inner circle."

"How do you know I'm not in his inner circle?"

"That whole frisk and gun removal upfront meant he doesn't trust you. Why would he trust you with the information that he intends to kill the President? I can tell you why."

Gregory thinks some. "He *is* going to kill me."

"Bingo." Hopefully, I can get to Gregory and turn him so he'll help me out of this mess.

"Yeah, I just don't agree with you. Mr. Jacobs hired me for a few jobs, and I don't think he's finished with my services quite yet."

"Would you kill the President for him?"

"You crazy? The person doing that wouldn't last three seconds."

"Then, he sees you as expendable since he needs another assassin."

"Aw, come on. Nobody would do that number."

"He thinks I will."

"From what I've seen, you won't have much choice if you want those other folks to live."

"And with this information, you think Jacobs will let you walk out of here to tell all your friends what you know?"

"Hey. I have a great reputation for keeping my mouth shut."

"So does Jacobs. He has ways to make sure everyone keeps their mouths shut. Think about it."

With a tight jaw, he says, "It's time to go. You first."

We step through the doorway. Maybe Gregory has some things to think about now. I can't count on him to come around but, at the least, I've opened up one option. With any luck, as the evening progresses, more will present themselves. Gregory steers through a couple more doorways until we come to an opening with no door. The lights inside the room glow dim, and it appears to be an intimate dining area. A guy in a tux meets us. "Good evening, Mr. Cannon. Allow me to show you to your table."

I follow the guy, and he seats me at a table set for three. "Mr. Jacobs will be here shortly. Our chef has prepared some surprises, which I'll explain once Mr. Jacobs arrives. Would you care for something to drink?"

"Tanqueray on the rocks with two olives, please." I need to take the edge off this situation. The guy gives a little bow and backs away. The room holds four other tables. By the appearance of things, and the lit candles on each table, more people will join us.

The server comes back with my drink and tells me, "Mr. Jacobs has been delayed. Would you care to see the menu while you wait?"

With a nod, I say, "I would. Bread would also be good, please." Gin on the rocks can get to you when you have nothing in your stomach. He bows again and is gone. What other matters does Jacobs have to take care of that would make him late? He isn't the kind of person to keep guests waiting, and anytime he is late, it throws off his careful timing. Being a driven man, this kind of thing isn't to his liking.

The server leaves a menu and a basket of hot bread. I take a piece, tear off a bite-sized chunk, and put it in my mouth. The bread has that yeasty smell and unmistakable sour taste that you find only in San Francisco sourdough. The crust proves crunchy, and the bread dense and resistant to gumminess. It must have been quite a while since my last meal, and I have to resist shoving the whole slice in my mouth. I pull off another piece, and then take a sip of my drink. Right now, I can't think of any combination more pleasing.

While I'm wrapped up in enjoying my gin and bread love fest, Jacobs comes in. I don't actually see him enter, but can feel the change in the vibration of the room. I look up in time to see him and Sarah walk toward the table. I rise as they reach me.

"Good evening, John. I hope your accommodations are satisfactory."

"Yes, quite. Thank you again for the clothes."

"Not a problem. It's the least I can do considering I pulled you away before you had a chance to pack. Please, sit."

I retake my seat, and Sarah sits beside me, with Jacobs taking the chair directly opposite me. "How are you, Sarah?" I say. Best to act normal. My inclination is to smack her across the face, but then I remember that she *was* the one who called Ned to tell him where we were in South America.

She offers a soft smile. "I'm good. How about you?"

"Couldn't be better. Of course, not being here would be an improvement."

Matt laughs out loud as the server approaches. "Would you care for something to drink?" he says to Sarah. Then he looks at me. "What are you drinking? That famous gin drink of yours?"

"Yep, Tanqueray on the rocks. I would recommend it. Of course, it's probably against your religion."

Jacobs ignores me and addresses the waiter, "I'll have a ginger ale, and please, bring a Viognier for the lady."

The server leaves the menus and disappears to get the drinks.

Jacobs fixes his gaze back on me. "You think life would be better if you weren't here, huh?"

"What I mean is that every time I come in contact with one Matt Jacobs, he puts me in a position of worrying about my longer-term survival."

"Well, why don't you just give up and help me conquer the world?"

Appalled, I look at Sarah. "I can't believe you're still hanging around this guy."

She looks at me with annoyance on her face. "Did it ever occur to you, I'm here because I want to be?"

I shake my head. "Not given the way Matt, here, has coerced you into behaving."

"He's made up for that many times over."

"You've got to be kidding. He killed your best friend."

"I've seen no evidence of that. Also, he made sure my little sister is well cared for."

"You mean she's no longer a hostage?"

"I told Matt I would be his if I could be sure my sister is okay. He's putting her through college and pays for her apartment and whatever she needs."

With a scowl, I bang my glass onto the tabletop, and a bit of gin splashes my hand. "The money talks and the bullshit walks."

"John, I would appreciate it if you would mind your manners," Jacobs says.

"Oh, that's good coming from a guy who repeatedly forgets his manners."

Jacobs grows red-faced and says, "Maybe this social hour was a mistake. Why don't we get straight to business?"

The server arrives with the drinks and places them in front of Sarah and Jacobs. He doesn't look at his drink or the server, and tells him we will order later. Now he locks me in a staring contest as if we were kids. Not being nice just cost me dinner. Who cares? I take a sip of my Tanqueray. Jacobs keeps his eyes on mine.

"What have you decided to do?" Jacobs picks up his drink and takes a sip.

"I can't help you without assurance that the people I care about will be okay."

"What the hell does that mean? I remember, you took advantage of me the last time when I met your demands for the safety of your friends."

"You have to believe I would try again."

"So, what makes you think I would do a deal with you?"

"Because you know I won't help you without one."

"Like, what kind of deal?"

"Like letting Ned, my parents, and Stephanie go now."

"And what would be in it for me? You would resist if I didn't have some of the people you care about under lock and key."

"You'll have to take the chance or I won't help you." I shrug. "Kill me. Like you probably have Gregory."

"I love how you tried to get Gregory to join forces with you. Good try."

"So, he's gone, right?"

"Let's not say 'gone.' I prefer to think of him as a martyred soul."

I glance at Sarah. "I can't believe you simply sit there and listen to the fact that your benefactor has murdered a person."

"Gregory was a nasty man and deserved to die."

"Hello? You still in there? I can't believe you're thinking just like this maniac." I hook my thumb toward Jacobs.

Sarah shakes her head. "It's true, though. He wasn't a nice person."

"You think people that aren't nice, as you put it, should die?"

"This is getting tedious," Jacobs says.

I turn away from looking at Sarah and fix my glare on Jacobs. "So, what do we do now?"

"Sorry to say, I don't have much of a choice. You want to tell me who should go first?"

Furious, I jump to my feet, plant my hands on the table, and lean in close to Jacobs' face. "Oh, fuck you. I refuse to play your game. Kill me, why don't you?"

Other than leaning back a couple of inches, Jacobs appears unruffled. "You could be a tremendous asset. I will be sorry to have to kill you. Just know, you will be the last to go."

I try to think fast of some way I could pretend to work with Jacobs and then try to thwart whatever he is going to try to do. Then it comes to me. With a loud sigh, I make a show of dropping back into my seat. As in any conflict, time makes for a precious commodity. If I could buy some time, maybe I'll find a way to get an advantage over Jacobs. To sit here and blatantly tell him he can't have what he wants is foolish. Such folly would only force him to kill innocent people. And I see no use in doing that right now. We could all die later if a plan to get Jacobs can't be worked out. Right now, the advantage of staying alive hinges on what I say next.

"Okay. I think we ought to cool off for a minute."

Jacobs watches me, and then says, "That sounds better. What do you have in mind?"

"You know I want my friends to be safe, and I think your plan is diabolical. Now I find myself in the position of having to

choose between saving them by helping you kill the President or
…"

"Or what?"

"Or, I do not help you, and they die."

Jacobs smiles. "You have a good grasp on where you stand."

I want to hit him with something heavy, and actually look around for something, but know it would be futile. I sigh and continue speaking, "I've decided to help you, but I need some assurance that Ned, Stephanie, and my parents will be safe. I propose that you let them go now, and if I do anything to hurt your plan, you kill me."

"I respect the offer, but you must know that I can't accept those terms. I need all of my hostages as a guarantee of your co-operation."

I figured he'd say that. To make him buy the fact that, reluctantly, I will help him, I try to act confused. If he believes me to be insincere, he will kill us all anyway. Oh yes, and not to forget, me last.

I look at Jacobs, wanting to sell him on the idea of acquiescing to his will. "Okay, Matt. You have me right where you want me. I'll help you, and once the plan is done, we're all free."

"Well, I need you to help execute the plan, too. I would modify your offer to the effect that you will all go free after the plan is executed successfully."

"I don't see that I have any other choice but to accept your terms. I would like to see an order, drawn up by you to whomever you need, to direct the release of Ned, my parents, and Stephanie at the successful completion of the mission. I can't take the chance that things get confused, and your folks don't follow through."

"I can do that. Once I've written out the order, I'll give you a copy. You'll be assured your friends will go free for certain when you complete your commitment."

"Sounds good. Now, if you don't mind, I'd like to turn in for the night."

"Of course. Someone will show you to your room."

"Nice way of saying one of your goons will lock me up." Jacobs gives me a smile and claps his hands. Out of nowhere, the biggest guy I've yet seen around here comes close and stands next to my chair. I bid Sarah a good night and get up. The guy takes my arm, and we leave.

Chapter Nineteen

With a start, I awaken and can't remember where I am. Then, in a nanosecond, it all comes back. The memory of my untenable situation makes me groan, and I swing my legs over the side of the bed. I almost wish I'd dreamt this whole thing, and that it was just part of a PSTD attack. By now, with everything that's gone on, I must be a PSTD victim; however, the reality of the mess makes that excuse unlikely.

I can do almost nothing about Jacobs and his wishes to bring America to its knees. He is totally insane and has the money and power to do exactly what he wants. In what scenario could I ever get the best of him and his goons?

I take a quick shower and can imagine someone will be coming to get me soon. A knock on the door confirms my belief. "Who's there?"

A mumble comes in response, which can only belong to someone big on muscle and small on brains. The lock turns, and as I pull on my underwear, the door opens.

"Mr. Jacobs would like you to join him for breakfast."

"I will be ready in about five minutes." I can't tell if the guy heard me or not. He stands there for a couple of minutes and then goes out into the hall. I assume he'll wait. Dressing in haste, I go out in the hallway. The guy grunts and steps out of my way. He gives me an "after you" gesture, and we move down the hall. Presumably, we'll go back to the same place we sat down to dinner last night. Light-headed and hungry, I look forward to food. I can't recall the last time I ate. It had to be my homemade chicken with Stephanie back in Port A. Not that it matters at this point. Had I watched my tongue last night, I would have been able to get something. This morning, I shall be more careful. Jacobs is such a weasel, and it makes having a meal with him unpleasant.

We arrive at the same room, and a different server shows me to a table. I sit, and then order coffee. Though I'd like some of Jacobs' blend, I'll take anything right now. My burly escort stands at the entrance—his job to make sure I don't bolt. I lean back in the chair, pull a folded cloth napkin off the table, and put it in my lap. Being normal won't be a bad thing. The server comes to the table with a silver pot of coffee and pours me a cup. The smell identifies it as Jacobs' blend. I add some half-and-half and Splenda and take a gulp. Lost in the taste, I look over the cup to see Sarah standing by the table. I set the cup down, and half rise. She gives me a smile and lowers onto a chair.

"Can I have some of your coffee?"

"Of course, this is your boyfriend's stuff. I'm just borrowing it for an hour or so."

Sarah laughs, and I have to say, she looks beautiful. Life with Jacobs has treated her well. I like that she can laugh. Still, after everything, I find her an interesting person. Sure wish she wasn't part of this crap Jacobs is concocting, though. "Where is his lordship?"

"He won't be joining us this morning. He has a meeting and won't be able to talk to you until around lunchtime."

"Gee, does that mean you have to entertain me by yourself?"

"Entertain is a funny way to describe joining you for breakfast."

"Is that all you have to do?"

"I volunteered to join you so you wouldn't have to eat alone."

"I sure thank you for that."

"John, if you would rather I left, I would understand."

220

"No. You have to excuse my attitude. Your boy has worked me over hard ever since he tried to blow up the Annapolis Midshipmen. Also, that trick of sending photos of our lovemaking to Stephanie was low."

"I agree. I had no idea he was going to do that."

"You did know that us having sex had some other motive, right?"

"I had no idea. You and I had a wonderful moment. No one told me to do it. You have to believe me."

"Why do I have to believe you?"

"I want you to believe that I wouldn't want anything to happen to you."

"You're so confusing. You're the girlfriend of a monster, and you're trying to tell me that you care what happens to me. What do you think will happen? Jacobs will kill me, Stephanie, my parents, and Ned. How in the hell can you overlook those facts?"

"Believe me, I can overlook those facts since I don't believe that Matt will hurt you or your loved ones."

"How are you so sure?"

"Why don't we order and have a halfway decent breakfast? This conversation isn't going where I wanted it to go."

"Where did you want it to go? You want me to forgive the fact that you're sleeping with a pirate? Or should we just be buddy-buddy until Matt assassinates the President?"

"Please, let's change the subject."

Sarah looks upset. Her large brown eyes swim with tears like they might overflow any second now. The mannerly person in me drops the subject. I almost told her about Matt drugging and raping Stephanie, but then something inside balks at the thought of sharing Stephanie's shame with this woman. All I say is, "Okay. Let's order."

Sarah smiles, and I melt. She makes a wonderful agent for the other side. I feel guilty for bringing her near tears, and can well imagine what happens to Jacobs when he refuses to give her what she wants. The server arrives. Sarah orders an egg-white omelet and dry toast, and then pulls her cellphone out of her purse. I go the grand slam route—two eggs over medium, sausage, bacon, hash browns, and an English muffin. Just saying the words makes my mouth water. The server leaves, and I say, "So, what's up for the rest of the morning?"

She looks up from her cell phone, and I can tell she wasn't listening. "Oh, sorry, John. I wasn't paying attention."

"That's all right. What's up for the rest of the morning?"

"I'm not sure. We could walk around."

"Might be nice to know where I am."

"Don't you recognize this place? You've been here before."

I shake my head. "Tell me."

"This is the corporate headquarters for Taft International. We're in downtown San Francisco."

"How can we just walk around?"

"Matt doesn't believe that you'll run away; not when your folks are under lock and key."

"Hmm, he sure has me pegged. Do you know where he's keeping them?"

Sarah shakes her head and drops her gaze.

I press, "Could you find out?"

"Please, John. I can't help you."

"I don't see how you can say that."

"It's true."

"You're just going to let this madman kill the President?"

"I didn't say that."

"What did you say, then?"

"I can't help you. Matt is interested in having you join him. He won't allow any interference. If I were to do something to help you, he would—in all probability—kill you and your loved ones."

"So, you're helping to keep me alive by not helping me out of this mess?"

"That's one way to look at it."

"Seems warped to me. You help keep me alive only to die later."

"At least, it won't be today. Take my advice, John. Try to play along while you can."

I'm about to answer when the server arrives with the food. I look at my breakfast and admit that I need to eat whether I feel like it or not. Our discussion has destroyed my appetite, but I have to eat. Sarah says no more and picks at her eggs. I cannot understand what she's trying to say to me. If I didn't believe it would be more than I could wish for, I'd say she has a plan that she can't discuss. I have to dismiss the thought—every time I go down the nice Sarah path, I get burned.

"I'm going to pass on the walk around if you don't mind," I say.

"I don't mind, but I think it would be good for you to have some orientation as to where you are."

"In case of what?"

"Oh, nothing. You should be more interested in your surroundings, that's all."

I think about what she just said. Breakfast finished, I feel better—amazing what a little food will do. "Okay," I say. "I'll go with you on a walk around."

"You won't be sorry."

I won't be sorry. What does that mean? I swear Sarah is acting strangely. It will be an achievement to figure out what she's up to, let alone where I am. Sarah rises, and I do likewise. She indicates that I should follow her out of the dining room. We walk down a short hallway, through large doors, and back to the reception area. Sarah says something to the receptionist, who makes a call. In about thirty seconds, a big guy comes through the doors. Sarah explains that Matt wants us to have company. Is he worried I'll bolt, or maybe make a pass at his girl? Both thoughts are ridiculous, and the big guy seems unnecessary. I don't say anything, and we all make our way outside.

Taft offices run from the Number Two Embarcadero Center. This has to be one of the weirdest coincidences, as my law firm is at One Embarcadero Center. Embarcadero Street is so named since it runs along San Francisco Bay and has docks where ships can land. Embarcadero means *landing place* in Spanish. The centers are named after the street. It's good this isn't lunch hour, as I would be too likely to run into people I know. A lot of my colleagues take lunch along the Embarcadero. The spectacular views of the bay and the Bay Bridge make for a great lunchtime oasis. Also, the area has plenty of eating places. I follow Sarah when she turns down a side street, and we walk straight ahead until we come to the protected way across the Embarcadero to the Ferry building.

"This must all be familiar to you," Sarah says to me.

"Well, since I worked in this area for ten years, I would say so."

"I thought we'd go into the Ferry building and have a coffee."

Nonplussed, I say, "Sounds good."

We continue across the Embarcadero and enter the Ferry building, constructed in the late eighteen hundreds to accommodate travelers before the Golden Gate and Bay bridges were built. Now, it's the central point for those who ride the ferry to the affluent suburbs in Marin County. I loved to come to the Ferry building on Saturdays for the farmers' market. I would buy my produce and then take it to the office and put it in the refrigerator until time to go home. That seems like a lifetime ago.

Sarah sits at a small café table and asks me what I would like. I order a latte, which she conveys to the big guy with us. He came in handy after all. I snag the chair across from Sarah.

Sarah smiles. "I'm glad we could get out of the office for a few minutes. It feels good to be away."

"Don't you get out often?"

"I do, but while Matt is in the office, we don't get out too much. He has an apartment in the building, and I stay there most of the time."

"Do you find him attractive, really?"

"He's a fascinating man. He knows a lot about many areas. Although not self-made, he has the curiosity of someone who came from nothing. And, he speaks several languages. English isn't his native tongue, yet he speaks it so well."

"Okay, okay. I get it. You're in love with him."

"Let's just say, I am with Matt. I haven't given much thought to the prospect of love." Sarah jerks in her chair, and then says, "Oh, here come the lattes."

I take my drink from our escort, and he hands one to Sarah. We both take a sip, and Sarah appears lost in thought. I ask, "You thinking of something?"

Sarah smiles. "Yes."

"Anything you'd like to share?"

"Um, it's nothing that should concern you."

"I see. Keep my nose out of it."

"It's not like that. I just remembered a time when Matt lost his cool and spoke in Farsi. He sounded so different, I felt almost afraid of him."

"You should be afraid of him."

"I can assure you, I have no reason to believe that Matt would hurt me."

"I can see that. Still, you should be concerned about what he's planning to do."

"Please, don't go over that again. You're becoming dreary."

"Yeah, that's me, dreary John." I take a sip of my latte and sit back in the chair.

"Now, don't pout. I'm just saying."

I have to laugh. Sarah doesn't want me to pout over her being hooked up with a cold-blooded killer. I'd like to tell her where to go, but it's not worth the hassle. This woman is dead to me, and I might as well just give up trying to get her to see that the path she's on could lead to catastrophic ends. Instead, I sit and sip my latte in silence. Sarah doesn't try to engage me in any superfluous conversation. What's this whole "take a walk" thing all about? I break the tense silence, "Ned tells me that you were the one who called him to let him know where I was in South America. That true?"

My question takes her by surprise. She looks at her latte too long, and then says in a soft voice, "I can't talk to you about this."

"What's the matter? Are you wired?"

"No. It's just, there's no good place for a conversation like this."

I lean back in frustration. I can't believe there is any way we could be overheard in this large building. It must be that she doesn't want to talk about it. "Okay," I say. "Let's drop it."

Sarah avoids my gaze. At length, she asks me if I'm ready to go, and I tell her I am.

Without any further discussion, we get up and walk back to the building. I leave her in the lobby, and the big man takes me to my room. He tells me Jacobs would like to talk over lunch, and that he will come back for me. I don't know why, but I thank him before closing the door. Reminds me of saying thank you to a police officer after getting a ticket.

After throwing my sports coat on the bed and taking a seat by a small table, I think about what Sarah might have had in mind. Was she trying to get out of the building so we could talk openly? If so, what hints did she give me? Did she want to ask me something, or give me some information about the future? I didn't pull anything out of our discussion. Maybe all she wanted was a latte and someone to join her. If that were the case, then I made for one sorry companion.

I have to stop trying to figure out what Sarah is up to. This kind of thinking is a waste of time. Best to accept that she isn't on my side and forget about it. The woman is a big disappointment, but I need to get over it. Every time I'm in her presence, I turn to mush. Any other person would have me being as rude as possible to inflict hurt on them. When it comes to Sarah, I'm incapable of hurting her, no matter what she's done to me. Does she mean more to me than I've been willing to recognize? God, but I need to stop this. However, thoughts about her stay in my head like a tune I can't forget. I make a motorboat sound to try to get my brain to think of something else. A glance at my watch shows that I have about a half-hour until noon.

I go over to the bed and sit. Although he didn't say when, I assume the guy will come back sometime around noon. With nothing much to do, I lie back on the mattress. They're bound to have put cameras and microphones in this room, just like every other time they took me. This go around, I'm not interested in finding them. With a sigh, I close my eyes, take deep breaths, and start to relax.

The knock at the door, followed by the unlocking sound of the deadbolt, tells me that the big guy is here. I rise just as the door comes open. The big guy fills the doorway, and I pick up the sports coat and go to him. "You won't need that," he says.

I throw the coat back on the bed and follow him down the hall. We head back to the dining area, and I expect it will be another one of those 'threaten me' meetings. Jacobs alone at a table. We cross the room to him. "Have a seat." He waves his hand to the chair opposite his. "I trust your walk went well?"

"Yes, fine. I hadn't realized that we were so close to my office."

"Yes, your office is in Embarcadero One, I believe."

"Well, when I'm not on leave, you're correct."

"When does your leave expire?"

"Two months."

"Then what?"

"I go back or get an extension."

"Have you made up your mind which it's to be?"

"Not that it matters, but I intend to ask for an extension."

"What do you mean, ask for?"

"I have to request more time."

"You're a partner of the firm, are you not?"

"Yes, but it doesn't matter. My boss makes the decision."

"Can I help with that?"

"What?"

"I could give your boss a call and tell him that I'm considering selecting the firm and want to spend some quality time with you before I make up my mind. I could also say that I understand you are on leave for six months but would meet you anywhere."

"How would that convince my boss that I should have an extension on my leave?"

"You surprise me. Do you think a guy like Peters would be so audacious as to imply that I don't have my facts straight when I tell him you are on a six-month leave? He wouldn't have the balls. He would just say 'okay' and give me your address. I'd be willing to bet your extension would arrive the next morning by FedEx."

I have to stifle a smile, thinking of Gerome on the phone with a multi-billionaire and trying to soft-pedal the fact that they haven't granted the six-month extension. Jacobs is correct—Peters wouldn't even try. He wouldn't mention anything contrary to whatever Jacobs said. No, he'd be left with an ethical dilemma because the firm represents Avery Corp, a direct competitor to Taft. Though it would be interesting, I wouldn't want Jacobs helping me in any way. Who knows where that would lead? I can just see Gerome testifying in court about the conversation and looking at the jury in wide-eyed innocence when asked, "Why would Matt Jacobs want to talk with John Cannon?" His "I don't know," would be flavored with a tone of questioning disbelief, which would ensure his total credibility in the minds of the jury.

"Thank you, but I'll wait for their response."

"Have it your way. Before we order lunch, I want to have another conversation about your future."

"My future?"

"Yes, as it pertains to helping me."

"I don't know how you think I can help."

"By not doing much other than asking the President for a meeting, is how. Once you arrange a get-together, you won't be involved any further."

"Not involved? Who'll attend the meeting?"

"I will introduce you to him later. Just know, it won't be you."

"So that I have this straight: All I have to do is arrange a meeting with the President, and then my people go free?"

"That's it."

"Why don't you arrange it yourself? You have enough money to buy your way in."

"It is not the time, yet, for me to be a martyr. I have much more to do."

"The person who will play me will be martyred?"

"Yes. He will enter the kingdom of heaven along with the President."

"You're having an impersonator of me kill the President?"

"That is the plan."

"The world will think I killed him."

"They will until the DNA results rule you out. You will, eventually, be found innocent of the crime."

"But not innocent of plotting to kill the President as part of a conspiracy."

"Well, that may be the price you pay for saving your people, as you call them."

"I won't help you in any way."

"You want your people to die at your hands?"

"Not my fault. You kidnaped them, not me. Therefore, I can't recognize your appeal to my guilt to get your way. I'm sorry that we'll all die, but helping you is out of the question."

"You underestimate the kind of death you and your people face. Think of a long, drawn out affair with a lot of pain and an eventual plea to finish it."

"You have to be the most deranged person on Earth. I'd never believed there could be such a person until I met you."

"Okay, John. Let's do this. Why don't you take some time to think about it? You and I can have lunch, and then we'll go over to the monitors, and you can get a better idea of the kind of mission we're talking about."

"I'm not hungry," I say. In fact, I could eat something, but why let him know it? Besides, the moments I spend with Matt make my skin crawl. I couldn't make up the kind of evil this jerk is capable of pulling off. I should humor him, but even the ability to be near him has fled.

Unperturbed, Jacobs says, "Okay, then. Let's go. I can always grab something later, as you can if you change your mind." Matt gets up, and I follow. The big guy comes out of nowhere and takes up the rear of this morbid caravan. We take a brief walk down the hall and through a door. Then we enter a room that looks like a TV control room. Monitors line the control panel, all marked with a camera number. Jacobs takes a chair and waves me into the one beside him.

Chapter Twenty

Jacobs puts on a headset and adjusts a few knobs. The monitor marked number one comes to life. Ned sits bound to the same chair as earlier, although minus the gag or blindfold, and, apparently, unaware that we can see him. He seems calm if not bored. His head snaps up, and he looks straight into the camera. Jacobs talks to him through the headset.

"Hello, Chief Tranes, this is Matt Jacobs," he says. "How are you feeling?"

"Yeah, what's it to you, asshole?" Ned wears a fierce look on his face, which the harsh lights make even more threatening.

"My, my. We seem a little upset today."

"You would be if you'd been held against your will."

"I suppose I would. Although you can't see us, I want you to know your friend John is here with me."

"You bastard. What are you up to now?"

"I'm trying to make a deal. I need his help to pull off my greatest statement yet."

"I hope he told you to go to hell."

"He sure did. That's why I asked my associates to put you back in that chair."

"What does that have to do with John?"

"I told him that if he didn't co-operate, I would make your death a miserable and undignified affair."

"He still said no, I'm sure."

"Yes, he did. So, we need to demonstrate what will happen if he doesn't co-operate."

"Demonstrate how?"

Jacobs twists another dial, and Ned stiffens, and then slumps after Jacobs sets the dial back to its original position. "What do you think? Did that get your attention?"

I jump for Jacobs, but the big guy grabs me around the arms. I struggle, but there's no way I can break free. This guy is strong as an ox and has strength in reserve with which he could probably crush my ribs. I stop struggling, and he relaxes his hold but doesn't release me.

"Ned?" Jacobs says. "You still with us?"

"Y-yeah." Ned stirs. "I-I'm still here. That was some jolt."

"We have a lot more where that came from. If John co-operates, we won't go any further. After all, you are not permanently damaged. The next level will not kill you, but I'm sorry to say, if John decides to help me after I take you to that level, you will have symptoms as if you'd had a stroke. You will lose the use of one or both of your arms and, at least, one leg. You've seen stroke victims walking around, haven't you? They need help and don't seem to be all there. We will leave you now so you can think about what advice you want to give John when we come back."

"I-I don't c-care what you do. I'll still tell him to resist. John, if you can hear me, tell this asshole to go to hell."

Jacobs gives the knob a twist, and Ned stiffens again. Given it's the same reaction as before, I assume Jacobs repeated the level of the last jolt. As if Ned wants me to know that he's okay, he smiles broadly and says, "Clears the sinuses, though."

The screen goes dark, and the one marked number two flashes. As I feared even before the scene becomes clear, Stephanie sits strapped in a chair. As did Ned, she looks more bored than concerned. Jacobs' voice surprises her, and she straightens to attention, looking into the camera. And, like Ned, looks right at us. The big guy shoves me into the chair and secures my wrists behind me. No getting to Jacobs physically, then.

"Ah, Ms. Savard. How are you doing today?"

"Like you would care. Who is this?"

"I'm surprised you don't recognize my voice."

"Why would I?"

"Don't you remember when you and I had a conversation while you were recovering from that unfortunate bullet wound?"

"Yeah. You came to the hospital and told me you were an agent and took all the listening devices off me."

"That's right. I knew you would know me."

"But you're not an agent."

"No. In fact, I'm sitting with your friend John Cannon. He is my prisoner, as you are. He refuses to help me, so I thought you could talk him into it."

"My God. Matt Jacobs."

"Nice to meet you. I must say, the other times we were together, you were less fashionably dressed."

"You son of a bitch. You raped me, you pig, and weren't even man enough to do it while I could defend myself. I would have kicked your ass, not to mention your other parts. If John refuses to help you, then I support him."

"I'm sure you do. Since you are filled with such rage, we need to do something to convince you to change your mind, though. How does this feel?"

Stephanie stiffens and lets out a low-level cry. Not a scream but, whatever Jacobs is doing, it hurts her. She slumps in the chair when Jacobs turns the dial to zero.

"Well, John," Jacobs says. "The next level will turn the lovely Ms. Savard into a vegetable. What are you going to do?"

At last, I get a plan in the back of my head. I assume Jacobs will move to my parents next, and I want to save them from even the initial jolt, as I'm not sure if, at their age, they would survive even the low-level charge. I'll do some dramatics and then give in. I need him to buy the fact that I'm giving up on my principles to save Stephanie, Ned, and my parents. Worried that I might not be able to conjure a tear, I think about what Matt did to Stephanie and the danger she and Ned are in, and before I know it, I have an eyeful of tears that I have to be careful to let fall at the right time.

"I-I think I'm ready to think about what you want me to do," I say.

Jacobs turns to me, and I turn to him. With a blink, I let the tears run over the edge of my lower eyelids and down my cheeks. "What do you have in mind?" Jacobs says.

"I don't want you to give my parents a jolt. I don't think they'll recover."

"That is up to you."

I sigh deeply and pull what appears to be a sob from the inside of me. Since I don't have use of my hands, the tears run freely and drop on the floor. I hope it's a good enough demonstration of sincerity. "You win. I will do whatever you want. You have to assure me that my folks, Ned, and Stephanie will be okay."

"Have I ever gone back on my word?"

"Not that I know about."

"You have my word. Your people will be released after you do what I want done."

"Okay. I have one more thing, though."

"You are in no position to ask for anything, John." He shrugs. "Well, it won't hurt to hear what it is. What do you want?"

"I want to be the one to carry the bomb and die with the President."

"You are kidding me, right?"

"No, I'm serious. If I'm going to help you, even if just a little, I don't want to be around to face the consequences. I don't think I could live with myself, anyway."

"We've chosen our martyr, and he looks forward to his reward for doing his duty."

"I'm sure he can be talked out of martyrdom. Tell him, next time."

"You are not a believer, so this martyr opportunity will be lost on an infidel."

"You can explain that away, right? You are the grand poobah of this operation."

"Okay." Jacobs rubs his chin, deep in thought. "I will allow you to carry out the mission. If you think you might be able to warn the President or otherwise interfere with the explosion, understand that it will be a remote detonation, and I will still have your people as my captives."

"Oh, I understand completely. I'm tired of being under constant threat of elimination by your goons and will look forward to ending this nightmare forever. You will consider whatever is between us as finally resolved in your favor, right?"

"I will consider your debt paid in full."

"Great, then let's get started. I assume there have been some preparations that I will need to be brought up to speed on."

"Yes. I'll shut down here, and you and I can start the briefing immediately."

I nod and turn to look at Stephanie. Awake now, she appears pale but beautiful. I think I sold Jacobs on my co-operation. I threw in being the bomber as a last thought. My reasoning was to get more involved in the plan in hopes of subverting it. Also, the longer I'm involved, the more time I can buy. When I run out of options, the moment of truth will come, but by being actively engaged, I hope to put that time off for as long as possible. I am alone completely. No Ned will ride in at the last minute to save my bacon. How do I find out where he's holding Stephanie, Ned, and my parents?

With the setup here, I suspect that they might be close by. "Any chance of seeing my friends or family?"

Jacobs doesn't look at me and takes no time to contemplate. "Out of the question, John. They aren't anyplace near, and we don't have the time to take you to them."

"Don't you think it's going to take some time to get me on the President's meeting schedule?"

"I think he will be delighted to see you. So, no, I think it will be a matter of days."

"How about before the mission so at least I can say goodbye."

"Let's see how things go. I won't make a promise, but it might be possible."

"Thanks, Matt."

Jacobs looks at me at last, trying to read my face for insincerity. Hopefully, I pull off the sincere look of the decade. If the son of a bitch lets me see my folks, one part of my plan might come together—the bit where I grab them and fight our way out. A whole lot of other parts have to fall in before then, but at least it's a start. Maybe, I could get deeply involved and then refuse to do any more until I see everyone. It might just work. If I know where they are, I will be in a better position to get to them and pull off a rescue. At least, that's what I hope.

"All finished here." Jacobs' voice breaks my thought stream. "Let's go." He gets up and motions to the big guy to cut me free. With my hands released, I rise, and Jacobs leads the way, talking over his shoulder and explaining what needs to be done. The big guy follows behind me. Only listening with one ear, I hope I don't miss anything that might be useful to my escape plan. However, I'm more interested in checking my surroundings. We pass a set of doors that have studio numbers on them. I'd bet that these lead to rooms holding my folks and friends. I can't imagine having them too far away from the control room. There must be a holding area around here somewhere. Perhaps they have a room like mine, which would mean they're on a similar floor to me.

We reach what looks to be a conference area. Small rooms surround a large one, which sits in the center. Through the double doors, we come to a full conference setup, including a large screen on the far wall. "Is this where the money is made?" I ask.

"This is a private room. What I call my war room. Here is where we make the plans that, hopefully, will someday bring the mighty Satan to his knees. My team and I have everything we need. Here, let me show you."

Jacobs walks to what could be taken for a wall-to-wall closet. He picks up a remote and presses the button, then smiles when the cabinet disappears into the ceiling. In its place, sit four consoles with monitors and an array of equipment that resembles NASA launch headquarters, which I've seen on TV. At the first console, Jacobs hits a switch, and the equipment comes on. A large screen forms the central piece and looks like it is capable of providing a lot of information. The question is what kind? Almost as if he read my mind, Jacobs asks me to step closer. "This central monitor is for tracking targets anywhere in the world."

"What kind of targets?"

"Almost anything. Here, let me run a digital copy of the last target we tracked." Jacobs selects a CD and inserts it into a small slot under the monitor. A large green wave appears on the screen, sweeping three hundred and sixty degrees. The wave makes two revolutions, and then a small white dot appears from the right. An audible tone sounds when the wave passes over the dot. While the dot moves closer to the center of the screen, several numbers generate.

"That dot is the jet on which you and Ms. Savard left the Greenbrier. Notice all the numbers? Those are the call out positions for the missile that you'll see launched shortly. This is a playback, but it is just as exciting as if it were happening right now. Don't you agree?"

"Real exciting. Especially if you were in that jet. How did you guys find out where we were?"

"No harm in telling you. Not now. While Ms. Savard was in the hospital with her head wound, we had the opportunity to slip a tracking device into her body."

My blood runs cold. "You did what? ... You've tracked her since then?"

"Yes. Cool, wouldn't you say?"

"Son of a bitch. You knew where we were all the time?"

"Yup. Like I said, cool. Oh, watch this. See that little dot rising from the bottom of the screen? It's the missile. Watch now; it's going to correct its path. Look, a hard left turn. This is like a watching video game."

"Except you killed two people."

"Collateral damage. Doesn't mean a thing."

"What would have happened had your little missile hit amidships instead of blowing up by the windshield?"

"Never happen. We gauged Ms. Savard's location on the plane and calculated how far to the windshield."

"Why didn't you just bring it down?"

"What, and deny Ms. Savard the pleasure of saving you from a fiery death?"

"Oh, I see. You think a little drama like that would guarantee my co-operation, seeing as I would be grateful whether conscious or not."

"Worked, didn't it?"

"Come on, Jacobs, there has to be another reason."

"Well, we figured if there were a threat en route, you two would be more willing to stay together, and that the experience of surviving a major threat would bond you like nothing else. This would guarantee that we would know where you were. The helicopter and missile to the airplane were for the same reason."

"Seems like a lot of trouble. What about that disgusting video of you and Stephanie? How were you certain that stunt wouldn't drive us apart?"

"A gamble, but I figured it would be a nice quid pro quo for your, erm, dalliance with Sarah. I did you a favor. Since Stephanie since had a dalliance of her own, you don't need to apologize to her."

I don't know how to answer. Matt's rationale is sicker than I thought. I glance over my shoulder. Big guy stands at the door. I'd like to grab Jacobs by the throat but know I won't get to finish him before his goon knocks me silly. Instead, I bite my lip and work hard to keep from saying or doing anything rash.

Jacobs seems oblivious to my turmoil, totally absorbed in looking at the monitor. "Here it goes. The missile is almost there. Five, four, three, two, one. Blam. Look at that. Beautiful. I have another view of the nose camera in the missile. Do you want to see that one?"

"God, no. You forget I was there. I don't need to see anymore."

"Suit yourself. Now, take a look at the firing center over here." Jacobs talks while he walks to the next console. He touches a couple of buttons, and the center electronics light up. Once again, Jacobs motions me over. I sigh and comply. "This is the fire control center. We can launch missiles and any other kind of drone or aircraft."

"You can fly planes remotely?"

"Yes. We can also use the craft to launch bombs and other ordnance."

"Why don't you just fly something into the White House and be done with it?"

"We could never be sure we'd take out the President. So many things could happen. I admit, it would be easier than having someone up close and personal, but not as sure."

"You have people working these consoles?"

Jacobs chuckles. "I don't do all this myself. Yes, I have loyal followers as committed as I am."

"Where are they? All these committed people?"

"At prayer. We have prayer five times a day."

"You pray and kill people. I just don't get it."

"We pray and smite our enemies, as it is written."

"Yeah, in the Jacobs' book of life, I imagine."

"No need to be blasphemous. If you would rather sit this out, I understand. Can't say the same about your people."

"Okay, let's skip a repeat of the threats. I said I would go through with it and I will. What am I to do?"

"You will have two jobs. First, get an appointment with the President."

"Not sure I'll have the juice to do that."

"I'm certain the President feels bad for not giving you your medal. And equally certain he will bend over backward to help you."

"Did I ever tell you how well you speak English?"

His eyes widen. "Why mention that right now?"

"That idiom 'bend over backward' reminded me that English isn't your primary language. You're sophisticated in its use."

"Thank you." He studies me for a moment longer. "Now, back to your job. The second thing you will have to do is carry a bomb into the presence of the President."

"Sounds difficult. He has a ton of security."

"This has been the hardest thing to figure out. We finally got a breakthrough with the mixture of a C4-type explosive and silicone. We can make a bomb as thin as skin. Once we get your measurements, we will construct a second skin, which we will apply to your body. It is virtually undetectable under present screening methods, including a pat-down. We build in the detonation device—a simple wiring and detonation mechanism, which you will have in your iPhone, attached to your belt in a normal holder. Wait until you see this stuff. Amazing."

"I would be more excited if it didn't mean I would blow along with this skin thing."

"You will be the first martyr to use this system. I envision hundreds, if not thousands, of my warriors getting on airplanes and, in one major action, watching them fall from the sky. You can imagine the public panic. It will be such an overwhelming victory that it will make nine-eleven look like a kindergarten exercise."

"You're mad, you know."

"John, John, John. I may be passionate, but I can assure you, I don't have a mad bone in my body."

"Another idiom. Good job."

"I wish you would stop the English lesson. We have important work to do. We should get to the lab now."

My thoughts turn to the terror and panic that all those airplanes crashing would bring. The law of averages dictates that some would fall in major population areas. It would be unexpected and without precedence. An unthinkable number of passengers would perish, let alone those on the ground. Instead of limiting my focus on just saving Ned, my parents, and Stephanie, I need to give serious consideration on how to kill Jacobs. It may come to using my bare hands, and I need to figure a way to do it.

Chapter Twenty-One

Jacobs leads the big guy and me through a couple of doors, which open onto a space that looks like a hospital emergency department. They open to a series of rooms where people in white coats work over benches, which indicates that we are, indeed, in a laboratory situation. Sophisticated computer layouts replace the classic test tube lab setup. We enter one of the first doors.

"This is the compound lab," Jacobs says. Pride fills his voice, and he looks in my direction to see my reaction. I smile and give a slight nod to acknowledge the impressive array. "Come over here," he says.

I join him at a table by the wall. He picks up a manikin's hand and passes it to me.

"This is what I described in the other room. See, the skin looks and feels just as it should on a manikin. If you notice, it is difficult to detect. What do you think?"

I turn the hand over and over. "I can't see any skin. In fact, this just feels and looks like an ordinary dummy's hand."

"Just like I told you. Try to pull the skin off."

I attempt to pinch a piece of the skin and have no luck. "I can't get a hold of it."

"Here, give it to me." Jacobs takes the hand and looks at the wrist. "Here it is." He pulls near the wrist and strips the skin off the hand, just like removing a latex glove. "Here, take the skin and look at it." He hands it back to me. "Turn it inside out, so you can see what it looks like on the outside."

I pull one of the fingers through the opening, and the skin pops into the shape of a hand again, resembling a glove. "This is light," I say. Jacobs looks pleased with my observation. I press a little further, "You're saying you can coat a whole body with this stuff?"

"That is the beauty of it. It starts as a liquid, and then dries quickly into what you see there."

"What about the body being able to breathe with this skin in place? Seems like it would be hot and cause the body to suffocate."

"I'm impressed with your knowledge of the body's function. You are right, of course. If the skin were choked off with this substance, it would not be long before problems set in. Let me show you something. Give me the skin."

I hand it to Jacobs, and he walks to another table, where he opens a glass box and puts the skin onto a hand inside. Once he closes the door, he goes over to a panel of switches. After throwing one, he walks back to the glass box. "Watch."

Smoke seeps out of the skin and floats to the top of the glass. Jacobs retraces his steps, and then hits the switch one more time. "The smoke shows that the skin is permeable. Air flows through as if it were really a skin. One of my people could wear this for months with no adverse effects."

A chill goes up my spine as I witness the sophisticated weapon. With a smile, Jacobs comes back to my side and opens the glass case, and then pulls the skin from the hand. "I'll bet you are wondering if it works like a bomb."

"No, really, I'll take your word for it."

"Very funny. Come with me."

We move to another bench, and Jacobs puts the skin on another hand in another box. He attaches a couple of alligator clips to the skin and shuts the door. The inch-thick glass on the door tells me that we're about to have an explosive demonstration. Sure enough, Jacobs flips a switch, and I jump when the skin disappears in a flash and smoke.

With the door open, Jacobs holds the stand, which no longer has anything recognizable on it and is frayed at the end where the hand used to be. He gives me a proud smile. "This tiny piece of skin destroyed the entire hand, which we made out of aluminum. Think of a whole body of this stuff sitting next to the window on an airliner."

I shudder at the thought. This could be the ultimate weapon. "Why isn't the skin detectable with x-ray or other methods?"

"Good question. It is made out of a compound that has no metallic content. This will show up in x-rays as skin, and metal detectors will not register it either. The beauty of this weapon is that there is no way, other than through a close examination, to detect it as synthetic skin. The funny part is, your country's stand on political correctness almost guarantees none of my followers will be strip searched. Yes, if a fairly alert security person actually laid his hands on the synthetic skin, there could be a discovery. I'm betting no one will touch our followers as they pass through security. I also bet that no one at the White House will ask you to remove your clothes for a check before entering."

Sadly, Jacobs is right. They'd have no reason to check someone with an appointment with the Present closely enough to determine if his skin was real or not. "How long does it take to have a phony skin deployed on a body?"

"About an hour. Once it's on, about another two hours to dry fully. It is a little uncomfortable since you will have to stand with your arms outstretched for those two hours. Once dried, you will be able to move freely, and it will feel no more uncomfortable than a tight-fitting wetsuit."

"Does the stuff go over the face?"

"No, we stop at the neck. We conceal the seam, though. It is difficult to find it once dried. We also try to match the hue and tint of your skin just in case someone gets suspicious and asks a follower to take off their clothes. All in all, we think we have looked at every eventuality."

"When do you plan to coat me in this crap?"

"We can start as soon as we get the appointment with the President. This will give us an idea of exactly how much time we will have to prepare."

This is the time to take Jacobs. When I glance toward the door, I see the big guy grow more interested in me. He must have a sixth sense that tells him I have murder in mind. He steps closer. It will be impossible.

So that I can, maybe, learn more, I ask more. "When do we get the appointment?" This feels like pulling teeth, getting Jacobs to lay out his plan. Irritation creeps into my voice, although I try hard to keep it under control.

"We can make the call today. We have arranged a cell phone with the proper caller ID so there will be no alarm at the security level. Let's go and get it over with."

Jacobs goes through the door, and then the two double doors. I follow close behind, with big guy behind me, and feel quite surprised at the speed he walks. It seems as if he's late for an appointment. It may be that he's anxious to secure the meeting with the President and wants to do it before I change my mind. That might explain the rush. We walk past several doors, and then turn left into another wing of the building. Another two doors and we reach a sizeable office.

"Have a seat," Jacobs says. "Let me get the cell phone." He moves over to a large desk, pulls open a drawer, and retrieves a box, which bears the phone company's logo. Then he heads back to me and smiles broadly. "Okay, here is your phone. We programmed the number of the appointment secretary already. Let's talk about what you're going to say."

"Good idea. We don't want me stumbling around with the White House."

"Too right. Now, what I would do is go ahead and ask to speak to the President."

"What? He's not going to get on the phone with me."

"I know that. If you just call and ask for an appointment, you will be shuttled off to someone whose job is to bury calls like yours. If you ask to speak to the President like you have every right to do so, you will be a force to be dealt with and the easiest way is to take your number and find out if the President wants to see you."

"So, you don't think I will get an appointment on this call?"

"Would be a miracle. These things take time, but we have to start the process. Okay, once you ask to speak to the President, you will get passed to someone who will ask the nature of the discussion. Just say that you want an appointment with him and that you want to discuss security concerns."

"Security concerns?"

"Yes. You're not going to say much more. You won't have to. You, after all, are a hero who would be qualified to discuss security. Don't forget, once you give your name, someone will be entering it into a database search. They will know all about you before you get off the phone. So, you got it?"

"I think so."

"All right then, pull that phone out of the box and hit the contacts list. The White House number is under White House."

"Well, that figures." I pull the packaging off the box and pick up the phone. The power button brings it to life, and it is fully charged. I look at Jacobs, and he gives me a "what did you expect" shrug. With shaky fingers, I touch "contacts" and then the "Ws," and the number comes on the screen. Next, I touch the phone icon, and it rings.

"Good afternoon, The White House, how may I help you?"

"Uh, could I have the President, please?"

"Whom may I say is calling?"

"John J. Cannon."

"Can you please hold, Mr. Cannon?"

"Y-yes, I can hold." I roll my eyes in Jacobs' direction. He just smiles, and it looks like this is all going as he suspected it would.

"Mr. Cannon?"

"Yes."

"May I tell the President what this is in regards to?"

"Yes, please, tell the President I would like to arrange an appointment to come in to see him and discuss some security concerns."

"Thank you, sir. Please hold for a minute." They're transferring me to another person. The line stays deathly quiet. I wouldn't expect some music on hold, but this is like being in a huge black hole.

"Mr. Cannon?"

I jump. "Yes?"

"I'm Ms. Gonzales, the President's appointment secretary. The President has some time available on Thursday the fourteenth. How much time will you need?"

"Um, time?" Jacobs flashes 'five' three times. "No more than fifteen minutes."

"Perfect. The Present can see you at one-fifteen. Is that good for you?"

"That is perfect for me as well. Thank you so much, Ms. Gonzales."

"You are welcome. To confirm, you will see the president at one-fifteen Eastern Daylight time. One more thing, Mr. Cannon. May I have your date of birth to confirm your identity?"

"Yes, of course. March thirty-first, nineteen-eighty."

"Thank you, sir. You will need to be here no later than twelve-forty-five. Be sure to bring a photo ID, and be prepared for security screening."

The words 'security screening' cause my scalp to break out into a sweat. "Thank you, Ms. Gonzales."

"No, Mr. Cannon, I thank you for your service to our President. He will be looking forward to seeing you, as will we all be. Next Thursday, then. Goodbye, Mr. Cannon."

"Goodbye, Ms. Gonzales." My heart lodges in my throat. This seems way too easy, as Jacobs thought it would be. Now, I have an immense problem. I need to figure out how to subvert this plan since I'm an integral part of it.

"Now, was that so hard?" Jacobs says. He has a big smile on his face.

"Unfortunately, it was way too easy."

"We only have four days to get ready. A tight schedule, but sooner is better than later." Jacobs gets up, and I follow.

We leave the room and go back to the lab, where Jacobs picks up a phone and makes a call. "The date is set. The team should meet me in the lab." Without saying goodbye, Jacobs hangs up and turns to me. "We are going to start right away. It will take us only a few hours to apply, and although we have four days, I think a couple of tests will be in order before we actually put the skin on you. After all this planning, we need to know if you'll have a reaction to the material. If so, we will need to put it on a little nearer to the event. You ever had contact dermatitis or any other allergic reaction?"

"Not that I remember."

"Good, maybe we will luck out, then. This stuff can be tricky. Sort of like gasoline on the skin. We have developed a pre-application cream, but people have broken out in hives. It won't stop the mission. However, we would like you to be as comfortable as possible."

"Much appreciated."

Jacobs laughs one of his deep guffaws. "Sometimes, John Cannon, you are a funny man."

Not seeing the humor, I say, "That's what Winther used to say."

"Yeah, and look at him now."

"Where is he?"

"No idea. The Feds took him. He could be in Guantanamo, as far as I know. You saw him last in South America."

"I would've thought a big important guy like you would have figured a way to free him."

"Ran out of ideas. Besides, he failed me twice, so I'm not so enamored with trying to get him released."

Jacobs' coolness toward his former number one feels chilling. He's a psychopath and sociopath all rolled into one. I wish I'd paid more attention in Psych classes in college, and then I'd have more idea how to handle him. All I know is that his attitude gives me the creeps. What else is new?

My thoughts about the evilness of Jacobs have me distracted, and I don't notice that several people have entered the lab until Jacobs calls everyone to order. It startles me to see them here. Jacobs thanks them for coming on short notice. Then he lets them know that he's pleased to announce that the mission is a go for Thursday. They all seem happy at the news, and a couple of them shake hands. With a stern expression, Jacobs says, "We have a lot of work ahead, and the planning and execution process is in phase red." Not sure what that means. More excitement and applause greet his words. This feels like a pre-game pep talk, except we're talking murder, not scoring points.

"John Cannon, here, has graciously volunteered to carry the weapon when he meets the President. It will not be necessary to arrange a stand in, so we can release him."

One of the white coats raises his hand.

"Yes, a question?"

"Yes, sir. Mr. Watkins was looking forward to his role as a martyred soul. Does this mean he will not fulfill his destiny?"

"Not at all. Please, kill him in the name of Allah."

"Yes, sir. It will be done. Praise Allah."

No other comments come, and all of these people seem to be at ease with one of their team being eliminated. I look at Jacobs, who shows no emotion. How did these people get this way? They're so committed to destroying America that not even death will turn them from their objective. They remind me of a mythological monster. Any one of the arms, or all of them for that matter, could be cut off and still the monster would come. Only a fatal strike to the head would be effective. Jacobs is the head. He must be eliminated.

Jacobs looks at me. "You seem tense. Is there something about a man being given the ultimate gift of eternal life that bothers you?"

Resolved, I hold his stare. "Almost nothing surprises me. Everything bothers me."

"I see. Well, we are ready to begin. These gentlemen will take you for a test of the skin. We will apply the material to several places on your body to see the reaction. We will leave for

Washington on Wednesday. We have a suite at the W, which I think you will enjoy for your last night on Earth."

"Yeah, a little too much information." I roll my eyes. "Leave me to guess the various outcomes. Okay?"

"Suit yourself. I thought you would like to know what's going on. But I'll not bore you with details." With a nod of dismissal, he addresses one of the technicians, "Take him to begin."

Jacobs turns and leaves the room. A quiet-voiced guy comes up to me. "Please, follow us, Mr. Cannon. We will use that room over there."

I go with him, and three more scientific-type people join us. One is a woman, and I flash on the prospect of being stripped for the test. "Do I need to take off my clothes?" All three laugh, and the leader says, "No, just remove your shirt."

I comply and sit where they tell me.

The room feels cold on my bare skin. A young woman comes over to me and takes a bunch of pictures. She says, "We'll enter the digital pictures into this machine, which will give us a plan on how to manufacture the skin."

Not caring to understand what they do, I settle for a shrug.

The woman goes to what looks like a printer, where she attaches a USB cord to a laptop. Then she types. Another technician monitors a screen. He holds up his hand, and the woman stands with her fingers off the keyboard. A grinding noise sounds from the printer, and after a few moments, the technician takes what looks like a skin-colored piece of paper out of it. They both walk over and ask me to lift my arm.

The woman holds my raised hand, and the technician applies cream to my arm. He then wraps the skin thing around my arm. To my surprise, it feels warm and, once in place, I can't see a seam. The woman lets go of my hand, and I drop my arm. Dense. It feels like clay. This small piece might weigh as much as a pound. "Seems heavy," I say.

The technician looks at it, and then rips it off. He walks back to the printer. More grinding noise produces another piece.

He comes back and slaps the sheet back on my arm. This time, it hardly feels like it's in place. "That's better," I say.

"Lift your arm," the technician says. I do, and he inspects the piece closely. Satisfied with the results, he doesn't smile, but says, "You will wear this tonight, and tomorrow we will check on it." Then he turns to the printer, occupied with whatever's on the screen. The machine produces another piece, which he picks off and brings to me. "I want to put this on the upper arm. If you have any sensitivity, it should show up on the upper area."

I nod and offer my arm. He wraps the piece around my bicep and, other than the warmth, I don't feel it in place. "You may put your shirt back on," he says.

I grab the shirt and fasten it up. While I'm doing that, he says, "Someone will take you to your room."

"What am I supposed to do with this stuff? Can I shower?"

"This is just like your natural skin. You can shower or even go swimming. You won't hurt it. Don't try to take it off, though. The seam is almost invisible, and if you try to take it off yourself, you could damage it."

"Okay. Hadn't thought of taking it off."

"If it itches, or you see swelling around it, call this number." He gives me a card with just a number. No name or anything else.

"I don't have a phone."

"You have one in the room. Except for few numbers, it is restricted. This is one of those numbers."

"Okay, thanks." I tuck the card into my shirt pocket. While I do so, the technician looks past me and nods. The big man waits at the door. The technician tells me to go with him. I walk toward him and say, "You ready, chief?"

He grumps something and holds the door open, and then we walk down the hall. Where am I in relation to the torture studios? Not expecting much of a reply, I ask the gorilla, "Where are the studios from here?"

"The what?"

"The studios where the broadcasts are made."

"Don't know what you're talking about."

"I saw a few rooms that looked like studios. I passed them somewhere today."

"We are here."

"Where?"

"At your room." The big guy opens a door, and sure enough, there is a full room. The same as I had last night. Which confuses me, as I'm positive Jacobs took me a different way before. I can't be sure, but I don't remember the room being this close to the lab. Of course, all these doors look alike, so it could be that I was as close before. "Is the dining room to the left down that hall?"

"Yes."

"Thanks. Just trying to figure out where I am."

The big guy backs out of the room and leaves me, then throws the lock into place. The phone rings, and I pick it up. "Hello?"

"Matt Jacobs."

"Yes?"

"Would you care to join Sarah and me for dinner?"

"My pleasure. Thank you." I want to tell Jacobs to take himself and his whore and take a flying leap, but doing that won't accomplish anything. Who knows, more information at dinner might be a good thing. And, a person has to eat, after all.

"Good. We'll have dinner in my suite. Someone will come for you at seven. That will give you some time to relax."

"Thank you." With me almost gagging, it's fortunate that Jacobs is too busy saying goodbye and detects nothing. Why the fascination with meeting me for meals? Jacobs must have a fixation on breaking bread with his victims. Such a weird situation. Sarah being there makes it more awkward. No, make that a lot awkward.

Chapter Twenty-Two

At seven o'clock on the dot, a knock sounds at the door. "Come in," I say. Not much other option, seeing as I can't open the door myself.

Another of the big, ubiquitous, rough-looking guys pokes his head in through the entryway. "You ready?"

"Sure am. Lead on, McDuff."

"Name's Francis." He looks at me as if he's waiting for me to make fun of his name. I wasn't raised to be stupid, so I just nod and go through the door, which he holds open. It wouldn't surprise me if he'd never heard the "lead on" phrase from Macbeth. If I pulled out something from a Marvel comic book, he'd probably get it. Why do I give a shit? Anything to keep from thinking of the nightmare situation I'm in. I still struggle to accept that Jacobs has me embroiled in yet another drama. Seriously. This stuff doesn't happen to normal folks, let alone three times. My lucky star must've been a falling one.

We walk a few more steps to an elevator. Francis punches a button, and the door opens. Once I'm in, I turn. My companion hits the floor marked fifteen. The top floor. The trip up takes little time, which is surprising given the distance. The door opens, and the big guy holds it until I get off. He surprises me by not following; he just stands and watches the door close, and that leaves me at a loss for what to do next.

"Welcome, John," I spin around, and Matt Jacobs stands in an opulent foyer, which must lead to his personal space. Drink in hand, he looks relaxed. "Please, follow me."

We walk through two heavy doors and into an open area—the living room. The far wall is glass from floor to ceiling, and beyond, I can see the glow of the city night lights. "Nice view," I say.

"Yes, the city is beautiful at dusk. The sunsets are spectacular. I find it the most peaceful time of day. May I get you something to drink?"

"What are you drinking?"

"Believe it or not, Tanqueray on the rocks. Something I picked up from you, actually."

"That sounds good. I'll have that. If you have olives, I'll take two."

"Coming right up." Jacobs turns and walks over to a bar on the wall. It looks well stocked, but its small size surprises me. I would have thought that Jacobs would have a huge bar for entertaining. He follows my gaze and says, "I don't do much entertaining up here. This is my private space. Not too many people have been here."

"Your man didn't get off the elevator."

"Yes, he is well trained." Jacobs crosses over to me and extends the hand with my drink. "Why don't we go over to the couch where we can be comfortable." He leads, and I follow.

The couch, as he calls it, is in fact, a large sectional facing the window view. A coffee table, set with an assortment of cheese and snacks, sits before us. "Please, help yourself." Jacobs nods toward the food.

After a sip of my drink, I ask, "Why dinner in your private quarters?"

Jacobs studies me for a moment, and then says, "My beliefs dictate that, since you are going to be martyred, it is up to me to make sure your last days on Earth are spent as enjoyably as possible. This includes the finest food, accommodations, and company. I realize you would rather be with your loved ones, but I still feel I should do what I can to make you comfortable here."

"I understand that. You're right, I'd rather not be here, but as long as I am, here's to comfort." I raise my glass, and Jacobs does the same. We each take a sip, but I notice Jacobs only touches the rim of the glass with his lip—avoiding the liquor. Did he only get the gin since he knew it was my favorite? While his warped view of kindness shocks me, I appreciate where he's coming from. It reminds me of pet owners who spoil their animals on the day before they euthanize them. Most likely, it's more for him than me. Perhaps, I can use his feelings to get out of here. My best bet is to play it cozy and see how it goes.

"This drink sure hits the spot."

Jacobs nods. "Let me know when you are ready for another."

"Thanks. I thought Sarah would be here as well?"

"You know women. She is running a little late. She'll be here shortly."

I pretend to be pleased and reach for a cracker. Just as I pop it into my mouth, Sarah enters the room. When you need to say something, a cracker is a tough thing to handle. I try to melt it with a big mouthful of gin. With my mouth full of wet mush, I stand.

"John. Please sit," Sarah says, and then takes a place next to me on the sectional.

Finally, I get rid of the cracker. "Nice to see you."

With some suspicion in her eyes, Sarah says, "Good to see you as well. After all, it's been so long."

I laugh out loud. "Yeah, I guess being in captivity makes me a little needy."

Jacobs asks Sarah if she would like something to drink. I think it is more to stop the current conversation path, as opposed to concern about Sarah's needs.

"I would love white wine, thank you."

Jacobs moves over to the bar. Sarah takes my hand. I almost jump and pull away until I feel the paper nestled between our palms. With a quick breath in, I fold my hand around it and slip it into my jacket pocket. Sarah's expression doesn't alter, and she sits with a smile on her face.

"Have you seen my new skin?" I hold out my arm.

Jacobs calls over from the bar, "Okay, John, one rule. No talking about the mission."

"I get it," I say. Sarah's expression remains fixed. She nods toward my pocket. Has she written something that will help me get out of here? It could be a macabre version of a Dear John letter, but I doubt she'd go to the trouble of concealing it from Jacobs. I have a good feeling about this and think on how I'll be able to read it without being seen by the cameras, which I'm sure watch my every move. To indicate that I understand, I give her a slight nod. She relaxes a little, and I grow warm. Must be the gin.

Jacobs comes back and hands Sarah a glass of wine. She thanks him and takes a substantial sip.

I look up at him. "So, what shall we talk about if not the mission?"

"Oh, how about something interesting about you? Let me ask, what made you decide to become a lawyer?"

Where's this going? I have nothing to hide, so I answer, "I graduated from high school and decided I wanted to be a lawyer. It sort of hit me as I was watching a courtroom scene in a movie. I don't even recall which one. I applied to Stanford and studied hard for five years and then took the bar exam. And that was it."

"How did you come to work in the firm?"

This is getting tedious, and I still wonder where Jacobs is taking this. "I was an intern there for four years, and they made me an offer."

Jacobs nods. "The rest is history. You were an excellent litigation attorney and made a ton of money."

"Well, not a ton in relation to your fortune."

"But you are well off."

"I guess. As if that's important now."

"What are you going to do with your money?"

"It will go to my parents. I don't have anyone else."

"Quite so. Do they need money?"

"No, they've set themselves up for retirement."

"You might want to think about giving your money to a worthy cause."

The utter crassness of Jacobs has me flustered. Him giving me advice on how to handle my affairs after he blows me up is almost more than I can take. I clench my jaw and attempt to stay calm. Besides, I'm hungry, and if I say what I want, I will be sent to bed without any dinner—the son of a bitch. "Yeah, I could give that consideration." I take a big swallow of Tanqueray.

"I could suggest leaving it to the cause, but I'm sure you'd find that rather too bold of me."

Then it clicks—Jacobs is trying hard to get my goat. Leave money to his cause? I'd rather die first. Hmm. I look at Sarah, and her lip twitches. She shares my embarrassment with this conversation. "Why don't we change the subject," I say.

"Yes. I'm afraid I am sticking my nose into things that are not my business. My apologies. Why don't we have dinner now? John, would you like another drink?"

I look at my glass. The ice has melted. I shake my head. "I'll wait for the wine. Thank you."

"Very well." Jacobs rises, and Sarah and I follow. We all go into the dining room, which is part of the great room. Wine glasses and silverware adorn the well-set table. It looks like the meal will be a major event with numerous courses. Seated where I'm told—on Jacobs' left—he sits at the head of the table, and Sarah to his right.

As we sit, a server comes out of a door, which I assume leads to the kitchen. He pours white wine while another man sets a plate of what looks like seafood but not quite. Jacobs explains that we will have the same meal that will be served to the Presidents of France and the USA the night before my meeting with him.

"You might as well have the same meal, even though you will not be invited to join the Presidents," Jacobs says.

Bemused, I ask, "What's on the menu?"

"Ah. To start, we have American Caviar with fingerling potatoes and Quail eggs. This is served with a nice French Pouilly Fume."

Jacobs has slipped deeper into his obsession; however, I have to admit, the first course tastes delicious. I refrain from asking about the other courses. Can I take Jacobs' ostentatiousness for much longer? The second course, and the rest, are delivered without much discussion. The dinner moves along with general conversation. Jacobs gives his opinion on several subjects, and the meal comes to a merciful end without any controversy. After coffee, we rise.

"I will walk you to the elevator. It has been a pleasure, John."

"Yes, thank you for the lovely dinner. It was nice seeing you again, Sarah."

She nods. "Yes, thank you. Good to see you, too. Goodnight."

Jacobs walks me to the entryway, and Sarah stays at the table. The elevator opens when he touches the button. Big guy Francis stands in the way, and then moves aside. When I get on, Francis punches the button. I can hardly wait to get to my room so I can read the letter. A good place to read it would be in the closet. Whoever is watching me will think something is up if I disappear, so I'll have to be quick. The shower might have been an option, but I already took one before dinner, and I'm sure some alarm will go off if I take another. Besides, I'm not sure the water will do the note any good, and if I spend time in there without the water running, that's sure to raise suspicion.

The elevator reaches our floor, and I get out. Francis escorts me to my room. Upon entering, I look around to see if anything is disturbed. The only change is that the bed is turned down, and a mint sits on one of the pillows. Francis bids me a goodnight. Then he says, "We are meeting Mr. Jacobs for breakfast at eight o'clock." After I thank him, he locks the door. I look in the mini bar to see if it holds Amaretto; I want to make sure the guys watching don't have a reason to believe I have this note burning a hole in my pocket. I would love to go into the closet and read it, but that would look weird. The mini bar has what I want, so I grab the miniature of Amaretto. A small tray on the chest of drawers holds glasses. I open the bottle and pour the liquor into the glass, pull out the mini bar ice-cube tray, and fill my glass with ice. The tension kills me, but I reach in for a second bottle of Amaretto, open it, and add it to the glass. Hopefully, this will calm me down. I take a sip and roll the liquor around in my mouth, and then I glance to see where the cameras are located. So hard to tell, but going to the closet should look like a natural enough move.

While sipping my drink, I rise and stroll across the room. At the closet, I set the drink on a table. Then I pull off the sports coat and open the door. It's not a walk-in and no way can I go inside without raising questions. A better idea comes to me, and I walk back to pick up my drink. As casually as I can manage, I reach into the sports coat pocket, palm the piece of paper, and throw the jacket on the couch. With the paper in my pants pocket, I take a seat. A magazine on the low table catches my attention, and I grab it. When I lean back, I pull the paper out of my pocket and slide it between the pages of the glossy. With another sip of Amaretto, I turn the pages as if I'm interested. The paper waits sandwiched in the next few pages. I glance up and over my shoulder, and don't see any evidence of a camera. With a deep breath in, I go for it and open the paper. Sarah's handwriting is easy to read.

John,

I have taken a great deal of punishment at the hands of Jacobs. I hope you understand by now that I have no control over what he does to me. He has my sister, and <u>daily</u> threatens her harm. He is an evil man, but I have given myself to him if only to prevent him from harming her.

Your people are being held in this building in cells near the broadcast studios. I will help you get them out, but you must promise me to help take care of Matt Jacobs. This is the only way my sister will be free since I know where she is as well and, without an order, no one is going to harm her. If you can't or won't, then I will have to keep their exact location and my help to myself. When next I see you, just use the word ROSE in any kind of context, and I will know you will assist.

I'm sorry about everything that has happened, and that you and I have been pitted against each other. This was not my doing, and I'm greatly saddened.

Fondly,
Sarah.

After folding the letter, I close the magazine, get up, and go to the bathroom with it tucked under my arm. No way can I let them find this letter. It would mean the instant death of Sarah and, probably, me as well. I lay the magazine on the vanity, and then turn on the faucets and pull the sink stop. Then I pull a towel off the holder and lay it on top of the magazine. Next, I reach under the towel while looking in the mirror. When I feel the paper, I pull it out along with the towel, which I bring near the sink and dump the paper into the warm water. I put the cloth down and turn the faucets off. Then, grabbing the soap, I make a show of lathering my hands. I reach into the sink and feel the paper. It hasn't dissolved, so I tear it into the smallest shreds. Hopefully, all the pieces will be small enough to go down the drain. When I think they are, I pull my hands out of the water and release stopper. To my relief, a bit of swishing and a little more water and they all disappear.

I dry my hands and move to the closet, where I find a pair of pajamas, and am in bed in less than two minutes.

Once I've turned out the lights, I think of a plan. If I tell Sarah that I'll kill Matt, I assume she will give me further directions. I don't know how she'll accomplish freeing my parents, or her sister, Ned, and Stephanie while Matt remains alive. No, I would take care of Jacobs, and then we would go and free our loved ones. What about all the people who work for Jacobs? Won't they try to prevent us from freeing the hostages and then leaving? Maybe they're all like Sarah and have been forced to do what they're doing. That would be a break since once the wicked witch is dead, they will be free. I caution myself not to get my hopes up.

Wide awake, excitement at the possibility of getting the best of Jacobs chases away the relaxing effects of the wine and Amaretto. If I can pull it off, I won't have to blow up the President and myself to get out of here, and Jacobs will be finished for good. Could it be that I consider this a contest and the winner of it will be the victor, as opposed to thinking living is important? Not taking the life of the President should also be high up on the list of welcome outcomes. Getting the best of Jacobs should be way low. Maybe he's pushed me over the edge. For sure, this feels personal between the two of us. Does he feel the same? If so, he will be disappointed when Sarah delivers his downfall. I see how he looks at her, and feel he is in love. How can he continue to threaten the sister? Maybe he's scared he'll lose her.

Okay, I've thought this thing through enough for one day. I need to sleep. Tomorrow will be a big day. With my hands under my head, I take a deep breath. It won't be easy to find sleep under the circumstances. Instead, I try to think of something pleasant, but am still caught in the moment. My mind keeps coming back to Jacobs and his personality. How did he get on this terrorist track? I turn over onto my side and, before long, am not thinking anymore.

My dream involves being caught in a giant spider web and then falling, and I lurch awake. Sweat coats my forehead. A look at my watch shows me that it's six-thirty in the morning. Not believing I actually slept, I double-check to make sure the time is right. Then I pull back the covers, sit up, and turn on the light. Since breakfast with Jacobs is scheduled for eight, I have plenty of time to get ready. Coffee would be great, so I pick up the phone. "Yes, Mr. Cannon. How may I help you?" The voice sounds like the same guy from when Jacobs held me captive here before.

"Any chance of getting coffee?"

"Why, yes, sir. Would you like anything else?"

"A bottle of water would be great."

"Yes, sir. The water and coffee should be delivered in ten minutes. Anything else?"

"No, thank you." I place the receiver back on the hook. Does this headquarters building have any legitimate business? I remember attending one of Jacobs' meetings, and it did seem that he had regular stuff going on. He keeps his other life of leading a terrorist cell a secret. Why wouldn't he? You don't go around telling everyone you're trying to destroy America. Even if folks work for you, there's no guarantee they'll keep their mouths shut.

With no time to get into the shower before the coffee comes, I might as well just wait, so I go to the closet, where I pull out a shirt and slacks. Then I decide to wear the sports coat again, so I lift it off the couch and hang it up—allowing it to hang out a bit can't hurt.

The knock on the door startles me, and I step back away from it. The lock turns, and big man Francis comes into the room. A much smaller person, who looks rather nervous, follows him. Probably, they've told him I'm here as a guest, but I think he knows better. Equally, I'm sure he doesn't want to let on, as otherwise ole Francis here might just do him in.

The server puts a tray on the desk and leaves. Francis gives me a once over and also leaves, locking the door behind him. The coffee smells heavenly, and I pour a cup. First, I take the bottle of ice-cold water, snap off the top, and drain it in several swallows. After the alcohol, I should have had some water last night. Another bottle on the tray means I have more should I need it.

The coffee tastes as good as it smells. I take the cup with me to the bathroom. A nice hot shower and one more cup of coffee should have me ready for the day. When I turn on the shower, another thought comes into my head. What if Sarah is doing a double-cross, as ordered by Jacobs? She has in the past, and I have no reason to trust her now. She is, after all, beholden to Jacobs for the safety of her sister. With the cup on the vanity, I step into the hot water and allow it to help me sort out the variables. If Sarah is double-crossing me, I can't do much about it. I shall have to work out a way to say the word rose and see where we go from there. Coming to this conclusion gives me a temporary respite from the agonizing worry and tension I have been living with over the last few days. The hot water helps as well.

I grab the towel, step out of the shower, and take another sip of coffee. Looking in the mirror, I can only sympathize with the pitiful person staring back at me through the condensation.

John W Howell

This has been one hell of a ride, and knowing it is not over yet burdens the soul. Sighing, I pick up the shaving cream and begin my morning ritual.

Chapter Twenty-Three

The knock on the door, followed by sounds of the bolt unlocking, tells me the hour has come to see Jacobs again. Big Francis comes in and *actually* smiles. What's on his mind? Concerned, I say nothing. He waves me out into the hall, and we return to the dining area.

Jacobs and Sarah are already seated, and Francis leaves me to join them.

"Good morning, John. I trust you slept well."

"Yes, very well, thank you. How are you, Sarah?"

She looks down at her menu and mumbles something like fine or good.

I turn to Jacobs, "I noticed the flowers in the reception area, and have to say, they're beautiful. The rose is one of my favorites."

The word brings Sarah's head up, and her eyes lock on mine. She gives me a little upturn of her mouth, which could be the start of a smile, and then returns to her menu. Jacobs stares at the menu and says, "What was that? I wasn't paying attention. My bad."

"Oh, nothing. I was just admiring the flowers in the reception area."

"Ah, yes. We have fresh flowers every day. It sets off the day with a positive feeling. Don't you think?"

"I really do think they are lovely."

Sarah looks up again and says, "Roses are my favorite as well. I wonder, Matt, if it would be possible after breakfast if John and I take a tour of the roof gardens? I think we both would enjoy it. John, you have to see these gardens. They are under glass, and Matt's team grows some of the most beautiful flowers."

Matt frowns and says, "I'm sorry, I have some things that need attention this morning. I'll have Francis take you up there. You will only have about a half-hour, and then John needs to be in the lab to check how he is tolerating his new skin."

"I understand. We will miss you. Well, I will miss you; I know how proud you are of the gardens. However, having Francis take us will be fine, and a half-hour should be adequate."

"Very well then, are we ready to order?" Jacobs snaps his fingers, and a server jumps into place. We order, and I ask for more coffee. Jacobs smiles. "You like my coffee, don't you?"

"I have to admit, it's one thing about you that I truly like."

"Now, now. We were having such a good time." Jacobs wears a slight smile, so I'm sure he didn't take my dig personally. I look at Sarah, and she confirms my opinion with a calm expression, devoid of alarm.

Not having much to talk about and hating the silence, I ask how Jacobs came to build a garden on the rooftop. He thinks a minute, and then opens what becomes a long ramble about loving nature and flowers. He also mentions a concern for the environment, which is quite strange coming from someone who tends to blow things up. Massive explosions can't be good, environmentally speaking. He talks long enough so that, when he's finished, the server shows up with the food.

We eat and talk about inconsequential things. I learn that Jacobs has a collection of rare cars, which I didn't know from my research.

"Yes, I love the older cars. Usually, they make them by hand, and the craftsmanship is extraordinary."

"What's your favorite?" I ask the question not out of curiosity but to keep Matt engaged.

"I like the 1962 Ferrari 250 GTO Coupe the best. Of course, it was the most expensive."

"I've heard the Ferrari's are becoming quite the collector's items."

"If it is in pristine condition, almost any Ferrari can fetch a great price. Some not in pristine condition still do well."

We continue to chat idly about cars and finish breakfast. None too soon for Sarah, as she looks bored. If I weren't trying to keep Jacobs off guard, I would be as well. The more he thinks he and I have in common, the better my chances to take advantage of him. I only know enough about cars to keep asking questions. I'm glad Jacobs is such an ego maniac and could care less about what I think and, therefore, asks me nothing that would expose my ignorance.

We rise and walk out to the reception area. Big guy Francis waits there. Jacobs tells him to take Sarah and I up to the roof, and then after, just me to the lab. He tells him to give us thirty minutes or so to look around. "Forty minutes at most," he says. Then he turns and gives Sarah a hug, and says, "See you at lunch." With a glance my way, he says, "I will see you in the labs." And then he walks down the hall.

Francis takes us to the elevator, which stands open. This seems like a private elevator, and I guess that no one waits for it on the other floors. We get in, and Francis punches the top button. Sarah and I avoid looking at each other on the way up. When we arrive, Francis gets off first, and Sarah and I follow him down a hallway to a pair of doors. We go through the doors and then through another set.

The scent of thousands of flowers takes my breath away. Rows and rows of raised beds hold all manner of flowers that should only bloom in the spring and others that bloom in the fall. I ask Sarah about them.

"Yes, Matt has this greenhouse so he can grow anything he wants whenever he wants. Come over here and look at the vegetable section. He has tomatoes, asparagus, melons, and all manner of root vegetables and fruit trees. The restaurant grows all of its needs here. The flowers that you see in the building are grown here as well. He has ten full-time caretakers for this space. Unlike the rest of the building, Matt doesn't have eavesdropping equipment in this space. There are cameras, sure enough, but his valued nursery workers couldn't accept being overheard. They explained to him that sun and chatter form a big part of their workday and that they would feel constrained if they knew someone was listening. So, keep smiling and try not to look directly at the cameras."

"Where are they now?"

"They have a day off today. It is Matt's birthday, and he gave them the day off in celebration."

"His birthday? I didn't know."

"No reason you should, and besides, it's not going to make a difference since it's fitting that this is his last day too."

Nervous, I glance around. Francis stands next to me and must have heard what Sarah said. He has no expression on his face whatsoever. "Francis is helping me." Sarah looks at him and smiles. "He's being held against his will. We've formed a little club, which has as a charter, getting rid of Matt Jacobs."

"My God. I had no idea." This is all I can say. To trust all this as the truth might be a stretch. My heart wants it to be, but my head thinks it's too easy to be believed. "How did you two find each other?"

"Francis was assigned to guard me early on when Matt decided to take me. We got the idea that each was being manipulated, so I came out and asked if he was a prisoner. He said he was and didn't want me to share the information with Jacobs. I knew at once that we could be partners."

"So this has been a while?"

"Oh, I don't know, maybe a month or so. He's guarded me for a while, but it's only a little over a month as a co-conspirator, so to speak."

"And you trust Francis?" I look at him again, and he smiles.

"Of course, I do. He's kept our mutual circumstances completely quiet."

"How do I trust you? No offense, but you have a record of not being the most reliable."

"John, I'm sorry about that. As I said in my note, this was not my doing. I'm a victim and, certainly, not an ally of Jacobs. I want to see him dead for what he's done."

"I'd like to see him brought to justice. You didn't mention killing him in your note."

"I don't see any other way. He won't stand still to be tied up and gagged. There would be no way to get him out of this place without his people knowing. If he were dead, most of these vultures would run away and try to save their skins. If you can think of another plan, I'm all ears."

I need time to process. What Sarah just said gives me some hope that an alternate plan can be worked out. I don't think I could go through with killing Jacobs in cold blood, which is what Sarah envisions. "Give me some time," I say.

"We don't have much. You'll be going into the lab and will be occupied for the rest of the day. Once you're in the explosive skin, there's no telling how mobile you'll be."

"I see that. Hold on a minute. I think that we could make up an excuse as to why Jacobs should meet us in the suite. Then, we could overpower him, and Francis could stuff him in something and then put a gun on me, and all of us walk out with Jacobs. The only problem will be how to free the captives. Maybe, we could take Jacobs with us and free them."

Sarah thinks for a minute. Then she frowns and says, "No way can we free the captives without a direct order from Jacobs."

"How does he issue orders?"

"He visits and gives the order in person."

"How about on the phone?"

"Yes, he's done that sometimes."

"Couldn't we force Jacobs to give the order from his suite?"

Sarah chews her bottom lip. "We could try. He's nuts, you know. Even threatened with death, he might not want to co-operate."

"Well, we can always kill him and then do what we want. I just think we should try to bring him out alive. That way, we can live guilt free. I'm not a killer and don't think you are either."

"Okay, I see your point. Francis, what do you think?"

Francis looks embarrassed at being put on the spot. He looks down and then says, "I think we ought to kill the son of a bitch. If you don't want to do it, I can. With pleasure."

I study him. "Do you have a weapon?"

"No, Jacobs doesn't trust me that far."

"So, how would you kill him?"

Francis grabs me and places his forearm around my neck. He increases the tension, and I can feel the squeeze on my neck. I croak, "Okay, I get it." Francis lets me go, and I cough to regain my breath, which takes a moment. When I can talk, I say, "Would you be willing to try, at least, to take him out alive?"

"Yeah, I could go along with taking him alive."

"Okay, then it's settled. We get him to come to the suite and grab him. How do we get him to the suite?"

Sarah looks at me like I'm the dumbest person on the planet. "It's his birthday. I'll just call him and tell him I have a present for him and to come up."

"He won't be suspicious since I'm not at the lab yet?"

"You and Francis can go to the lab, and then follow him shortly after to the suite. I can keep him busy until you get there."

"He'll wonder about who's at the door when we get there."

"I'll tell him I've ordered a surprise and to stay comfortable. Then, I let you two in, and before he knows it, we have him."

"Does he carry a weapon?"

"No, not on him. He does have one in the suite, in the desk drawer in his office, but that's a distance from the living room, where I'll have him sitting comfortably. Yes, he may jump up at the sight of you two, but he can't get too far."

I think it over, and then nod. "Sounds like a good plan. So, after we get him under control, we call the guards in the holding area and force Jacobs to tell them that we're coming down to release the captives. Do we dare ask for a van?"

Sarah smiles. "Wow. Great idea. I'd figured we'd just go out into the street and stop the first police officer we see. If we had a van, we could go right to the police station. Let's do it. There's a garage on the other side of the holding area. We can tell them to have the van there."

"Okay. What do we put Jacobs in?"

Francis speaks up, "We have laundry carts on wheels. We could use one of those. If we have a van, it will be a simple matter of lifting the cart and dumping Jacobs into the back. I don't think anyone will bother to watch us in the garage."

"Won't there be cameras?"

"Yes, but dumping a load of laundry isn't something the guards care about, and they certainly won't put it together that Jacobs is in the basket."

"Okay, you sold me. Laundry cart it is. What happens if we have to kill Jacobs?"

Francis gives me his usual frown and says, "Then, we just walk out and try to stay out of the way of all the people running out of there as well."

"If we have to kill him, how do we broadcast that to the population?"

Sarah says, "I call the front desk and ask them to ring the police. I'll tell them that Mr. Jacobs is dead, and we need someone to come and investigate. Believe me, no one will want to be questioned. The place will empty so fast it will make your head swim."

"You're talking about all of Jacobs' cohorts. What about the regular workers?"

"They won't stop us from doing anything. They're innocent and will behave that way. Don't forget, they see me as Jacobs' girlfriend, so in most cases, my orders will hold water with the regular workers where it means nothing to Jacobs' team."

We look at each other and, since we have no more questions, we move to the elevator. Sarah uses her phone and gives a soft invitation to Jacobs to meet her in the suite. She listens for a few seconds, and then says, "Be sure you come alone. I have a birthday surprise for you." Sarah disconnects and gives me a wink.

I smile. "Everything okay?"

"Yup," she says. "He'll come up right after you two get there, and he's given instructions to his boys in the lab."

Without further conversation, we get on the elevator. Sarah leaves at the suite level, and big guy and I go down to the lab level. We get off, and Francis takes up a position behind me as if he's on guard. Casually, I stroll toward the lab and hide my nervousness well. Hopefully, I won't do or say anything to give our plot away. Years of keeping a straight face in front of juries have prepared me for this moment. My feelings seem like stage fright before a big trial. I always thought of this nervous feeling as a method to prepare me for the fight to come.

When I go through the lab door, Jacobs stands with his hand outstretched. "Nice to have you in the lab," he says. "We have much work to do." Jacobs almost sounds like we haven't seen each other this morning. Oh well, he has to act for the general lab population, I guess. Maybe they're not in on the plot. They might think they're developing a weapon for the armed services. That wouldn't surprise me in the least. Jacobs is such a good liar, he could pull that off with no trouble. It makes no difference now, of course.

"Good to see you." I pull my hand out of Jacobs' grip and say, "What are we doing today?"

"We will fit you with a complete skin and make sure you feel comfortable during the procedure. Why don't you have a seat while I give my staff instructions?"

With a nod, I take a soft leather chair, and Francis slumps in the other. Jacobs smiles and goes over to a group of white coats gathered around another version of the printer I saw yesterday. I need to think of something to say to the white coats so that I can get away without raising an alarm. I could tell them I left something in the restaurant and ask Francis to go with me to get it. That should be okay, as it's close enough, and they won't think it will take any time at all. Not wanting to tip off Jacobs, I don't say anything to Francis—I'll wait until Matt leaves.

Jacobs comes back and makes some excuse about having to take care of business. The fact that he makes up a story leads me to believe he has no idea Francis and I were present when Sarah made the call. A guy in a white coat accompanies Jacobs.

"This is Doctor Hsiang," Jacobs says. "He knows what needs to be done. I'll be back as soon as I can." With a smile and bow, Jacobs leaves the lab.

I get up, and Dr. Hsiang says, "You need to take off your clothes so I can apply the skin. Did you experience any problems with the test strips?"

I shake my head, and then plant a shocked expression on my face. The Doctor asks, "Do you have a problem?"

"I left my wallet in the restaurant."

He nods and says, "No problem. I can call the restaurant and have them bring it here."

Francis gets up and says, "John and I will go and get it. Mr. Jacobs wants Mr. Cannon to be fully at ease." He frowns. "If my wallet were sitting in a restaurant, I would want to go get it straight away. Don't you have things you can prepare while we're gone? It won't take us a minute."

Dr. Hsiang agrees that his team can start without us. That's all we need to hear, and we head for the door. Dr. Hsiang calls after us, "Be sure and be back in no more than fifteen minutes and don't drink any liquids." We wave our understanding and go out through the doorway.

"Shit," Francis says. "I wish you'd let me in on that scheme. I was flat-footed."

"Yeah, but you played your part superbly."

We reach the elevator, and Francis hits the up button. The indicator shows that the elevator is on the suite level, and it seems like forever until the doors open. My heart rises to my throat as I rush into the elevator. By this point, we've been gone from the lab for about a minute. I have this counter in my head and want to get to Jacobs before the good doctor grows suspicious. We still have a lot of time, but the elevator seems to take too long in the ascent. Francis looks at me, and a nervous twitch flicks the corner of his mouth. "You okay?" I say.

"Yeah. What about you?"

"I've been better."

Francis gives me a smile and, under different circumstances, he might have laughed out loud. His apprehension makes me a little less tense. Finally, the doors open on the suite level. Neither of us wants to be first off. Finally, I take the lead and go to the double door of Jacobs' suite. My hands drip sweat like I've run a couple of miles. After a deep breath, I knock on the door.

No response comes. Did they hear my knock? My hands twist while I try to decide whether I should rap on the door again or wait. Francis shrugs when I look at him. Some help he is. Just when I'm ready to knock, the door opens quietly, and Sarah has her finger to her lips. "Matt's in the bedroom getting comfortable. You'll have to be quick." She steps aside, and Francis and I go through the door. Sarah points in the direction of the bedroom. "Wait outside the door," she says. "I'll call Matt out, and then you can jump him."

Francis and I take up a position on either side of the bedroom entrance. I'm relying on Francis to be the heavyweight here. Hopefully, he has skill at this kind of thing. Too late, now, to question his qualifications. Fingers crossed and hoping for the best, I crouch, ready to spring. How will we restrain Jacobs? We don't have a rope or anything else. If necessary, big guy can sit on him.

Sarah speaks softly and breaks into my thoughts, "Matt, darling, your surprise is ready. Come on out."

The bedroom door opens, and Matt comes through in a hurry. Francis swings his arm and catches Jacobs' nose. Jacobs falls as if clotheslined on a football field. I jump on him so that he won't be able to get up. He doesn't move, and blood pours from his nose. "You knocked him out," I say.

"Sure he's not dead?" Francis nods down at Jacobs. "That was a solid hit."

I look at Matt's face, and then climb off him. His chest heaves. "He's breathing." I look at the prone man and notice his stone-naked state. No need to wonder what the surprise was going to be. We need to get him secured and do something about his nose. I ask Sarah to fetch towels. As she leaves, I ask, "Could you bring something to cover him as well?"

Chapter Twenty Four

I nod at Francis. "We need to find something to tie him up. Take a look around."

Francis grunts and goes to the kitchen. Sarah returns with towels and a sheet. After putting the sheet over Jacobs' nakedness, I turn to his nose. It looks broken. I could give two shits about helping Jacobs, but I want to stop the bleeding so that we won't have a mess dripping all over the place when we leave. The bleeding won't stop until I straighten the nose. Not that I want to I grab it and pull it straight. Jacobs thrashes about and makes a bubbling, groaning sound. With the towel, I wipe up the blood, and then ask Francis, "Can you bring ice?"

Francis returns, a bucket of ice in hand. I grab a handful and put the cubes in a towel. Then I hit it on the floor to take some of the sharpness out and place the pack on the bridge of Jacobs' nose. "We better raise his feet, so he doesn't go into shock on us."

Sarah grabs his legs and puts his feet on a low stool. "Where did you learn first aid?"

"Boy Scouts. Never leaves you."

Francis finds cord, which he wraps around Jacobs' wrists. I turn to Sarah and tell her to place the call to the guards, as Jacobs is in no position to talk. She nods, pulls her phone out of her pocket, and places the call. She talks for a minute or so. The guards must be asking questions, but I think Sarah puts an end to them when she says, "Mr. Jacobs is in the shower. Shall I go in there and tell him you don't want to follow my directions? Directions that he gave me to give you. I will let you talk to him then." Sarah ends the call with, "Fine, please have Ms. Savard, Mr. Tranes, and the Cannons in the van in a half-hour. Mr. Jacobs' party, including myself, will come down then. I will not report your reluctance to Mr. Jacobs, but if you would like to call him, please do." With a frown, she looks up. "What a chicken shit."

I grin. "Looks like you got him on the right track."

"These people are afraid of anyone in power. I sure am glad they don't have any balls."

After a chuckle, I say, "You have the market cornered."

The three of us share a laugh and prepare Jacobs for transport. When we're all done, I ask, "Where can we get a laundry cart?"

Francis says, "One of the rooms in this suite should have one." He goes to look for it. Sarah and I go into the master bedroom to find something for Jacobs to wear. We agree that, given that his hands are tied, we'll need to release him temporarily to put a shirt and pants on him. The way he is now, he doesn't even need to be tied up, but I don't want to take any chances. We pick out a shirt, sports coat, and a pair of slacks.

"We better get shoes," I say.

Sarah goes into the shoe-rack section of the huge closet and pulls out Loafers.

"He doesn't need socks," she says.

The thought of the powerful Jacobs sitting in a police station with no socks amuses me, and I nod in the affirmative.

With a handful of clothes, we return to the lounge. Jacobs still lays on the floor and remains out cold. I remove his bindings and roll him so I can put his arm in the shirt. His elbow comes over and hits me in the eye socket, and before I can stop him, Jacobs jumps to his feet. Lucky for me, the elbow hit the bone and not the eye. I get up, alarmed that I'll have to take Jacobs on man to man. "Get Francis," I say. Sarah runs to the back of the suite where I assume Francis is still looking for a laundry cart.

"You don't stand a chance, John," Jacobs says through his dry lips, spitting blood. "I'm going to kill you."

"Matt Jacobs, you are an evil son of a bitch, and it will give me pleasure to personally bring you to justice."

I barely finish talking when Jacobs makes a swift move, crossing the room then pulling open a drawer in a table by the wall. He twirls around with a gun in his hand, aimed at me. He breaths hard, and blood runs from his nose.

"Looks like you're hurt," I say.

"It's nothing. When I'm through, you'll have a lot more serious wounds than this little thing. I wouldn't make a move if I were you."

Sarah and Francis come into the room and stop in their tracks. Sarah wears a horrified look. "Matt, what are you doing?"

"What am *I* doing? I could ask *you* the same thing. So, our love was nothing but a sham. You helped these infidels with their bloody work. You have betrayed me and need to be punished."

"Hold on, Mr. Jacobs," Francis says. Jacobs looks at him, and then—without warning—an explosion goes off, and Francis falls like a tree. Jacobs shot him in the head, and he doesn't make any further movement. The only sound is a hissing from the air leaving his lungs.

Jacobs shakes and screams, "This is what traitors deserve."

I hold my hands in the air. "For Christ's sake. Stop the madness."

"You dare ask me to do something to please that heathen? You are a big disappointment to me. I thought we were going to help each other. Now, I demand that you call me by my birth name."

"Your birth name? I don't know your birth name. All I know is Matt Jacobs."

"A name chosen from the book of Abraham the Jew. A cursed name, and one I was forced to use. My name is Aahil Tabatabai."

With effort, I force my breathing to slow. "Aahil. Put down the gun."

I move to grab him, and another explosion reaches my ears, followed by a red-hot punch to the leg, which causes me to lose my footing. Stunned, I fall to the floor, clutching my leg. The bullet hit me in the thigh.

"Damn you, Jacobs."

"Tabatabai. You swine."

I can't think of anything else, and a wave of nausea sweeps over me. I need to stay conscious, and so I scream—not from the pain but to keep me alert. With the aid of a chair, I ease up onto my good leg.

"Better stay down." Jacobs waves the gun. "The next one will be between your eyes, infidel."

I laugh out loud. "You mean you'll kill me quick? I don't think that's like you, *Matt*."

He smiles and points the gun to my other leg. The sound seems far away, and the bullet hits like the kick of a horse. Down again, I can't help screaming now. Those shots hurt. Thoughts of bringing Jacobs to justice fade as the red-hot pain gives my body a mission to try and overcome. Barely with it, I say to Sarah, "Those folks we were supposed to meet? Tell them to go ahead without us."

Matt screams, "What folks? You have let the captives loose, haven't you?"

The effort of fighting off the mercy of unconsciousness leaves me choking and unable to answer. Sarah yells at Matt that it's too late. "All the captives have driven out of the building. I phoned while you were unconscious and made arrangements. I just called back while in the other room with Francis and told the guards to give Ned Tranes the keys and to have the group leave."

"You ungrateful bitch. I loved you, and you turned on me. You've betrayed me. You never gave yourself fully to me, did you? In the eyes of Allah, you are a whore and a defamer. You came to my bed on one pretext, yet you were planning to take advantage of me all along. You deserve to go straight to hell. No, make that straight to hell's hell."

Sarah plants her hands on her hips. "You threatened me. You've had others killed. You raped Stephanie Savard. You're on some misguided mission to destroy those who don't share your beliefs. You're a monster and deserve your place in hell."

I wish Sarah would stop antagonizing Jacobs. From where I lie, he looks less rational as the moments pass. His breathing comes heavily. A loud slap sounds, and I can't tell if she hit Jacobs or if he hit her. I roll over to see Sarah throw herself at Matt. The gun goes off, and Sarah and Jacobs hit the floor together.

Paralyzed, no matter how much I want to move, I can't. Jacobs sits up. He has Sarah in his arms and cradles her like a sleeping child. I'm not sure he meant to kill her, but that point doesn't matter now. Sarah is dead. Jacobs has killed the one person who meant something to him. Although he held her against her will, he loved her just the same. And, I'm certain, he also thought she felt the same for him.

"It's over," I say. "The police will be here soon, and you'll have a tough time explaining all this carnage."

Matt says nothing, but lifts Sarah and moves toward the couch. Her head swings like she's made of cloth. A trail of Sarah's blood follows them across the room. Her pain and suffering have ended. Jacobs sobs and lays her down. Then he takes a moment to brush a strand of hair from her forehead. Eyes blazing and bloodshot, he glares at me.

"You have destroyed the only person I could love. She was the reason I wanted to go on and fulfill my destiny. Now, I have nothing. I have disgraced my heritage and my God. I hope you rot in hell. I would love to kill you right here, but to allow you a hero's welcome into the kingdom is something I will not do. You will die like a butchered hog. You will bleed out slowly with no dignity or prayers of supplication. Satan will welcome you."

Sleep ready to claim me, I say in a whisper, "Please, come closer so you can hear me. I have something you need to know." Slowly, I drift away, but want to bring my hands up to surround Jacobs' throat. Matt shuffles over and leans in just close enough for me to grab his neck and gun arm. With the last of my strength, I make maximum use of his Adam's apple to block his windpipe. Jacobs hasn't paid enough attention to his upper body strength. Although, he has a certain advantage in that he can use his lower body as leverage.

Jacobs lays top of me, and I tighten my grip on this throat. He struggles to get away and turns the gun in my direction. His other fist beats me, harmlessly, on the side. The pain in my legs makes his beating fist all but useless. Blood from his face drops into my eyes, and I have no choice but to close them. Overcome with a new sense of movement that I feel rather than see, I strain against the gun pointed at me. Slowly, I overpower Jacobs' effort. I rob him of air, and his arm gives way to my pressure. In an attempt to breathe, Jacobs spits more blood and has no spare air to do any talking. I continue to squeeze, and his neck muscles soften. A series of grunts escape his constricted throat. It won't be long until Jacobs will succumb to the lack of oxygen. All I have to do is hang on and keep the gun pointing away. He stops beating me with his other fist—a sign that he can't keep going on all fronts.

Jacobs tries one more time to get the gun into a position where he can put another bullet into me. I squint and see his ear close to my face. I rise, grab his lobe with my teeth, and hold tight. He jerks back, which causes his lower lobe to separate and remain in my mouth. He screams and his arm goes limp. I apply pressure to the limb and bring the gun up to his temple. My hand wraps around his wrist, and I don't dare let go. I wave his wrist until the gun bashes his head repeatedly. Then I spit out the lobe and squeeze his throat as tight as I can while flailing at him with the gun. He slumps and feels like dead weight.

His body drives the air out of my lungs. Still, I hit him over and over. Then more heat comes, followed by the explosion of the gun firing. Jacobs crumples on top of me, and the warmth of his blood flows like a running faucet over my face. I pitch with all my strength to free myself from his crushing weight. His body rolls away, and I breathe in with such force that I inhale some of the blood. To clear my lungs, I cough and have trouble getting my hand off his throat. It almost feels like part of him. I feel sick and turn my head so as not to add to my misery by mixing

Jacobs' blood with my vomit. I don't think I'd survive both on my face. As nausea hits in racking waves, my thoughts go to Sarah and her bravery. I haven't fully grasped the fact that I've killed Jacobs with my bare hands but know my justice is complete. Make that Stephanie's and my justice. Our justice.

Blessed darkness hits me like a rock.

Chapter Twenty-five

I bring the cold can of beer to my lips and take a big drink. The sun is quite hot, and I feel as if I've been without moisture for days. In reality, Stephanie just brought this beer and picked up the one I finished two minutes ago. Will I ever want to leave this porch? Unlikely. The sea looks wonderful with small whitecaps set against a deep blue canvas. The sky and water meet somewhere on the horizon, and not a sound reaches me, other than the surf. I could stay here forever.

"Don't forget we're having dinner at Ned's house tonight," Stephanie calls through the screen door.

"I won't. It will be good to see him and Geneen again after their trip."

Stephanie comes out carrying a tray with snacks. "Sorry, we missed lunch. Maybe these will hold you over."

She sits in the deckchair next to me and places the tray on the small table.

I hold her gaze. "I love you."

"Good to know." She grins. "I love you."

"Man, those are the sweetest words on Earth."

"You're a hopeless romantic. Here, have some cheese and crackers."

"Thanks. You not having any?"

"The doctor told me to lay off the carbs, so no. She said to try and keep my weight down for the first trimester. I'd love to eat that whole tray, but no can do."

"You tell your commander about the baby?"

"Not yet. Plenty of time for that. By the way, there's a letter sitting on the counter from the law firm. You going to open it?"

"Maybe some day. I'm sure it's a form letter telling me my leave is extended."

"How do you know?"

"When the President of the United States called Peters and told him I deserve another extension, I don't think he said no."

"Can you imagine his face?"

"I sure can, and it's beautiful. You want to go on the boat tomorrow?"

"Sounds lovely."

"It does, doesn't it?"

End

Thank you so much for reading Our Justice. I hope you enjoyed the story. It would be nice if you could give the book a review on Amazon. This is one way authors receive feedback from their readers and are so thrilled to find out what you think about their story.

You can also catch up with *My GRL* and *His Revenge* by going to my author page on Amazon. Here is the link.

https://www.amazon.com/author/johnwhowell

You can contact me at my e-mail address johnhowell.wave@gmail.com

You can also reach me at johnwhowell.com

My next novel is titled *The Circumstances of Childhood* and should be out mid-year 2017.

www.ingramcontent.com/pod-product-compliance
Lightning Source LLC
Chambersburg PA
CBHW070320260626
47160CB00003B/905